UNLAWFUL HARVEST

UNLAWFUL HARVEST

A KENZIE KIRSCH MEDICAL THRILLER

P.D. WORKMAN

PD WORKMAN

ISBN: 9781989415283 (IS Hardcover)
ISBN: 9781989415276 (IS Paperback)
ISBN: 9781774685181 (KDP Paperback 2 ed)
ISBN: 9781774685198 (KDP Hardcover)
ISBN: 9781989415252 (Kindle)
ISBN: 9781989415269 (ePub)
ISBN: 9781774683705 (Lulu Paperback)

ALSO BY P.D. WORKMAN

Kenzie Kirsch Medical Thrillers

Unlawful Harvest

Doctored Death

Dosed to Death

Gentle Angel

Zachary Goldman Mysteries

She Wore Mourning

His Hands Were Quiet

She Was Dying Anyway

He Was Walking Alone

They Thought He was Safe

He Was Not There

Her Work Was Everything

She Told a Lie

He Never Forgot

She Was At Risk

Auntie Clem's Bakery

Gluten-Free Murder

Dairy-Free Death

Allergen-Free Assignation

Witch-Free Halloween (Halloween Short)

Dog-Free Dinner (Christmas Short)

Stirring Up Murder

Brewing Death

Coup de Glace

Sour Cherry Turnover

Apple-achian Treasure

Vegan Baked Alaska

Muffins Masks Murder

Tai Chi and Chai Tea

Santa Shortbread

Cold as Ice Cream

Changing Fortune Cookies

Hot on the Trail Mix

Recipes from Auntie Clem's Bakery

Parks Pat Mysteries

Out with the Sunset (Coming Soon)

Long Climb to the Top (Coming Soon)

Dark Water Under the Bridge (Coming Soon)

High-Tech Crime Solvers Series

Virtually Harmless

Stand Alone Suspense Novels

Looking Over Your Shoulder

Lion Within

Pursued by the Past

In the Tick of Time

Loose the Dogs

AND MORE AT PDWORKMAN.COM

For those who speak for the voiceless
and for the rights of all who are vulnerable

1

MacKenzie reached for the ringing phone, trying to drag herself from sleep, but her hand encountered only the empty base of the phone, the wireless handset missing.

She pried her eyes open while feeling for it on the bedside table, knocking off keys and a glass and an empty bottle and other detritus. She swore and blinked and tried to focus. Where had she left the handset and who was calling her so early in the morning? The phone rang five times and went to her voicemail. Too late to answer it. She sank back down onto her pillow and closed her eyes. Whoever it was would have to wait.

But no sooner had it gone to voicemail than it started ringing again. MacKenzie groaned. "Are you serious? Come on!"

She turned her head and squinted at the clock next to her. It was hard to see the red LED display in the bright sunlight. It was almost eleven o'clock. Certainly not too early for a caller, even one who knew that she would sleep in after a party the night before. She rubbed her temples and scanned the room for the wireless handset.

There was a man in the bed next to her, but she ignored him for the time being. He wasn't moving at the sound of the phone, so he'd probably had more to drink than she had. She slid her legs out of the bed and grabbed a silk kimono housecoat to wrap around herself. The caller was sent to voicemail a second time. MacKenzie took another look around the bedroom without spotting the phone, then went out to her living room, also bright with sunlight streaming in the big windows. Outside, the pretty Vermont scenery was covered with a fresh layer of snow, which reflected back the sunlight even more brilliantly. MacKenzie groaned and looked around. The newspaper was on the floor in a messy, well-read heap. The remains of some late-night snack were spread over the coffee table. Some of their clothing had been left there, scattered across the floor, but no phone.

It started ringing again. Now that she was out of the bedroom and away from the base, she could hear the ringing of the handset, and she kicked at the newspaper to uncover it. She bent down and scooped up the handset. She glanced at the caller ID before pressing the answer button and pressing it to her ear, but she knew very well who it was going to be.

No one else would be so annoying and call over and over again first thing in the morning. She couldn't just leave a message and wait for MacKenzie to get back to her, she had to keep calling, forcing MacKenzie to get up and answer it. Her mother didn't care how late MacKenzie might have been up the night before or how she might be feeling upon rising. It was a natural consequence of MacKenzie's own choices. MacKenzie dropped into the white couch.

"Mother."

"MacKenzie. Thank goodness I got you. Where have you been?"

Her mother had been calling for all of two minutes. Where had MacKenzie been? She could have been in the bathroom, having a shower, talking to someone else on the phone, or at some event. Granted, she didn't go to a lot of events at eleven o'clock in the morning, but it *could* happen. Mrs. Lisa Cole Kirsch had a pretty good idea where MacKenzie had been. In bed, like most any other morning.

"What is it, Mother?"

"It's Amanda. She's sick."

MacKenzie nodded to herself and scratched the back of her head. One of the things that would definitely set Lisa into a tizzy was Amanda being sick. She worried over every little cough or twinge that

Amanda suffered. She had good reason, but it still made MacKenzie roll her eyes.

"What's wrong with Amanda?"

"I don't know. Maybe it's just the flu, but I'm really worried, MacKenzie. The doctors said to just wait and see, but they don't understand how frail Amanda is. They think that I'm just overreacting and being a hypochondriac. You know that I'm not just a hypochondriac."

"I know. So, how is she?"

MacKenzie had to admit that even though her mother worried about Amanda, her worry was well-justified. Amanda's health could get worse very quickly, and with the anti-rejection drugs suppressing her immune system, she was prone to picking up anything that went around.

"She's not good. She was up all night, throwing up, high fever, she's just not herself. I called an ambulance at eight o'clock. She just can't keep anything down and I don't like the way she's acting. So… weak and listless."

MacKenzie felt the first twinge of worry herself. Amanda had spent much of her life sick, but she was a fighter. She usually did her best to look like nothing was wrong, not letting on unless she was feeling really badly. She would laugh and brush it off as just a bug and smile and encourage MacKenzie to tell her about what was going on in her far-more-interesting life. MacKenzie closed her eyes, focusing on Lisa's words.

"But the doctors don't think that there's anything to worry about?"

"No, but you know… they never do. She has to be at death's door before they'll admit that there might be a problem."

"Have they given her anything or did they just send her back home again?"

"They've got her on an IV and have said that they'll keep an eye on her. But you know they don't really think there's anything wrong. They're just humoring me."

"Yeah. Do you want me to come?"

"Would you? I'm really worried."

"Okay. I'll need a few minutes to get myself together. I'll be there as soon as I can."

"Thank you, MacKenzie. I don't know what I would do without you."

The sad thing was, Lisa would do just fine without MacKenzie. Even though she said that she needed MacKenzie, MacKenzie wouldn't really be able to do anything that Lisa couldn't do herself. She'd been dealing with doctors for a lot of years, and though she didn't pick up on the medical jargon as quickly as MacKenzie did, she could hold her own very well and was stubborn as a mule when it came to Amanda's care. She would protect her baby at all costs, and Amanda would get the best of care whether MacKenzie were there or not.

But if Lisa wanted the extra comfort of having MacKenzie around, who was she to argue? She didn't have anything else going on that prevented her attendance, and even if she did, it was easy enough to beg off of any event with an excuse, especially if the excuse were that Amanda was sick. MacKenzie had used it as an excuse even when it wasn't true. Although technically, even when Amanda was feeling well, she was still sick, so it wasn't really a lie.

MacKenzie hung up the phone and put it down on the brass and glass side table. She scrubbed her eyes with her fists, and when she opened them again, Liam was standing in the front of her.

"What's up?" he asked. "Everything okay?"

He hadn't yet recovered anything more than his boxers and, for a minute, MacKenzie just let her eyes rove over the piece of eye candy, remembering the night before through a slight haze of alcohol. They had gone to the Cancer Society fundraiser, had made the rounds there and let themselves be seen, and then had returned to MacKenzie's apartment for more drinks, some real food, and private entertainment.

"MacKenzie? What's up?"

"Amanda. She's in the hospital and Mother wants me to go over there and reassure her." MacKenzie yawned.

Liam bent over to pick up the various items of clothing he had dropped the night before. "Is she okay?"

"I'm sure both Amanda and Mother will be just fine. But she sounded pretty worried, and she said that Amanda was listless, which isn't like her. A really bad flu, maybe. I hope that's all it is."

"I was going to have a shower before heading out. Do you want it?"

MacKenzie weighed the options. Amanda was in the hospital, so she would be getting the best of care. Did it really matter whether MacKenzie had to wait an extra ten minutes for Liam to shower before she got herself ready?

"Or," Liam suggested, a dimple appearing in his cheek, "we could shower together and be done twice as fast."

"I have a feeling I wouldn't be out of here very quickly if we did that," MacKenzie laughed. They could easily be another hour, and Lisa would be on the phone again, ringing insistently, demanding to know where MacKenzie was and why she wasn't at her sister's side yet.

"Okay," Liam agreed. "So, do you want it?"

"Yes. I guess so. I need to pull myself together even if I am just going to the hospital." Lisa would not want her to show up looking bedraggled. She'd expect MacKenzie to be well turned-out even if it were the middle of the night, which it wasn't.

Liam nodded agreeably. He pulled on his white shirt from the night before, but didn't put on the pants or the rest of his outfit. "Shall I make you some breakfast while you're in there so that you can get out more quickly?"

"Would you? Just a couple of pieces of toast and some juice," MacKenzie requested, heading toward the bathroom. She looked back over her shoulder at him. "And coffee."

He smiled. "I think I know by now that you don't start any morning without coffee."

"Well, I need to fortify myself with *something* this morning before facing my mother."

She had a quick breakfast while Liam got into the shower, but he wasn't out by the time she was finished. She poked her head into the bathroom.

"Will you be much longer?"

She could see his shadow through the shower curtain as he turned his head toward her. "Oh… I can just lock up when I leave. You can go ahead."

MacKenzie shook her head. "I don't like to leave people here when I'm not around. Sorry. Can you be quick?"

"Yeah, sure." His tone was agreeable, but clipped. He obviously didn't appreciate that she didn't trust him enough to leave him alone in her apartment. But MacKenzie had been burned in the past by people who didn't respect her privacy, and she wasn't about to leave him there without supervision. She didn't know him well enough. Just because she could go with him to an event, and maybe bring him home afterward, that didn't mean she knew enough about his essential character to leave him there alone. She valued her privacy and there were a few things around the apartment that were quite valuable. Not that she thought Liam Jackson was going to steal them. She knew where to find him if he did. But it just wasn't good policy. If she didn't notice that something was missing right away, she might never be able to track it down again.

"I'll just be two more minutes," Liam promised.

"Thanks."

She went back to the bedroom and, since she had the time and couldn't leave until he was finished, she actually went ahead and pulled her bed into some semblance of order. It didn't look as good as when the maid did it, but it was better than leaving it all rumpled. She would appreciate it when she got home later.

If Lisa could only see her now. Twenty-seven years old and actually making her own bed. On a roll, she went into the living room and picked up the newspaper, which she threw in the garbage, and her clothes, which she threw in the laundry. Liam was out of the shower but not yet out of the bathroom. She threw a random assortment of dishes into the dishwasher and had the place looking pretty tidy when Liam made an appearance, dressed, hair wet but neatly combed, and his face still stubbly, not having taken the time to shave. She stood on her tip-toes to give him a kiss. "Thanks. Sorry about having to rush you out of here. It's my sister. Mother wants me there, so I have to make sure she's okay."

Liam nodded, looking down at her and letting his fingers linger on her jaw for a moment. "That, or you got one of your girlfriends to call to break up the party so that you could get rid of me."

"Ugh. I wouldn't do that when I was still in bed."

He smiled. "Give me a call later, then. Let me know how it goes. And we'll see each other again… soon."

They didn't have anything lined up, no dates, no fundraisers, nothing on the horizon. Liam was a nice guy, good looking, and MacKenzie might add him to her regular coterie of admirers, but she hadn't made up her mind yet. She wasn't one hundred percent sure that he was her type. Whatever that was.

After seeing him out the door, she put on her coat and winter gear and headed for the hospital.

When she managed to find her way to Amanda's hospital room, not in the renal unit where she usually was, Amanda was asleep. Lisa sat next to the bed, watching her sleep. Not reading a book. Not looking at her schedule for the week. Just watching her sleep. MacKenzie would have gone crazy. She couldn't stand to have people staring at her.

"Hi, Mom," she said softly.

Lisa looked over at her, automatically making a motion for her to be quiet before she evaluated MacKenzie's voice and the deepness of Amanda's sleep and decided that she probably wasn't being too loud after all.

"How is she doing?" MacKenzie looked over her kid sister. Amanda was twenty years old, but when she was asleep, she looked about ten. She was shorter than MacKenzie, and MacKenzie wasn't exactly an Amazon herself. Amanda was small and elfin, and people often mistook her for a kid if they weren't paying attention. She had a beautiful face, when she was feeling well. She wasn't looking too bad. Her weight was good, her cheeks round rather than sunken like they had been when she'd been through her worst times. She had long, dark hair that got tangled if she didn't take care of it, which was hard to do when she was in a hospital bed all day, but she didn't like to cut it short so that it would be easier to take care of. She said she needed her strength, like Samson.

Amanda was pale, and that bothered MacKenzie. But if she had the flu and had been throwing up for hours, then of course she was going to be pale. It was just a virus. She would be feeling better soon.

"She's sleeping," Lisa stated the obvious. "She's been so sick all night… I'm glad she was finally able to drift off. Maybe she's on her way to feeling better."

"Probably just a bug."

"Yes. Hopefully."

There was an IV hanging, but Lisa had said that Amanda needed it to stay hydrated. It didn't necessarily mean that she was back on some treatment again.

MacKenzie pulled the other chair in the room closer to her mother's and sat down. Amanda had been given a private room, of course. There was no way she was going to be left in some hallway or emergency room curtain. Lisa would see to that.

"Do you want to go get something to eat?" MacKenzie suggested.

"Well…" Lisa's eyes flicked over to Amanda. "I don't know. I don't want to leave her alone."

"I'm here. And you haven't had anything to eat, have you? You've been with her since last night?"

"Yes, you're right."

"Well, you're not going to be any good to her if you're fainting from hunger or all angry and irritable from low blood sugar. So go. I'll be with her if she wakes up. She's not going to be alone."

"Are you sure?"

"Why don't you take advantage of the fact that I'm here, because I'm not going to be here all day. Go have something to eat."

"Okay," Lisa agreed, but she still made no movement to get up, watching Amanda with worried eyes.

"She'll be fine for now. I'll have them page you if something happens."

"Would you?" Lisa brightened at that suggestion. She could go have something to eat and still be sure that Amanda hadn't taken a turn for the worse. She clutched her purse on her lap, then nodded and got up. "Thank you so much, MacKenzie, I appreciate you coming and being here for your sister."

"And for you," MacKenzie reminded her. "Don't you try saying that I never do anything for you."

"I would never say that."

MacKenzie raised her eyebrows as her mother left. She might say it and she might not. But she would certainly imply it the next time she wanted MacKenzie to do something for her and MacKenzie had something else going on or didn't want to be there.

Lisa's heels clicked sharply as she walked away. MacKenzie watched her go. She leaned back in her chair and looked over Amanda once more. The hospital chair was far from comfortable. She was going to have to get used to it if she were going to be there for a few hours.

"I should have brought a book," she murmured to Amanda. She hadn't thought to bring anything with her. She'd just gotten herself together and headed over. And she couldn't go down to the gift shop to pick something up. Not after dismissing her mother and saying she'd stay with Amanda while Lisa was eating. MacKenzie sighed and resigned herself to just sitting there and napping while she waited either for Amanda to wake up, or for Lisa to return from lunch.

and their toys. Was that how her mother saw Walter's lobbying? As a hobby that occupied her husband and kept him out from underfoot?

"Does he have anything interesting going on right now?"

"I'm not sure what he's working on. I don't really pay much attention, unless it is something that could have an impact on one of my causes."

Lisa always had plenty of causes on her agenda. There were an infinite number of foundations, societies, and fundraisers that needed her attention and support. Lobbying kept her father busy and fundraising kept her mother happy. MacKenzie just didn't know what it was that kept *her* happy. When was she going to find her way in life? She didn't want to be a lawyer, lobbyist, or politician. But she didn't want to be a socialite or drum-beater either. She had done well enough in school and had taken enough classes in college to get herself a degree, but that hadn't helped her to find her place in the world. She wasn't passionate about anything.

Lisa's eyes were quick and perhaps took in more than MacKenzie had expected. She reached over and patted MacKenzie's hand. "You'll find something," she said. "You're just a late bloomer. You need to be patient and give yourself some time."

"When you were a kid, what did you think you would be when you grew up? Did you have any dreams?"

Lisa shrugged and looked away from MacKenzie. "I don't know. I wanted to be a wife and mother. I was never really interested in a job. I felt like children were my avocation." She shrugged. "I know that's not a very popular answer these days. We're supposed to think big and take the bull by the horns, to make our mark on the world. But I can't help but think… that the marks being made on the world wouldn't amount to very much if it weren't for the mothers."

MacKenzie gave her a smile. "The hand that rocks the cradle, and all that?"

"Yes. Exactly. Mothers shape the thinkers and the soldiers. The scientists and the astronauts and the Nobel laureates. They all had mothers. They all had people to help them along the way and give them support at various parts of their lives, like a mother would, even if they didn't have a mother. I happen to think that's a very important position."

"Of course," MacKenzie agreed. "I never thought that you should be required to give up your family and have a high-power job."

"I could have, you know," Lisa said. She obviously didn't want MacKenzie thinking that she had only stayed home to be a mother because she couldn't do anything else. She had chosen to be there and not to hire a nanny to raise them. That had been her choice, not a fallback position.

"I know, Mother. You have a brain. You're very organized and I'm always amazed at what you can accomplish. I know you could have chosen to do other things."

Lisa nodded, satisfied.

MacKenzie looked back at Amanda. They had been lucky to have a mother who stayed home to look after them. Amanda probably wouldn't have survived without a strong, proactive mother watching over her. How many times had Lisa been the one to take her to the hospital and insist to the doctors that something was wrong, and she wasn't taking Amanda home until they had figured out what it was? She had insisted that Amanda wasn't just a whiner or a hypochondriac, but that she was really ill. She could have died if they hadn't been forced to dig deeper for the answers.

MacKenzie and Amanda hadn't really been playmates. MacKenzie had been too much older than Amanda to consider her a real friend and peer. Instead, Amanda had been MacKenzie's baby as much as she had been Lisa's. MacKenzie had been fascinated with her care and had happily fed and changed her. It was like having a living doll. MacKenzie had never even liked dolls. But she liked having stewardship over the tiny new person in their home. Lisa had encouraged her interest rather than shooing her off to go play or insisting that she diaper her dolls instead of her sister.

At first, no one had known that anything was wrong. Amanda got sick a lot, but children picked up viruses everywhere, it wasn't really that unusual. As she got older, she didn't outgrow it, and MacKenzie realized that she was sick a lot more often than MacKenzie or her friends, or little Amanda's other friends. She remembered the day when she had been out at the playground with Amanda, about nine years old by then, and MacKenzie a teen. Amanda had been playing tag or grounders or some other schoolyard game on the climbing equipment with her friends, but she had to sit down at the edge of one of the platforms, her face white, trying to catch her breath and get up the energy to go back to the game. The other girls teased her for calling timeout too often and told her that she couldn't be safe, but there wasn't any point in tagging her while she sat out, because she wouldn't run after the rest of them and the game would grind to a halt.

MacKenzie walked over to Amanda.

"Mandy-Candy," she singsonged, "what's wrong? Don't you want to play anymore?"

Amanda was breathing shallowly, too fast. "I want to play," she protested, her arms folded across her stomach, "I'm just too tired. I need a break."

"Do you want to go home?"

Amanda looked at the other girls still playing and having a fun time on the playground equipment around her. She looked sad. Not just sad, but desolate, as if they had all run away and left her behind where she could not follow.

"I guess so," she said finally. "I can read, I guess."

"Do you really want to?" MacKenzie pressed. "I'm not saying you have to. If you want to stay and play..."

Amanda shook her head. "I can't," she said hopelessly. "I don't know how they can run around all day."

MacKenzie sat looking at her as the seconds ticked by, a knot growing in her stomach. She walked home slowly with Amanda, back to the big house on the hill. It was a long way for a child who didn't have any energy left. Partway there, MacKenzie boosted Amanda up onto her back and carried her piggy-back to the house. Amanda lay against her, body limp, arms around MacKenzie's neck.

When they got home and MacKenzie settled Amanda in bed with

a book, she went looking for Lisa. Lisa was, luckily, home for the evening and not on her way out to some fundraiser.

"Mother… I think something's wrong with Amanda. I mean… really wrong."

Lisa looked at her for a long time, then finally nodded. "I do too. And I think it's time we found out what."

So many doctors had said that Amanda was just a girly girl, that she didn't want to participate in activities and was overly sensitive to every little ache and pain that came along with growing up and roughhousing with friends. There wasn't really anything wrong.

But when they had insisted that it was time to figure out what was really wrong with Amanda and that they weren't going away until they got some answers, everything changed.

And it would never be the same again.

3

"Chronic kidney disease?" MacKenzie repeated what her mother had told her after the doctor met with her to discuss all of the tests that Amanda had been through. Anyone who thought that she was attention-seeking in order to get those countless vials of blood drawn and all kinds of imaging and poking and prodding should have their own head examined. Amanda didn't want to be sick. She wanted them to find out why she was sick so that she could get better. "What does that mean?" She understood the individual words, but not the impact that it would have on their lives. Not what it would really mean for Amanda and her future.

"It means that her kidneys are not working the way they're supposed to," Walter said. He was looking very serious and using his 'bad meeting' voice. Things always happened when he used that voice. People went out of their way to fix things when Walter Kirsch said that there was a problem in that grave tone. "In fact… at this point they're barely functioning at all. She needs to go on dialysis, so that a machine can do the job that her kidneys are supposed to be doing, cleaning her blood. That's why she hasn't had much energy and is always getting sick… her body just isn't working the way it's supposed to."

"But dialysis won't make her better, will it?" MacKenzie asked.

She was no idiot. She wasn't the one who was nine years old. She was old enough to know that kidneys didn't just suddenly get better after dialysis, and that a machine couldn't do the job of a person's real kidneys forever.

"No. At some point in the future, they're going to have to get Amanda a new kidney. If she can get a new, functioning kidney, then she won't have to be on dialysis. But until then… It's going to take a lot of time. She'll have to be on dialysis for several hours per session three times a week. She'll need to be quiet and still, and it's pretty boring. We're going to have to be understanding and flexible in our schedules. It isn't Amanda's fault. We're going to need to reshape our lives for her."

MacKenzie nodded, but didn't really understand what that was going to mean to them. How it meant spending so much time at the hospital, and traveling back and forth, and finding things for Amanda to do to entertain herself when she became so bored she threatened to disconnect herself and go home. MacKenzie spent her time at school and at the hospital and didn't have much time for friends or dating.

They didn't have too far to look for a kidney donor, since MacKenzie was a good match. But Lisa and Walter didn't want to rush into anything. They searched for any other solution. They didn't want to put both of their girls through surgery if there was any other option. There was talk of artificial kidneys being pioneered by some medical supply company. There were non-related donors and there was continuing dialysis so that they didn't have to risk MacKenzie's health for Amanda's. They put Amanda on a special kidney diet. They tried herbal cures that were supposed to improve kidney function. Vitamins and minerals. Drugs that were being trialed.

And things did improve. With some of the load being taken by dialysis, Amanda's kidneys were no longer so stressed and recovered to some degree. All of the little things that they were doing helped, and to begin with, her function inched up.

But then an infection had turned one kidney to mush, and things were getting critical.

When MacKenzie turned eighteen, she announced that she was donating one of her kidneys to Amanda. As a legal adult, Lisa and

Walter no longer had any say in MacKenzie's medical decisions. She could donate without their permission. MacKenzie couldn't stand to see Amanda suffering any longer.

MacKenzie was eighteen and Amanda was twelve. Old enough and experienced enough with kidney disease to know that she wasn't like the other little girls and that the illnesses that had dogged her all of her life weren't going to go away. Old enough to understand that MacKenzie didn't have to take the risk. They were both fully informed about the surgeries and risks that they were facing and were prepped for surgery. Then they lay on gurneys, waiting, as the team assembled and did whatever last-minute jobs and briefing they needed to do before beginning. Amanda reached over the raised sides of her gurney to take MacKenzie's hand. For a while they just lay there in silence, overwhelmed by emotion, unable to find the words to say to each other.

"Thank you, MacKenzie," Amanda said softly. "This is… really nice of you to do. Thank you."

"I would do anything for you, Mandy-Candy." MacKenzie hadn't called her by the nickname for a long time, a name intended for a much younger child. "Anything I have is yours."

"I'm a little scared."

MacKenzie was a little scared too. And she wasn't the one who was facing the greatest danger. She was strong and healthy and would be left with one fully functioning kidney. Amanda was the one who was weak and would need to take anti-rejection drugs for the rest of her life, the one who could be pushed over the edge by an infection or by the doctors making a mistake in reattaching one of the tiny vessels. She was so young, and so small. MacKenzie wanted to pull Amanda onto her lap and rock her, like she had when Amanda was a little girl. She knew Amanda must be terrified.

"It's okay to be scared," MacKenzie assured her. "I am too."

"What if something goes wrong? What if they make a mistake or it just doesn't work? What if my body rejects it right away?"

MacKenzie squeezed her hand. "I don't know. We have to focus on the positive. On how great it is going to be when it works. No more dialysis!"

Amanda made a little moan. "That would be so great. I can't imagine what I'll do with all that extra time!"

"You can do things with your friends. Have a social life."

"Get my homework done," Amanda said with a little laugh.

While MacKenzie had originally thought that Amanda would be able to do her homework during the dialysis sessions, since she was sitting there with nothing to do anyway, it hadn't worked out that way. The nurses advised against doing anything stressful during that time. If Amanda tried to do too much, she would end up feeling sick during or after the dialysis.

"Yeah. It won't be so hard for you to keep up. You'll have more time for yourself."

"Maybe I'll take up a sport," Amanda said.

Turning her head to look at her sister, MacKenzie could see Amanda closing her eyes as she daydreamed.

"Tennis, maybe. Or speed cycling."

MacKenzie shuddered at the thought of her frail sister racing around a tennis court or a track, something tearing loose inside her because she was being so rambunctious. She knew Amanda was just fantasizing and would never take up something that would put her transplant in danger, but it still made her queasy and anxious.

"You can do whatever you want," she promised Amanda. She wasn't the one who would have to tell Amanda to curtail her activities. She would leave that to the doctors. "It's going to be so nice for you not to have to be in hospital anymore, to be able to just live a normal life."

"Yeah."

They lay in silence, waiting for someone to take them into the surgical theater. MacKenzie had butterflies in her stomach, worried about how everything would go and if it would all turn out right like they all hoped. What if Amanda *did* reject the kidney right away?

"What if Amanda is rejecting her graft?" MacKenzie blurted.

Dr. Proctor, seated to her right at the dining table in the event room of the Resort Inn, looked over at her in surprise. "Sorry?" He looked at her as if she had two heads.

MacKenzie was impatient. She had taken her mother's place at the charity auction, since Lisa wanted to stay with Amanda until they were sure she was going to be okay. She had already explained to Dr. Proctor, a friend of the family who was also in attendance, why it was that she was there instead of Lisa. He wasn't a transplant surgeon, but he was one of the top doctors at the hospital and knew more than MacKenzie ever would about such matters.

"What if Amanda is rejecting her kidney? What if it isn't the flu? What would the symptoms be?"

He laid down his fork and considered her seriously, giving her his full attention. "If she was rejecting her kidney, she would probably have a high fever, vomiting, and decreased urine output. Very similar to flu symptoms to start with."

"Then how would we know? What if the doctors all just say it is the flu, but it isn't? Is there a test to see if she is rejecting the kidney?"

"I'm sure that her doctors are being very careful to watch her kidney function and all of her bloodwork to make sure that she is not. They know her history. Your mother wouldn't let them forget; I can promise you that."

"But it happens all the time. Doctors overlook symptoms and think that someone isn't really sick when they are. People get sent home from the hospital, told that they're just fine, and then die in the night. People die in the emergency room because the triage nurses think they aren't really sick."

"You can ask her doctors or the nursing staff if they have done the tests to make sure she's not rejecting her kidney. They would be very aware of her situation, but that doesn't mean you can't ask."

"They won't think that I'm just being a worrywart or interfering? I'm sure Mother is already driving them crazy."

"Does it matter?"

MacKenzie shook her head. "Amanda's health? Of course it does."

"No, I mean, does it matter what anyone thinks? Why does it

matter if her doctors think you're being a worrier? Are you concerned about your sister's health care or about what they think of you?"

"Her care. Making sure they treat her properly if it's not just the flu." MacKenzie considered. "I guess it doesn't matter what anyone thinks, does it?" She had been raised by Lisa to always consider how others perceived her, how to do the right thing socially and make sure people saw her in a good light. If people stopped inviting her to events, she wouldn't have the opportunities to advance herself and to help the causes and charities that she wanted to. She wouldn't make a good marriage. She wouldn't be happy in life. And while she had often rebelled against her mother's viewpoint, it was deeply ingrained. It had been repeated so many times that it was part of her thinking. Her default.

But Dr. Proctor was right. It was Amanda's health that was important in this case, not what the medical staff at the hospital thought of MacKenzie. She needed to get her priorities straight.

"So just ask them if they have tested to see if she's rejecting her kidney?" she asked.

"They should have done basic blood panels and be monitoring her urine output levels. From that, they should be able to tell whether she is rejecting the kidney or whether it is something else, just a virus or something that she will get over quickly."

"Okay. I'm going to ask. She wouldn't reject it this late, would she? I mean, after eight years, why would her body suddenly reject it?"

He opened his mouth to answer her, his brows drawing down, and then he stopped himself. His lips pressed together and he considered her question and formulated his answer. MacKenzie waited. There were other conversations going on around them. Other people talking about the weather and local events and issues, about things that really didn't matter. It seemed strange to MacKenzie that life should just go on for the rest of the world when, for MacKenzie and her family, everything revolved around Amanda's health and what she needed from them.

"A transplant can fail at any time," Dr. Proctor said. "It isn't predictable. Immediately, one year, ten years. Or it can lose function suddenly, and we don't always know why. We just do the best we can to treat a patient who is in crisis."

"What if she needs another transplant?" MacKenzie asked. "I can't give her another one."

"No," Dr. Proctor agreed with a smile. "You need to hang on to the one that you've got. If there are no other compatible donors in your biological family, then they will need to look for a compatible donor in the database. A stranger donation. They don't have the same success rate as a familial donation, but they can be successful. And, of course, she could survive on dialysis for a while, as they tried to track down another compatible donor. It's not easy, as your family knows, but the chance of finding a match is still good, on a three- or four-year scale."

"Three or four years," MacKenzie repeated. She remembered those years that Amanda had been on dialysis before. It had been a long time, and Amanda's quality of life had not been good. She rubbed her temples. "I don't know if she can handle going through that again."

"Amanda is stronger than you think. She's always had a good attitude. She's a fighter."

MacKenzie thought of how listless Amanda had been when she had weakened. Her mother's alarm was justified. MacKenzie felt the same panic when she looked at her sister and worried that she had given up the fight. She shook her head at Dr. Proctor, unable to put it into words.

Dr. Proctor looked at her, frown lines between his brows, then shook his head. "I'm sorry, MacKenzie… I'm sure it's just the flu. It can affect a person emotionally more than we think. I'm sure she'll be back to her usual self within a day or two. Right now, her kidney is fine, as far as we know. It's just a matter of nursing her through this virus. Lots of rest and fluids, and she'll be feeling better before you know it."

4

And it seemed that Dr. Proctor was right. MacKenzie slept restlessly that night, and after a few hours got up and drove to the hospital, worrying over Amanda and ready to quiz the medical staff about her condition and to demand to see the blood tests that would prove that she wasn't rejecting the grafted organ. Instead of finding Amanda asleep or listless, MacKenzie walked into the hospital room to find Amanda sitting up, eating her breakfast and talking to Lisa. MacKenzie stopped in the doorway, looking at them for a few minutes and was smiling when Amanda looked up from her breakfast tray to see her standing there.

"Well, good morning," MacKenzie greeted. "You're looking a lot better today."

"Just a twenty-four-hour bug, I guess," Amanda said, shrugging. "I'm still feeling it a little this morning… but it's not so bad." She gestured at the bowl of green Jell-O with her spoon. "I'm not ready to try pizza, but I've been able to have a few bites without throwing it back up again."

Lisa beamed at MacKenzie. "I guess it was just the flu after all. Chalk one up against the overly concerned mother. It's a case where I'm glad to be proven wrong."

MacKenzie walked the rest of the way into the hospital room and sat down in the other chair. "I'm glad too. I was ready to do battle with the doctors this morning. Quizzed Dr. Proctor all evening on what they should be doing and whether it could be something to do with Amanda's kidney."

Lisa sat back in her chair, smiling. "How was the auction?"

MacKenzie thought back over the evening. "I… don't really have any idea. Everybody seemed happy, so I assume they raised the money they were hoping to. I was too worried about Amanda to really pay attention to anything else."

"I'll have to make some calls to apologize again and find out how it went," Lisa said, pulling out her agenda to make a note of the fact. "I appreciate you going to stand in for me. Did you find someone to go with you?"

MacKenzie shook her head. "I just went myself. I didn't really have the time to chase down a date. And I wasn't in much of a mood to be good company, worrying about my kid sister here."

"You don't want to be seen at these things without a plus-one too often," Lisa advised. "People will talk. And they won't include you if they have to worry about pairing you up with another… single. It causes all kinds of complications with the fundraising when it is all focused so much on couples. The seating, the catering, dances, all kinds of things are impacted if you have odd numbers and unaccompanied guests."

"I'm sure they'll understand that I was only standing in for you. They'll be happy that I was able to make it so that at least your dinner didn't go to waste."

Lisa nodded. "Of course. I'm just saying… you don't want to be seen alone too often."

"People will talk," Amanda chimed in.

MacKenzie glared at her. "This is all your fault. You'd better be careful what you say. Next time, I'll be sick, and you'll have to go out to be on display."

Amanda smiled.

MacKenzie felt warm and comfortable. Everything was right with the world. They would keep Amanda in hospital for one or two days, to make sure she was stable and everything was in working order, and then she'd be back home again and things would fall back into their usual routine.

She couldn't have been more wrong.

It was the nightmare she had imagined at the auction while talking to Dr. Proctor. The hospital cleared Amanda, saying that it had obviously just been a virus and she was fine as long as she just didn't try to do too much too soon. She went home with Lisa and everybody was happy. And then sometime in the night, Amanda had suddenly taken another bad turn. Once more, she spiked a fever and was sluggish and unresponsive, complaining of hot and cold and that she hurt all over. Lisa again called an ambulance and had her taken in. She called MacKenzie in the night, startling her out of a sound sleep.

"I'm at my wits' end, MacKenzie. I don't know what's wrong. She was just fine. Everything seemed to be just fine. And it isn't like she did too much and tired herself out. She was just sleeping!"

"What do the doctors think?" MacKenzie asked groggily, trying to marshal her thoughts. "Are they still saying it's just the flu?"

"Yes. I told them she was doing better; she was back to normal. But they're saying it's perfectly normal to have a relapse. I don't know what to do!"

"Did you ask them to do any tests? Or to call Dr. Proctor? What about her nephrologist?"

"They'll do all of the consults tomorrow… tonight there isn't anyone available. Don't people ever get sick during the night? Why aren't any of these people in until morning?"

"I don't know. I guess if they thought it was an emergency, they would get someone out of bed, so it's good, isn't it? It means that they don't think it's too serious."

"But I do. This isn't normal for Amanda. You know how she usually gets sick. This isn't her usual pattern."

"No," MacKenzie admitted. While Amanda frequently came down with whatever was going around, she was usually unwell for several days, getting gradually worse, before a virus really hit her.

Then she kept a good attitude, ordered her family around, and kept a smiling, brave face throughout the course of the illness. These sudden attacks in the night, bouncing back again, and then suddenly coming up sick once more, so lethargic and apathetic were not like her. "But this is probably just a virus she hasn't had before. One that has more of an emotional impact on her. Sometimes bugs are like that."

"I hope that's all it is," Lisa sighed. "I'm sorry for bugging you in the middle of the night. I didn't know who else to talk to."

"Where is Daddy?"

"He's in Montpelier. He had some people to talk to, and we thought that Amanda was on the mend again."

Even if he was away, MacKenzie thought he should still be answering the phone when his wife called. He had a cell phone, even if he was out having late drinks with some other lobbyist. Had Lisa called him and he hadn't answered? Or had she just automatically called MacKenzie because he wasn't in Burlington? MacKenzie liked that Lisa felt like she could call her, but she worried about the relationship between her parents. Was Walter really on a business trip? Or was he seeing another woman? It seemed like he was away from home an awful lot and was too often unavailable even though she should be able to reach him on his cell phone.

How could he be away when Amanda was so sick?

MacKenzie knew she was being unfair. As far as he knew, Amanda was fine, just like the rest of them had thought. When you had a chronically ill person in the family, you had to make the most of the times when they were feeling better.

"Is everything okay between you and Daddy?"

They didn't have an ideal relationship, but who did? They pursued their separate lives, and MacKenzie wasn't sure how often he was actually home. He kept busy with his business and lived out of business suites in hotels. She knew he had a modest apartment in Montpelier for those times when he couldn't leave the capital while something was going on.

"Why do you ask?" Lisa returned.

MacKenzie frowned at the phone. That wasn't an answer, but at the same time, it was. If there were no problems between Lisa and

Walter, she would have just said so straight out. Instead, she wanted to know what it was MacKenzie suspected, so as not to give away anything she didn't have to.

"Are you and Daddy having problems?" she persisted.

"You know your father and I have different interests. We're not always together, like some couples."

"I know that."

Lisa hesitated and MacKenzie waited, not willing to leave it at just that vague comment.

"It doesn't affect you and Amanda. Nothing has changed in our relationships with you."

Their father had never been that big of a presence in their day to day lives anyway. They loved him and made sure to stay in contact, but he had frequently been absent when they were growing up. No *Father Knows Best.*

"Have you... separated?"

"We haven't actually been together for quite some time."

Kenzie's grip tightened on the phone. She hadn't lived at home for years, but Amanda had, and she had never hinted to MacKenzie that anything had changed in their parents' relationship.

"Mother... can you just give me a direct answer? I don't understand why you're beating around the bush."

Lisa sighed. "You always did want everything to be black and white. No shades of gray for our MacKenzie."

MacKenzie didn't laugh or agree. She didn't accept a segue to her childhood and the many times she had insisted on knowing the exact parameters of some story or principle. She preferred to think of herself as detail-oriented rather than demanding.

"Mother."

"MacKenzie... we restructured our affairs three years ago."

"You separated."

"We had not been living as husband and wife for some time before that."

"And I'm just hearing about it now? That's crazy! What's the big secret?"

"We prefer not to have the details of our private life out there for everyone to gossip about. Especially not when Amanda was still a minor. It can be very hurtful to hear people speculating on your parents' lives. We tried to protect you children from any… negative consequences of our relationship."

"So, you've been legally separated for more than three years. And this restructuring you're talking about…?"

"That would have been when you were in Europe. A lot was going on at the time."

MacKenzie felt the stirrings of guilt over that comment. She had been convinced that she would never be able to truly find herself unless she went away. And not just on a vacation, but really living away from her family, cutting off all of their influences. Which meant cutting off most of their communications. She had still made weekly phone calls so that they knew she was still alive, but it had been her attempt to break away and really become her own person. And during that time, her parents had done what, exactly? Her father had moved out of the house for good? Had transferred his business operations to the apartment in Montpelier? And what else?

"We divorced, MacKenzie," Lisa finally said. "It was all very quiet. We divided our assets, worked with the lawyers on a fair division of all of our property and affairs, and then signed the papers to legally sever our relationship."

"You're divorced," MacKenzie said in disbelief.

"Legally, yes. But we're still friends. And he still has a room here and stays here when he has business in town. It isn't like I have lied to you."

"No… not at all… you got divorced three years ago, when I was out of the country, and didn't bother to tell me."

"That's… yes… that's how it worked out."

"And what about Amanda? Does she know?"

"She's been with me the whole time. She couldn't exactly not know."

"She never said anything about it to me."

"We don't talk about it."

"Why not?"

"It's private. I prefer not to be discussed."

"I really think..." MacKenzie was having difficulty putting her stuttering thoughts into words. "I wish you would have told me."

"I tried, dear... but you cut yourself off. You were very remote. You didn't want to talk about it."

MacKenzie tried to remember what her mother might have said in trying to bring the subject up.

Your father and I met with our lawyers this week...

Daddy is moving his business to Montpelier...

Since your father left...

How many hints had she missed, so focused on herself and her own satisfaction and personal growth? She'd blocked the family out and refused to listen to anything they might have to tell her. What else had she missed?

"I'm sorry, Mom..."

"There's nothing to be sorry about. It's all for the best. We each wanted to be free to make decisions on our own. This way, we could operate independently."

"I mean for not being there for you. Not even paying any attention to what was going on."

"You had your own concerns, dear. I expect you girls to have your own lives. To pursue your own dreams."

If only MacKenzie actually had a dream to follow. And what about Amanda? She was still living at home and if she kept getting so ill, she wouldn't ever be able to be fully independent. She would always need someone checking in on her, dealing with emergencies, making sure she was taken care of.

They both had trust funds and, as far as MacKenzie knew, they hadn't been restructured during the divorce. Not that she'd heard.

But then, that obviously didn't mean anything.

"Do you want me to come to the hospital?"

"Not tonight. Go back to sleep, if you can. I'm sorry for waking you up. I'll sit up with Amanda tonight, and tomorrow if you feel like coming by the hospital, I could use a sounding board... if you think

I'm overreacting… I just don't know what to think. They said she was fine to go home."

"They don't always know. Hospitals and doctors make mistakes all the time. That's why they have malpractice insurance. If you feel like Amanda needs to be in the hospital, then you're probably right. I think you have a pretty finely-honed sense of what she needs the most. You've had twenty years with her. The doctors spend all of five minutes asking questions and taking her temperature."

"You're right. I'll ask them to re-run the blood tests tomorrow. Make sure they didn't miss anything the first time. Maybe it's just something that takes a while to show up."

"Okay. I'll come by and see how she's doing in a few hours then."

"Thank you, MacKenzie. I always feel better if it's not just me. It's good to have a second opinion, just like with the doctors."

5

MacKenzie knew that her mother could be a bit of a hypochondriac. She did tend to worry about Amanda more than was necessary, worrying about the smallest cough or pallor. She did work for so many of the disease-specific charities that she often worried about MacKenzie or Amanda getting cancer or diabetes or having a stroke.

But she had been right about Amanda being sick back before she was diagnosed. Lisa had taken her to doctor appointment after doctor appointment, just to be told that she was worrying too much and needed to give her daughter a chance to learn from her bumps and bruises and to develop a strong immune system by being exposed to other children regularly. She had been told so many times that she was just overreacting that she questioned herself and her motives even when it was obvious that Amanda was ill. She hated to take Amanda to the doctor or hospital when she was sick, for fear of being accused of being overly involved and attention-seeking.

But Lisa wasn't one of those moms who infantilized her children and got stuck in the role of a martyr. She didn't say that Amanda had a high fever when she didn't, or make up the bouts of vomiting.

MacKenzie stopped at the nursing station before going in to see Amanda and her mother.

"Can you tell me how Amanda Kirsch is doing?"

The stout nurse at with a purple smock looked up at her from the computer. "Are you family?"

"Yes. Her older sister. I was just going in for a visit, but I thought I would find out what I could before I see her. You know, reassure our mom that you're doing everything you can for her."

That last little gem seemed to put it over the edge. The nurse nodded.

"She's resting comfortably right now. We put her back on an IV and anti-emetics. Probably just released her a little too early."

"It seemed like she was doing fine. Her fever was gone, and she went a couple of days without throwing up or having any other issues. I actually thought she might have stayed a little too long last time. She seemed like she was back to normal."

"Transplant patients can be more fragile. She probably just pushed a little too hard. Did too much too soon."

"Okay. What about the fever?"

"She's still feverish, but that's her body's own natural defenses. We don't want to bring it down just for the sake of bringing it down. Give her body a chance to fight it off and produce antibodies so that she doesn't get it back again."

MacKenzie nodded her thanks. "Alright. Thanks so much." She walked down the hall to the room with Amanda's name beside the open door.

"Hello, Mother." She bent down to give Lisa a kiss on the cheek, wanting to reassure her that everything was fine. "The nurse said she's resting comfortably."

Lisa's lips pressed together. "I don't know if I would agree with that assessment," she said. "She's not throwing up right now, so that's an improvement."

MacKenzie looked down at Amanda to see for herself. Amanda's face was shiny with sweat, little tendrils of hair pasted to her damp forehead. Her pillow and sheets were mussed. She'd obviously had a restless night.

MacKenzie didn't want to wake Amanda, so she sat down on the other chair and took Lisa's hand, giving it a quick squeeze.

"The nurse said that they don't want to bring down her fever artificially."

"Yes," Lisa agreed. "They told me that. But she's so uncomfortable. And it's not just a mild fever. You know how it is when she's sick and she just gets warm. You have to take her temperature to actually be sure that she even has one. Not like this. She's burning up."

"It's just her body fighting the flu. It's a good thing. That means her body is doing what it's supposed to."

Lisa shook her head slowly. She sat there, watching Amanda, waiting for some change.

"Did you talk to the doctors about getting blood tests?"

"The ER doctor ordered some more. I'm still waiting to hear if anything showed up."

MacKenzie hadn't been able to talk her mother into going for breakfast and had eventually broken down herself to find Lisa some coffee and a granola bar she could consume while she was beside Amanda's bed. They didn't talk much, not wanting to wake Amanda up. She needed her sleep while she could get it. At lunch, Lisa made MacKenzie go get herself something to eat, and as five o'clock approached, MacKenzie finally managed to convince her mother to head down to the hospital cafeteria to get herself some real food. It was at that point that MacKenzie managed to get through to her father on his cell phone to report to him that Amanda was back in the hospital again.

"I'll try to get back as soon as I can, sweetheart," Walter assured her. "Tell Amanda and your mother both that I'll be there tomorrow sometime. How is Lisa holding out?"

"Daddy… why didn't you ever tell me that you and Mother got divorced?"

There was silence at the other end of the phone line. After a few awkward seconds, Walter cleared his throat uncomfortably. "Did Lisa tell you that?"

"Yes. When I pressed her. I don't understand why the two of you were keeping it a secret. Or how you thought you could!"

"Well... up until now, we've been pretty successful in keeping it under wraps. We didn't want to be in the spotlight, sweetie. That's all. And you were going through kind of a tough time. We didn't want to burden you with it. We were already pursuing our own separate courses, so nothing really changed... except on paper."

"You could have told me. I shouldn't have to find out by accident."

"I didn't think it would really make that much difference to you," he confessed. "It's like the difference between a common law relationship and getting married... does it really make any difference?"

"It obviously did to you."

He grunted an acknowledgment to this point.

MacKenzie heard voices and footsteps approaching in the hallway. "I think maybe the doctor is here. I'll call you back later, okay?"

"Sounds good. Leave me a message if you can't get through. I always pick them up."

She murmured another goodbye and hung up. A doctor in a white coat entered, followed by several other doctors, all looking too young to be the real thing and very intense. The head of the pack gave MacKenzie a reassuring smile of greeting.

"How's our patient?" he asked, in a hearty voice that MacKenzie was afraid would waken Amanda. But then, he was probably going to wake her up to examine her anyway. She wanted to know that they were paying attention to Amanda's condition and understood what was going on with her.

"She's mostly been sleeping... but she's still very hot and restless."

The doctor picked up the chart at the foot of the bed and looked over it. "Hasn't been throwing up since they started anti-emetics. Good fluid output. No signs of dehydration," he summarized quickly. He turned to his students. "Here we have a patient with a grafted kidney who has been admitted for observation. Fever and chills, achy, throwing up, general malaise. What are your observations and orders?"

Several of the students offered their opinions. The doctor nodded and shot back questions and made suggestions. He looked down at the clipboard at the suggestion of one of the young doctors that she might be rejecting her transplant.

"What is the average length of time that a kidney transplant will last?" he asked. "With the proper anti-rejection regimen in place, of course."

Several numbers were thrown around. MacKenzie was relieved to hear numbers longer than ten years. It had only been eight since Amanda's transplant, so she should still have a few good years left.

"In this case, it has only been a year since the graft, so we are very early on in the process, and if the tissues were a good match and the anti-rejection protocol is working, then we should still have—"

"Eight years," MacKenzie interrupted, amused. "It's been eight, not one!"

He looked back down at the clipboard. "Eight? No, I don't think so. It only says one year here."

"Then someone wrote it down wrong. I should know, I was her donor."

"You?" He looked down again. "According to the notes here, it was a non-related living donor. I just assumed..." He looked from MacKenzie to Amanda, studying the similarities in their features. They were pretty obviously sisters. Anyone who saw them together recognized the fact.

"I'm her sister," MacKenzie agreed. "They must have mixed up her history with someone else's."

He tapped the board with his thumb as he looked down at it. "I will follow up with the staff and we'll get it straightened out. At any rate, if she was rejecting her graft, whether after one year or eight, what would be the signs and symptoms?" he asked his little brood of doctors.

There was an ensuing discussion. He eventually put the clipboard back, nodded to MacKenzie, and headed out again. He didn't examine Amanda even to just check her pulse or her temperature. Then he was off and running again. As they left, MacKenzie saw that Lisa was standing outside the door waiting for them to leave. Once they were out of the way, moving down the hall to the next room, Lisa entered. She handed MacKenzie a cup of coffee and sighed.

"Did you hear that?" MacKenzie demanded, not sure how long Lisa had been waiting there. "They've got her history all screwed up. We need to talk to the nurses and get them to enter the right details. They can't make a good diagnosis and treatment plan when they don't even know her history."

"He probably just misread it," Lisa said with a shrug. "That was when she had her surgery."

MacKenzie was nonplussed at first, but then remembered the trip to a private clinic that was pioneering some new technique. Amanda had not been doing well prior to the clinic, and MacKenzie was pleased when Amanda had come back with much improved kidney function. She had not been sure about experimental treatments, thinking they should just stick to what was tried and proven, but she had to admit that they had made the right choice. Amanda had been on a dangerously steep downward slope, but the experimental surgery, whatever it was, had managed to stall the deterioration and improve her kidney function again.

"What exactly was it she had done?" MacKenzie asked, trying to remember the details. "They really did turn things around, didn't they?"

"It was a lifesaver," Lisa agreed. "I don't know if she would have lasted more than a few months without it."

Amanda had been back on dialysis at that point, and they had been talking about the need for another transplant. Whatever groundbreaking research that private clinic had been doing had been well worth whatever price her parents had paid.

Amanda had been shifting around restlessly for a while, and MacKenzie looked over at her, wondering whether she was hallucinating because of her fever, or getting closer to consciousness. Amanda had been babbling a few times during the hours that MacKenzie had been there, incoherent, rarely even forming words that MacKenzie could understand. She sweated with the fever, alternating with bouts of cold that left her shivering no matter how many blankets they piled onto her. Nurses came and went, taking her vital signs and pursing their lips and refusing to speculate on how she was doing or if the doctor would order a change in her treatment protocol. They were too full of assurances that Amanda was just fine and would get over this little bout of flu in no time. Fluids and time were all that she needed.

Amanda's eyes were open. MacKenzie leaned closer to her, turning her face sideways so that it would be right-side-up for Amanda.

"Hey, Mandy. How are you doing?"

Amanda's eyes went over MacKenzie's face, not appearing to recognize her at first. Then she gave a weak smile.

"MacKenzie. I didn't know you were here."

"Yeah. Just keeping an eye on you and making sure you don't go running down to the cafeteria or something. How are you doing?"

There was a delay while Amanda apparently thought this through and audited what she was feeling. "Good. I think I'm doing better." Amanda reached up and pushed hair away from her face. "Ugh. I feel like I need a shower."

"I'm sure you do. You've been sweating like you ran a marathon."

Amanda nodded. "I think I just did."

MacKenzie brushed hair back from Amanda's forehead, checking her temperature while she did so. "I think your fever finally broke. That was kind of scary."

Amanda frowned, wrinkles appearing on her forehead. "I thought I was doing better. Didn't I go home?"

"Yeah. But I guess you weren't quite over it yet, because you decided to come back here again."

"I did?"

MacKenzie smiled slightly at Amanda's confusion. "I mean you just weren't quite over it yet. The fever came back, and you ended up here again. I guess there are some nasty flu bugs going around right now."

"I should have gotten a shot. They said that I should, but they always end up making me feel so wiped out. I guess I should have."

"Your immune system just isn't very strong. I don't know if the flu shot would have prevented this from happening. They never really know which strain is going to be going around. They just guess."

Amanda nodded. She looked around the room. "Can I have a drink? My mouth is so dry."

"You've been sweating through everything. I'm not surprised. They should be giving you more fluids than they are."

"I'm sure it's fine," Amanda said, gazing up at the clear IV hanging above her. "I just breathe with my mouth open."

MacKenzie gave her a sip of the tepid water from the side table. "Do you want ice? I can go get you some."

"This is okay. Ice makes me shiver."

"Are you cold again? Do you want another blanket?"

"No, this is good, thanks."

Lisa returned and saw that Amanda was awake. "Hello, sweetie." She bent down and kissed Amanda on the forehead. "How are you feeling? Better?" She looked over at MacKenzie. "Didn't I tell you she'd wake up as soon as I left? I should have stayed here."

"If you knew she'd wake up when you left, then maybe you should have left earlier," MacKenzie teased. "You needed to get some rest. You aren't a help to Amanda if you let yourself get run down."

"Yes, you're right," Lisa agreed. She sat down on the other chair and gazed at Amanda.

MacKenzie too studied Amanda's wan face. "We'll make sure they don't release you so quickly this time. I want to make sure that you're really over this bug so that you don't end up right back here again."

"Okay," Amanda agreed, her voice barely louder than a whisper. "Sounds good."

MacKenzie glanced at her mother. Amanda was usually quite vocal about wanting to get out of the hospital and back home as quickly as she could after an admission. She insisted that she would recover faster in her own bed and didn't run the danger of getting a dangerous hospital infection there. MacKenzie didn't like that she was being so cooperative about extending her stay at the hospital. But then, she'd just barely woken up, and MacKenzie supposed she needed time to get her strength back before she would start to complain.

Lisa's eyes reflected MacKenzie's own concerns. Neither of them said anything, but they didn't need to.

6

MacKenzie pondered over her list of acquaintances, considering who she wanted to call. She was tired from the amount of time she was spending at the hospital, but it wasn't the kind of tired where she just wanted to go home and go to sleep. She wanted to go out and shake off the stresses of the hospital and the worry over Amanda's mysterious illness and to let loose. Maybe go dancing or clubbing, go home for a nightcap and further stress relief, and then sleep away what was left of the morning.

The problem wasn't that she couldn't find a man who would be happy to pursue this agenda with her, but that she wanted to keep it casual. Despite the common perception that men were happy to have a physical relationship without commitment, MacKenzie found that too many of them thought that one or two dates meant they were on a surefire track toward marriage. Whether they thought that the pot of gold at the end of the rainbow was her, her social standing, or her trust fund was sometimes difficult to discern. And it was harder than she would have thought to pick out which men were going to be interested in a more committed relationship and which would be happy to keep things casual and fun.

She settled on Roger, who had recently broken up with Anita, his fiancée of three years. MacKenzie figured he would be up for some rebound action without being ready to get back into another long-term relationship, which fit perfectly with her plans. A quick phone call to him brought a positive response, and she dressed and fixed her makeup while she waited for him to pick her up.

Their conversation was stilted at first, both of them smiling and talking about the weather and unimportant things that were going on in their lives while feeling each other out. They danced a little before dinner and then sat down to order. Getting more comfortable with her, Roger became more voluble, but his conversation all seemed to run along one track. Anita.

She hadn't figured in that he would fill the evening with Anita stories. Usually, when a guy had been recently dumped, he wanted to focus on just about anything but his ex. He could talk about her to his guy friends, but he should know better than to fill the ears of a new prospect with tales of the old.

MacKenzie did the best she could to change the subject, but he kept returning to Anita. He was ranting about the new guy she was seeing. How stupid he was, how lazy and undesirable a character he was, how inferior to Roger in every way. Why would she dump him just to go out with someone like that? It didn't make any sense.

MacKenzie cocked her head and put her hand over his on the table. "Roger."

He stopped and looked at her, almost as if he had forgotten she was there.

"Oh… yes? What is it?" He seemed slightly embarrassed. "Was I doing it again?"

"Doing what?"

"Uh… talking about Anita?" His blush showed even in the dim lighting of the restaurant. "I'm sorry. I'm over her, I really am."

"Uh-huh."

"No, really. I just forget myself sometimes, get carried away. Forget Anita, she's in the past."

MacKenzie watched his face and didn't believe it for a minute. "You're still in love with her."

"No. Goodbye and good riddance. I don't need someone like that in my life."

"Someone like what? You clearly cared about her. You were engaged for three years."

"We never got along that well. I was just lying to myself. I didn't know how to get out of the relationship, even when it obviously wasn't doing anything for me. I was just… too comfortable to get myself out. That's all."

His lips twitched as if there were more to say. Or as though his face didn't agree with his words.

"Then why are you mad at her for dating this other guy? Why aren't you happy she's out of your life?"

"I am. That's just the point. I'm glad we broke up so that we could both move on and find the right person."

"Then why do you care who she's dating?" MacKenzie persisted.

He scowled at her. "I don't care who she's dating, obviously"

She shook her head. People lied to themselves, so maybe he didn't actually know the truth, but it was plain to her. "You just spent ten minutes telling me all of the ways that this guy is inferior to you. Why would you do that if you were happy with her seeing someone else? You're mad at her for looking at someone who is not you. You still want her back."

"That's not why."

"Then explain to me why you care who she's dating now. What difference does it make to you?"

"It doesn't, obviously. She can date whoever she wants, it doesn't have anything to do with me and doesn't have any impact on my life. We're through."

MacKenzie let go of his hand and took a drink.

"Then show me."

In spite of how badly the evening was going, MacKenzie didn't have the heart to boot the already-injured Roger to the curb by the end of dinner. She continued with her plan, taking him back to her apartment for a nightcap. But the more he drank, the worse he got, and eventually he ended the night by crying himself to sleep over his memories of all the good times he'd had with Anita.

Not exactly the finale that MacKenzie had been hoping for.

Worse than that, the guy snored. Maybe he was just congested after crying so much and he didn't normally sound like a buzz saw, but MacKenzie was not at all impressed. She was awake much earlier than she wanted to be, unable to sleep with the racket he was making. She shook his shoulder.

"Roger. Roger, come on, wake up." She was not gentle about it, and it took several minutes of shaking to get him even partially awake. She was starting to consider the use of ice cubes. "Roger. Hey. You've got to go. Get up."

"What is it?" he mumbled.

"It's MacKenzie. You've got to go. If you still want to sleep, go home and sleep there."

He put both hands over his eyes, pressing into them. "I feel like crap. I've got a killer hangover. Just let me sleep it off."

"No. You have to go."

She suspected he was more hung over from crying than from drinking. She had not had enough sleep and was very irritable. He wasn't going to stay there and keep her up after she'd put up with his whining for the entire night. She could understand why Anita had dumped him. Why they had stayed together for so long and even gotten engaged was a mystery, but she wasn't going to pursue it. She wasn't spending any more time on the man. As much as she liked sensitivity in a man, she didn't like whining.

It took some more encouragement to get Roger sitting up, his eyes open a slit as he examined his surroundings and tried to remember the details of the night before. MacKenzie expected an apology when he realized that he'd talked about Anita all night long and then cried himself to sleep, but no such apology was forthcoming.

She shuffled into the kitchen to make some coffee. What she really wanted to do was to go back to sleep, but she had awakened herself even more than she had awakened him, and she probably wasn't going to be able to shut her brain off again. In the meantime, she needed some high-octane coffee to get Roger kickstarted and out of there.

"What time is it?" Roger groaned when she returned to the bedroom with a mug for him. He rubbed his eyes and squinted at his Rolex. "MacKenzie, it's only seven o'clock. We were up until dawn. I need more sleep. We both need more sleep."

"Then you can go home and sleep. Neither of us is going to get any more sleep while you're here."

She handed him the coffee. Roger sipped the scalding liquid. "Why are you being so hard-nosed? I thought we had a good time together."

"You tell me. You're the one who's been whining and crying all night. If you're looking for a good time, leave the tears at home."

"I didn't—" he started to protest, then stopped himself. He snuffled, apparently realizing how congested he was. He rubbed the puffy bags under his eyes and the middle of his forehead. "Did I really? Oh man. I must have really been sloshed. Not the way to make a good impression on a pretty girl."

"No," MacKenzie agreed. "And this girl needs some real sleep before she's going to even put on a semblance of pretty by the fundraiser tonight. So hit the road, Jack."

He grunted and drank more of the coffee.

"I wouldn't have such a problem with Anita if she hadn't started up dating as soon as we broke up," he growled. "She could at least have waited a decent interval."

"Don't start that again."

"But it's true! She was seeing someone the next week. How do I know they weren't already seeing each other before we broke up? While we were engaged and talking about wedding plans?"

"She probably was." MacKenzie was brutal. "And she's not even given you a second thought, so why are you still pining after her? Give it up."

"I'm not pining," he said sharply. "I'm glad she's out of my life and that I can pursue other avenues. I'm glad I broke up with her." He reached for MacKenzie, but she avoided his grasp. He was too late if he thought the date was going to lead to intimacy now. That ship had sailed.

"Come on! I'll show you," Roger protested. "She doesn't mean anything to me anymore." His face was red with anger rather than embarrassment this time. MacKenzie didn't care. He could think her a tease if he liked. She wasn't about to be a target for him to work out his frustration on.

"It's time for you to go, Roger," she said firmly, staying out of his reach.

"You accuse me of still being in love with her? I'll prove it to you. I'll show you that I'm not."

"No."

He threw his coffee mug across the room. He didn't aim it at MacKenzie, but it was still half-full, and she ducked out of the way to avoid the arc of liquid that sprayed across the room. The mug shattered on the wall. MacKenzie looked at the dent in the wall, the pieces of the shattered mug, and the coffee trail across her bedroom in shock and disbelief.

"MacKenzie, I'm sorry—" Roger started.

"You've got thirty seconds to get out of here before I call the cops."

"MacKenzie…"

"Twenty-nine, twenty-eight, twenty-seven…"

At first, he didn't move, trying to intimidate her with his glare. When it became obvious that she wasn't going to be pushed around and she kept counting down, he decided he didn't want to have to explain to the police what he had done. He was still fully dressed, so there wasn't any delay for him to get his clothes on. He got up and stalked out of the bedroom. MacKenzie heard him getting his coat and boots, and then the door slammed and he was gone. She shook her head.

"Good riddance."

She picked up the splintered pieces of the mug. She'd probably be finding bits of it through the room for months to come. She'd get the maid in to clean up the coffee and vacuum thoroughly in the hopes she would get all of the sharp slivers that were left in the carpet. And she'd have to get the handyman in to repair and repaint the wall. And Roger Milford would not be getting a return invitation.

7

MacKenzie arrived in Amanda's hospital room and greeted her mother, who was waiting for Amanda to finish changing into her street clothes in the bathroom so that she could, once again, head for home. The nurse came in with the discharge papers for Amanda to sign when she came back out.

"Now try to encourage her not to do too much right away," the nurse advised, giving Lisa a sage nod. "You don't want her to turn around and be back here again. She's been stable for a couple of days, no fever and no vomiting, so she appears to be in the clear now, but just be extra careful for a little while. She's not as strong as she would like to think she is."

Lisa sighed. "If I could tell her something and be sure that she would follow my advice, that would be one thing, but you know how daughters are." She gave MacKenzie a look that made them all laugh. MacKenzie gave a wide shrug.

"What are you talking about, Mother? Don't I always do exactly what you tell me to?"

Lisa shook her head and made a noise of disgust that clearly answered MacKenzie's query.

The mood was light. MacKenzie was glad that Amanda was in the clear once again and could safely go home. If she could stay quiet for a couple more days and not try to just pick up where she'd left off, MacKenzie was sure she would be fine.

"I'll just leave that with you, then," the nurse told Lisa, and took two steps toward the door.

From the bathroom, they all heard the unmistakable sounds of vomiting.

For what seemed like a long time, they just all looked at each other, not wanting to believe it. MacKenzie was the first to take a step toward the bathroom.

"Amanda? Are you okay?"

She wasn't sure why she asked that. It was obvious from the noises within that everything was not okay. Amanda was not throwing up just for something to do. After her two hospitalizations, one right on the heels of the other, Amanda was sure to want to go home, not to be wanting to throw up again. She didn't want to be sick.

Lisa dashed past MacKenzie and knocked on the door. "Amanda? I'm coming in."

Amanda knew from past experience not to lock the bathroom door. Of course, the nurse would be able to unlock it to get in, but locking it would cause a delay to Amanda getting help from her mother while she went to find someone who could unlock it. Lisa made the slightest hesitation before opening the door, as if waiting to see if Amanda would object or wishing that she didn't have to face this problem yet again, one more time. Then she turned the handle and swung the door outward. MacKenzie didn't get closer, not wanting to get in the way or to have to watch Amanda being sick if she wasn't yet finished. Lisa went into the bathroom.

"It's okay, baby. It's going to be okay."

MacKenzie could hear Amanda sobbing between heaves. Lisa swore. "Her temperature is back up again," she called out to the nurse. And she swore again, angry at the recurring fever, God, fate, or whatever kept making Amanda sick again.

The nurse looked at the IV, which she had just removed from

Amanda's arm half an hour before, shaking her head. They were all too stunned to believe it. How could Amanda be sick again, when she had been perfectly well for two days? She hadn't done anything strenuous. She hadn't been exposed to anyone new. They had all been careful not to cough near her.

When the bout of vomiting was finally over, Lisa helped Amanda to wash up and rinse out her mouth, then she and the nurse walked Amanda back over to the bed to lie back down. MacKenzie picked up the discharge papers and put them to the side, a wave of despair washing over her. How could Amanda be sick again? Why couldn't they figure out what it was that was making her sick? Food? A virus? An infection? It should show up in her bloodwork. It couldn't be that much of a mystery.

"What have you done to make yourself sick again?" the nurse demanded as she settled Amanda into bed. "Everything was going along just swimmingly. You were going to go home."

Amanda wept. "I know. I want to go home."

"It's not her fault," MacKenzie told the nurse, raising her voice in anger. "Don't you get after her for getting sick. She didn't choose to be sick!"

The nurse shook her head, looking as if she would argue with this statement. Did she really think that Amanda wanted to be sick? That she would have done something to herself to make herself sick again?

MacKenzie had heard of such things. Usually about mothers making their children sick. But Lisa hadn't done this either. It wasn't anything that any of them had any control over. Lisa wanted her daughter to get better more than anyone else did. She would never have done anything to put her daughter in danger.

The nurse said nothing as she reinserted Amanda's IV and made sure that everything was in order.

"I'll let the doctor know," she said curtly, and walked back out. MacKenzie and Lisa fell into the chairs, still unable to believe the sudden setback. Lisa was looking for something in her purse, and MacKenzie leaned closer, curiosity aroused by Lisa's frantic search.

"What is it, Mother What are you looking for?"

"I can't find my… it's just not here…"

Eventually, Lisa pulled a small cell phone out of her purse. Folded up to the size of a compact, MacKenzie could see how it could have been easily missed. Lisa opened it up and punched in the numbers for Walter's cell phone. MacKenzie thought fleetingly that she needed to show Lisa how to set up speed dial numbers so that she didn't have to remember everybody's numbers. But she suspected that Walter and MacKenzie were probably the only ones that she ever called on her cell. Anyone else could wait until her business hours, when she dealt with all of her social appointments and issues.

As Lisa waited for the phone to ring through to Walter, MacKenzie stroked the back of her mother's neck, hoping it would help to soothe her.

As soon as Walter answered, Lisa started crying.

She normally did not cry in front of the girls, and particularly not in front of Amanda. They were supposed to keep a stiff upper lip in front of Amanda. Never give away any doubts they had about her ability to fight for her life and survive. MacKenzie glanced over at Amanda. She was lying back, eyes closed, face shining, giving no sign that she heard her mother's weeping.

"MacKenzie," Lisa thrust the phone at her, gasping for breath. "Tell him."

MacKenzie took the phone, not sure what she was supposed to tell her father. Just what was going on, she supposed. So that he could make the decision as to whether to turn around and return home. Then she resolved not to leave it up to her father.

"Daddy."

"MacKenzie, what's going on?" His voice was heavy with concern. "Amanda was fine when I left. What happened?"

"I don't know. She just suddenly took another turn. I just can't understand it. She'll be sick for a day or two, and then better for two days, and then it comes back again. It's cyclical. But I can't figure out why. I don't know what's causing it."

"I'll be there as soon as I can. Is she okay for now? I'm worried."

"She's resting right now. They put her back on an IV, and I hope that means back on the anti-emetics again too. So that she won't be throwing up again. It just doesn't make any sense to me."

"I'll be back as soon as I can be. What about your mother? Can you calm her down?"

MacKenzie looked at her mother, a lump in her throat. Lisa was always so cool, always calm and rational and prepared to do just the right thing. It wasn't like her to get hysterical over a change in Amanda's condition. MacKenzie reached over and took her mother's hand and squeezed it.

"She's going to be okay, Mother. She's going to be fine."

But as MacKenzie took in Amanda's waxy pallor, fear gripped her chest. Would she be? Would she really be alright?

8

It was another longday and when she went home, MacKenzie was lonely and wishing for once that she had a companion, someone who would be there when she got home at the end of the day to rub her feet and cuddle in front of the TV and maybe get her a drink and a bite to eat so that she didn't have to think about it.

But from what she had seen of marriage, she would be the one who was expected to do those things, rather than her partner. And she didn't know how anyone could have the energy at the end of such a day as she had just been through.

She didn't want Roger this time, or any of his ilk. She wanted a real partner or best friend, but she didn't have anyone to call. While she'd had friends in school, most of them had gone in different directions, and she didn't have a crowd that she hung around with. She went out to some of the social events that her mother set up or asked her to go to. She spent time with Amanda, having nice long talks with her when she was better. She was pretty focused on her family.

So she did the next best thing she could think of. She didn't want to watch some inane show on TV. She didn't have the energy to read a book. She was worried about Amanda and wanted to help her. There was nothing she could do, but she was desperate for answers.

She booted up her computer and started typing search strings into Google. Recurring fevers. Cyclical fevers. Flu-like symptoms. Kidney transplant rejection. Unexplained fevers. For each search, she clicked on all of the possibly relevant links on the first page of results, and sometimes the second or even further. She looked for patterns, for diseases or disorders that fit with Amanda's symptoms. The doctors might still think that she just had the flu, but MacKenzie was on the warpath. They were obviously not giving her proper treatment, or she wouldn't keep coming back down with the same symptoms over and over again.

Her eyes burned from staring at the screen and she made an effort to blink more often. She took a break and put a cold cloth over her eyes for a few minutes to try to reduce the swelling. She started making some notes of the things that she was seeing repeatedly, frowning and trying to wrap her mind around the various possibilities.

She'd always had an aptitude for biology. She hadn't taken medicine in college, but when she'd been in high school, she'd gotten good marks and always been very interested in how bodies worked. She was one of the only girls who hadn't been grossed out or pretended to be grossed out by dissections. She loved dissection days and would participate whenever she could, even doing extra modules for more credit. Maybe it had started with her interest in Amanda's medical care and in understanding what was happening to her, and in her desire to donate her own kidney to Amanda even when her parents were leery of the idea. She hadn't fantasized about being a doctor, but she had imagined what it would be like to cure a fatal illness, especially Amanda's kidney disease. Someday, someone would find a way to reverse kidney failure, and the world would change, just like it had when insulin, antibiotics, or vaccines were discovered. She wanted to be there when it happened.

But she hadn't pursued science or medicine after secondary school. She'd done arts and other programs that were more suited to young ladies. The women who attended the social functions that Lisa prized so highly were not highly-trained and did not have an interest in dissecting things. They were students of the arts and maybe of business if they were expected to take over after their parents retired.

MacKenzie tapped her pen on the desk, looking at the screen. She looked at her watch and considered the time. It was late. But would that matter to a doctor? Doctors were used to being paged or woken up to take care of emergencies, weren't they? MacKenzie wanted to get done everything she could as quickly as she could. She didn't know how long Amanda would be able to last without the proper treatment.

Eventually, she bit the bullet. She might not be in the doctor's good books after this, but she had to at least try. She looked up his number and tapped it into her phone.

The phone rang a few times before it was answered. "Dr. Proctor," he growled.

"Dr. Proctor," MacKenzie used her most reasonable, more charming voice, "this is MacKenzie Kirsch."

"MacKenzie Kirsch," he repeated. "What's wrong? I do hope you're not calling to tell me that… something has happened to your sister."

"It is about Amanda. So far, she's hanging in there, but I'm really worried. We need to figure out what is going on with her before it's too late."

She could hear him moving around, the creaking of bedsprings, and the noise of cloth rubbing over the phone.

"How can I help?"

"I'm really sorry for calling you so late at night. I didn't know who else to talk to. Amanda just keeps cycling through these high fevers. But it's not the flu. I'm sure of it."

"What most people call the flu isn't even the flu," he provided unhelpfully.

"I know. But… I've been doing some research, and I was wondering about malaria."

There was a short bark of laughter from Dr. Proctor. "Malaria? My dear… I think it's time to go to bed."

"I know it's not likely. No one would look for it. And maybe that's why they haven't been able to figure out what she has."

"No one in America comes down with malaria. If they do, it's something that they picked up on a trip. Amanda isn't exactly a world traveler. She's been sheltered and coddled, she hasn't been anywhere there are mosquitoes that could be carrying malaria."

"She had surgery last year. I'm not sure where it was, but they went out of the country. To some kind of private clinic that performs an experimental procedure not approved in the US."

Proctor was silent for a moment, considering this. "Are you sure?"

"Yes."

"And you don't know what kind of procedure it was or where it was performed?"

"No. I can ask Mother and Daddy. They haven't said much to me about it because it's private, you know. Amanda's health and personal care are her business, not mine. But I know Amanda had to get a passport. And I know they went somewhere warm, because I helped to pack her suitcase, and it was all light summer clothing."

"Somewhere warm doesn't necessarily mean a tropical country. It could just mean that she would be indoors the whole time and wouldn't need to pack anything warm."

"I'll ask them. But if she did go to a country where there were mosquitoes infected with malaria, then could that be what she has?"

"I don't know. Tell me about her symptoms."

"She gets a high fever, throws up until they give her drugs to stop it. She's tired and listless. Then after she gets through it, she starts to feel better, like her old self. She goes a few days without any symptoms, and then it is back again. High fever, throwing up, tired. Flu-like symptoms, but it's not the flu."

"Surely they've done basic blood tests and would have found any parasitic infections."

"I know… but I don't know for sure if they've been looking for anything but a virus, and maybe they could miss it. Especially if they think that Lisa was just being a hypochondriac."

"It is possible to miss it. It might not show up in a smear, or it might be easily missed… sometimes it takes two or three tests before something like that shows up. If the person testing hasn't seen malaria before…"

"And they wouldn't, living here in the States, would they? They would hardly ever see a case of it."

"It's possible, MacKenzie. If she had this procedure somewhere tropical."

"So, what do I tell the doctors? How do I get them to test her for it?"

"You'll have to ask for a CBC panel and to check a blood smear for parasites."

"What if they don't want to do it?"

"You're going to have to be strong about it. You'll have to insist. Explain that she has been somewhere tropical and recurring fevers could mean malaria. Talk to your father. Tell him to insist."

"Okay. Thanks, Dr. Proctor. I really appreciate it."

"Good luck, Miss Kirsch."

"MacKenzie."

"MacKenzie, then. I hope it works out."

MacKenzie had not foreseen that her parents would present a bigger roadblock than the doctors. She drove over to the hospital early in the morning, having only had a couple of hours of sleep, to present them with her findings and Dr. Proctor's confirmation that Amanda could be dealing with a malaria infection. Walter shook his head adamantly.

"Malaria? No one gets malaria anymore, MacKenzie, it's a dead disease."

"A dead disease?" MacKenzie challenged. "Millions of people get it every year!"

"Not in civilized countries. Not in the US."

"But she wouldn't have gotten it in the US. Where was it she went for her surgery?"

He glared at her and didn't answer the question. "You have to be bitten by an infected mosquito to get malaria. Amanda was never bitten by a mosquito. She wasn't ever even outside."

"She must have been outside to get from the plane to the clinic," MacKenzie muttered grumpily. She had expected her parents to be happy to have a possible solution to Amanda's mysterious illness. They could stop the cyclical fevers.

"Don't be flippant, MacKenzie. It's not attractive."

MacKenzie gave him a glare as good as she was getting, and turned to appeal to her mother. "If it's malaria, it's treatable. We can get her out of the hospital and back home again."

Lisa looked at Walter, then back at MacKenzie again. "But I really don't see how she could have gotten it. We were very careful not to expose her to anything."

"I'm sure you were. I'm not saying that it was because you did something wrong. You can't foresee everything."

"I really don't think that's what this is."

"The symptoms fit. I asked Dr. Proctor and he agreed. He said to pursue it."

"If it was malaria, don't you think the doctors here would have figured that out already? It can't be."

"They wouldn't ever guess that's what it was if they didn't know she was in a tropical country."

The two of them continued to frown and shake their heads. MacKenzie was frustrated. "What's the harm in ruling it out?"

"Chasing after zebras instead of horses," Walter said. "Haven't you ever heard of Occam's razor? We need to keep the doctors focused on the likely causes of this fever, not rare tropical diseases that she could never have contracted."

"It's one test," MacKenzie insisted. "Maybe two. That's not distracting them. And maybe something else will show up in those tests. You never know."

"I'm going to have to put my foot down," Walter said stubbornly.

"Amanda can decide for herself." MacKenzie looked over at her sleeping sister. "I'll ask her when she wakes up."

"You don't need to be getting her hopes up with wild theories."

"It's not a wild theory. It's a logical hypothesis. It fits the facts."

"The facts are, she was never bitten by a mosquito. I can guarantee you that."

MacKenzie stared into his angry, unwavering eyes, at a loss as to how to deal with his certainty.

When the doctor came around, MacKenzie excused herself from the room to let her parents deal with him. She saw the relief in Walter's eyes that she wasn't going to stay there and cause problems. She waited in the hallway by the nursing station for when the doctor left Amanda's room to go on to the next one. He didn't have a group of students with him this time, and he didn't stay long in Amanda's room. Not long enough to examine her or to figure out what was really making her sick.

"Dr. Brady?"

He turned and looked at her as he left the room and headed away from her to the next one. "Yes?"

"I'm Amanda's sister. MacKenzie."

He nodded. "Yes, what can I do for you? I just talked with your parents. I have other patients to see."

"Well, they didn't want me to bring this up, so I waited until I could catch you alone."

He looked around, impatient to be on his way.

"I don't really have time for individual consults. If you want to talk to me, you should be in the room when I'm there to see your sister."

"I think she might have malaria."

He blinked at her. Then he shook his head. "Malaria is a tropical disease. We don't see much of it here in the States."

"I know that. But she was out of the country a year ago."

"Did she get malaria a year ago?"

"She didn't show any symptoms back then, as far as I know, but the stuff I read online said that it doesn't always show up right away. It can stay dormant for a few years."

Dr. Brady considered this. His dark brows drew down. He looked again toward Amanda's room.

"My father doesn't think it could be," MacKenzie confirmed. "He didn't want me to bring it up with you."

"He's right, you know."

"Nobody knows until you test for it."

"It would have shown up on the tests that we already ran."

"It never gets missed? You wouldn't have overlooked it if you didn't know that she'd been in a tropical country?"

"It would still have shown up."

"I read that they can do several tests and not see it."

He gave a small shrug, conceding the point. "That is very rare, though. And with a patient like your sister, who has so many other things going on with her health… It's far more likely to be related to her transplant than anything else."

"I know that's the most likely, but these recurring fevers… they sound just like malaria. If they're not malaria, then what are they being caused by?"

"An infection of unknown origin. Maybe hiding in her kidney."

"But then wouldn't her white blood cell count be up? It isn't, is it?"

"Her white blood cell should be up if she has a bacterial infection. But her immune system is suppressed, she might not be producing white blood cells like she should."

"What else is showing up in her blood tests? Is there anything to show that she's rejecting the kidney?"

"Not yet. We're watching pretty closely."

"So do one more test for malaria. Just to be sure. Looking for that specifically."

He pressed his thin lips together, thinking about it. Then he finally nodded. He turned to the nurse at the nursing station and gave her instructions on the blood to be drawn for the tests. He looked sideways at MacKenzie. "It might be best to do it while the parents are out of the room, if they go for supper."

MacKenzie nodded. "I'll try to get them to take a break while I sit with her."

The nurse looked from one to the other, raising an eyebrow. "You're going against the wishes of the next of kin?"

"See if you can get the patient's permission. That will override anything they can say. I don't want this to become a legal battle."

The nurse was hesitant, but finally nodded. "Alright. if you say so."

MacKenzie blew out her breath in a sigh. "Good. Thank you. I appreciate it."

"We want to find out what's wrong with your sister just as much as you do," the nurse said. "We don't like not knowing what's going on with a patient or how to treat it. Her parents should have mentioned that she's been out of the country. That makes a difference."

MacKenzie returned to the hospital room. Amanda was still sleeping. Her parents were talking in low voices, but stopped when MacKenzie entered the room. Lisa gave a strained smile. "Are you sure there isn't somewhere else you need to be?" she asked. "You don't need to sit with her, with both of us here."

"Just the opposite," MacKenzie said. "It's you two who need a break. You've been here all night and I'm here to give you a break. Go get something to eat and have a rest. Amanda will be okay with me here."

"Oh, you don't need to do that MacKenzie. You have other things to do."

"I don't know of anywhere more important than with my sister right now. Go get something to eat. Maybe find somewhere you can close your eyes for a while. Get some rest."

"We really can't do that."

"Of course you can. You can't sit by her bed twenty-four hours a day. Give me a chance to contribute."

Lisa looked at Walter, raising her eyebrows in a question. Walter finally nodded.

"I have my cell phone," he told MacKenzie. "You can call me if there is any change in her condition. Do you have your phone with you?"

MacKenzie checked her purse and nodded.

"Yeah, I've got it right here. I'll let you know if anything changes, but right now she's resting peacefully, so you guys go and get something to eat and take a breather."

They took a few more minutes to get on their way, but then finally left the room. MacKenzie flopped into one of the uncomfortable guest chairs and tried to relax. Whether her parents thought it could be malaria or not, she was still going to get it checked out. And she didn't need their permission to do it. If it turned out to be negative, there were still other things on her list that were less likely, but she'd keep looking. If it did turn out to be malaria, then her parents would forgive her for going ahead and having the tests done behind their backs. She was just a concerned sister making sure that Amanda got the best chance she could possibly get.

The nurse from the nursing station poked her head into the room to confirm that both parents were gone. She smiled at MacKenzie and shook her head. "Let's wake her up for a minute and get this done, then."

9

There was a sudden uptick in activity. MacKenzie had been keeping her ears pricked, on pins and needles while she wondered how long it would take for the tests to come back so that she would know whether her guess had been right or wrong. They were just blood tests, not ones that required any cultures to be grown or other long, involved processes. Just looking at a blood panel and looking at a single droplet of blood under the microscope. What if the parasite load wasn't large enough for them to see anything in the blood? What if it was a new lab tech who looked at the blood and didn't see anything or didn't know what he was seeing? What if they did a thin smear instead of a thick smear and there just weren't enough parasites for them to make a finding? So many things could go wrong, she didn't dare get her hopes up.

But it started as a murmur at the nursing station outside the door. There were low voices, gradually getting louder and more excited. There were people being paged and walking back and forth at an increased rate. Even Walter and Lisa started to sit up and look back toward the hallway, wondering what was going on.

She hadn't actually expected Dr. Brady to come in himself. She thought that the news would come from one of the nurses, casually mentioning that they had found something new and would be starting a new treatment. But she heard his voice at the nursing station, and it wasn't time for his rounds. She looked over her shoulder, waiting, praying silently that they finally knew what was wrong with Amanda and would be able to treat her and send her home. It was so simple. If it was malaria, they just had to treat the parasites, and she would get better. Of course, she would still have chronic kidney disease and be on anti-rejection drugs, but that was normal for Amanda. MacKenzie just wanted to get back to that normal.

Dr. Brady came in. He was looking at a clipboard, a pair of glasses perched on the end of his nose that MacKenzie hadn't seen him wearing before. Did he not need them the rest of the time? Did he not like the way that they looked on him? Maybe he thought he looked more authoritative with them on and this was one of those times when he needed to convince her parents of the veracity of what he was about to tell them.

He looked over his glasses at MacKenzie and then took them off, as if he'd just remembered he was wearing them and didn't actually want to be seen in them. He folded the arms in and put them into his breast pocket.

"There have been developments," he announced.

Lisa and Walter were both looking at him eagerly, waiting for the details. Finding something was good. Finding something meant that this new condition could be treated.

"Amanda *does* have malaria," Dr. Brady confirmed.

MacKenzie breathed out a sigh of relief. Her parents both looked stunned. They looked from the doctor to MacKenzie and back again, shaking their heads and trying to understand what was going on.

"Malaria? She can't possibly have malaria," Lisa said in disbelief.

"The slides are clear. She does have malaria. I'm not sure how it was missed on the earlier blood tests, but these things do happen. Maybe the parasitic load wasn't high enough to show up before, but it was enough to make Amanda sick, with her compromised immune system. Sometimes we just don't know why it doesn't show up. But now that we know, we can begin to treat."

"You'll put her on ACT?" MacKenzie asked.

Walter glared at her, like she had farted in public or done something else to sully their reputation. How could it be bad that they had figured out what Amanda's mysterious illness was? It means that she could be cured. Treating malaria was fairly simple.

"Yes, we'll start her on ACT and some other helper drugs. She should start to show improvement pretty quickly. It's a good thing that we caught it now. Malaria can be pretty devastating in someone with a compromised immune system. Millions die from malaria every year, and someone like Amanda is particularly susceptible."

"How could this happen?" Walter demanded. "I thought people don't get it here."

"She was out of the country for her transplant?"

Walter's eyes shifted sideways to MacKenzie and then away. His lips pressed tightly together and he didn't answer at first. "She has been out of the country for surgery," he admitted. "But that was a year ago. More than that. How could it just be showing up now? Are you telling me that she had it this whole time and we never knew it?"

"It can be dormant for long periods of time. Years, even. We don't know all of the reasons it hides. But we know what to do once it rears its head. She must have gotten infected when she was out of the country. Where was the surgery performed?"

"On an island," Walter said evasively. "But we were very careful of her exposure to anything that could have harmed her. We went to great lengths. She was never bitten by a mosquito; I can promise you that."

"There are other insects that can carry it. And she might not have even known she was bitten. She has a lot of health issues to be concerned about and might not have noticed a bite. With a compromised immune system, her body might not show the typical reaction. She might not get the usual bump and itching. Those are signs that your body is protecting you against a foreign invader."

"She was indoors at all times. The hospital was very clean. We would never have gotten the surgery done if there was any question of patient care."

"I don't doubt it," Dr. Brady agreed, though there was something in his manner that suggested he wasn't quite as confident of the conditions as Walter. It was beside the point. How his patient had gotten malaria was not as important as treating it and getting her healthy again.

"This is good news, Daddy," MacKenzie said, unable to stand their upset expressions any longer. "It means they can treat her."

He shook his head, scowling. "This is not good news," he argued. "And I was very clear that you were not to talk to the doctors about this and to distract them from their jobs."

"This is their job. They're supposed to find out what she has and treat it. They needed to know that it was malaria, or they couldn't give her the right treatment. I don't understand what you're so upset about. This is good news. This means that they can make Amanda better."

Dr. Brady nodded. "It is good that we figured out what is going on with Amanda at this point. Malaria can be fatal, and for someone like her..." he shook his head. "I want to be sure that she gets the best care possible, and I'm grateful to Miss Kirsch for pointing us in the right direction. I wasn't aware that she had been out of the country for her surgery." He took his glasses out of his pocket again and perched them on his nose to look at the information on the clipboard, flipping back several pages to look for some reference he had previously missed. "This gives the name of a *local* private clinic."

Lisa and Walter exchanged glances.

"It was facilitated by a local," Walter said slowly. "They are the ones who set everything up and supervised her care and all of the arrangements. It's just the surgery itself that is done out of the country. It isn't approved here, so..."

Dr. Brady took off his glasses and tucked them back into his pocket again. "The paperwork should have been filled out properly. You should have made it clear that she had been out of the country. You can't expect us to know when you are lying."

"It wasn't a lie," Walter protested angrily.

"You deliberately misled the staff into thinking that your daughter had not been out of the country. Wherever this private island is where the surgery was performed, you should have told us about it. Not obfuscated it saying that it was performed locally."

Walter clearly intended to intimidate Dr. Brady with his glare, but Dr. Brady wasn't having any of it. "We'll be starting the anti-malaria protocol immediately. You can look forward to your daughter regaining her full health soon."

Lisa put her hand over Walter's, and he kept quiet.

Dr. Brady gave MacKenzie a brief nod before he left, acknowledging her role in the diagnosis. He walked out of the room.

MacKenzie turned to her father. "Why does he think that the surgery Amanda had was a transplant?"

She was greeted with silence from Lisa and Walter. Lisa looked at her ex-husband for guidance, then dropped her eyes and said nothing. MacKenzie stared at the two of them.

"Are you telling me it's true? She had another kidney transplant?"

The silence ticked by. It was Walter who finally broke it. "Your kidney failed," he said finally. "That's not your fault; I don't ever want you thinking that your kidney should have been stronger and lasted longer. It gave her eight really good years."

"I… I don't care that my kidney failed. Why wouldn't you tell me that? Why would you keep something like this a secret from me? Why not tell me what was going on?"

"We thought you would be upset," Lisa said. "We didn't want you blaming yourself. And you couldn't give her another kidney, so there was no reason you had to be told."

"We did what we had to do," Walter said.

"You did what you had to do… I don't understand what that means. Why did she have to go out of the country to have a transplant? And why did it have to be such a big secret?"

"There is a shortage of transplant organs in America," Walter explained. "Other countries do not have the same restrictions and problems that we do. If we waited here, it could have been three or four years before she had the opportunity for a transplant. And in that time… well, you know that even with dialysis, kidney patients don't last forever. We couldn't take the chance that she would die while she was waiting for a transplant. We saw to it that she could get one right away."

"Some people think there is something wrong with going to another country to get a transplant," Lisa contributed. "We didn't want to have to deal with the stigma attached to transplant tourism, so we kept it quiet."

"But there isn't anything wrong with it. It's legal, right?" MacKenzie asked. "This isn't some black-market organ trade."

"You know better than that," Walter snapped. "You know there is no such thing as a black market for transplant organs. You've seen the statements put out by world health organizations. That stuff that you see on TV or hear repeated as an urban legend is just that, urban legend. There is no way that an organization performing black-market transplants could exist." He ticked points off on his fingers. "They need highly-trained medical professionals. This isn't something that can be performed by a regular doctor. They need specialized equipment and modern medical facilities. It would cost millions of dollars to run an organization like that. Maybe billions. There's just no way that it is feasible."

MacKenzie nodded. She had heard statements from the UN or WHO or local regulators assuring the public that there was no black-market organ trade. People didn't have to worry about getting drugged at the bar and having their organs stolen while they were unconscious, left in a bathtub filled with ice to bleed out. Such a crime had never been reported anywhere in the world. Certainly not in the United States.

10

MacKenzie held her breath as the ACT cocktail was started. She knew that nothing was going to happen immediately. No drug was instantaneous, and she wasn't going to be able to see the results right away. Amanda wasn't just going to awaken, sit up, and be her old self again. It would take time. A few hours or days—MacKenzie wasn't sure how long—and they would start to see improvements. But she still couldn't help holding her breath and watching Amanda for some sign that the ACT was working.

The nurse smiled and nodded at them cheerfully. "Well, that should do it, then. Just a matter of waiting for it to have effect now."

They were all there when Amanda woke up. She opened her eyes and stared up at the ceiling. Lisa, her eyes fixed on her younger daughter, was the first to notice. She stood up and leaned over Amanda.

"Hi, sweetie. How are you feeling?"

Amanda stared up at her, not responding immediately. She blinked and made a small movement with her head. Then she nodded a little and licked her lips.

"Mother."

"Yes. How are you doing?"

"Don't feel good."

"No, I guess not. But they're giving you a new drug, they've got it all sorted out now. You'll feel better soon."

"New drug?"

"You have malaria."

Amanda lay there looking up at Lisa, her face still slack.

"What's that?" she asked eventually.

Lisa laughed and smoothed Amanda's hair back from her face. "You pick it up in tropical climates. They think you must have somehow gotten it when you had your surgery."

"When? Back then?"

"It's been dormant until recently. Now it's making you sick with these fevers. But they're giving you the right medication now, so it won't come back."

Amanda nodded and closed her eyes, falling back asleep. Lisa continued to stand over her, stroking her hair and watching her sleep.

"She's looking better, don't you think? I think it's already helping."

Walter looked at her briefly, then back at his Blackberry. "I can't tell, Lisa. But I'm sure she'll be doing better soon."

"She woke up, that's a good sign." Lisa put her hand over Amanda's forehead. "Her fever is down… but of course, it's gone down on its own the last two times too. I just hope this is really the solution." Lisa turned her head to look at MacKenzie. "Whatever made you think of it?"

"Just searching the internet, looking for something that matched."

"Amazing. You really can find anything on the internet, can't you?"

MacKenzie shrugged. "I don't know about anything, but you can find a lot of things."

"Maybe you can find Amanda her next kidney on the internet," Walter grumbled without looking up.

MacKenzie saw her own frown reflected on her mother's face.

"Walter. That's really not appropriate. And I don't like you talking about her needing another kidney. I don't want to..."

"Jinx this one?" Walter gave a chuckle. "But you're not superstitious, are you?"

"What do you know about this kidney?" MacKenzie asked after a while, looking over at Amanda. It seemed unbelievable to her that for the past year, Amanda had had someone else's kidney doing the work of cleaning her blood instead of MacKenzie's, and no one had told her. A stranger's kidney in her sister. And MacKenzie's donated kidney no longer functional. She'd somehow always thought that once Amanda got her kidney, it would work forever. She had never anticipated it failing and needing to be replaced.

Lisa didn't say anything. Walter sat up, stretched, and looked questioningly at MacKenzie. "What do you mean, what do we know about it?"

"I don't know... I mean, do you know anything about the donor? Who it was? Where he or she came from? Was it... a live donor?"

"We have a profile somewhere," Lisa said. "They gave us a picture and a little write-up about her. I thought it was nice that they would do that. Makes you feel a little better about going through with it if you feel like you know the donor. Around here, they still refuse to tell you anything about the donor, afraid that you'll contact the donor's family and make trouble."

"What did they say about her?"

"She was a young woman, thirties. She was... where did it say she was from, Walter, do you remember?"

Walter made a face as he tried to recall details. "Germany, Sweden, somewhere like that. Blond girl. Very pretty."

"From Germany? But the transplant wasn't in Germany."

"No. They make matches all around the world, and you pay to have the donor flown in, pay all of their expenses."

"And that's legal?"

"Why wouldn't it be?"

MacKenzie had an uneasy feeling that her parents would have done anything, quasi-legal or not, to get Amanda her transplant. If it had been completely above-board, then why would they not have told her? She wasn't buying that it was just because they didn't want to break it to her that her donated kidney had failed.

MacKenzie had broken down and bought a couple of paperbacks at the hospital gift store, unable to entertain herself while she sat with Amanda and her parents, but unwilling to go home until she was sure that Amanda was better and wasn't just going to get sick again as soon as she left the room. Visiting with her parents was proving to be impossible, and Lisa didn't want them talking in the room and possibly waking Amanda up. She needed her sleep.

MacKenzie looked up from her book over at Amanda. She had started to snore a little as she slept. MacKenzie listened to her critically. She sounded like she had a bit of a cold. Was she getting something else on top of the malaria because her immune system was so fragile? Or was MacKenzie just worrying too much, jumping to conclusions?

Lisa caught MacKenzie's look and smiled. "Cute," she pronounced. "Like a little puppy snoring away."

MacKenzie smiled at the picture it brought to mind. She went back to reading her book.

But over the next hour, Amanda's breathing got progressively louder, until MacKenzie could no longer ignore it and pretend that she was just making cute noises while she slept. She put down her book and went out to the nursing station.

"Would you look in on Amanda, please? Her breathing is really loud."

The nurse sitting at the desk gave a sigh and hoisted herself to her feet. She went into Amanda's room without any sense of hurry. But she cocked her head as she heard the noise that Amanda was making.

"Sounds like she might have picked up a bit of a cold," she observed.

Lisa nodded. “It figures. You just get one thing under control, and something else pops up.”

The nurse put on her stethoscope and placed the diaphragm on Amanda’s chest. She listened for a minute, moving it around a few times as Amanda breathed steadily in and out.

“She is sounding pretty congested,” she said neutrally. “I’m going to get her on oxygen, and I’ll let the doctor know.”

They watched while she hooked up an oxygen cannula to Amanda’s nose and recorded her observations on the patient chart.

“It’s just a cold, though, right?” Lisa asked.

“I’m not sure. We’ll have the doctor take a look.”

She left the room again. MacKenzie sat back down slowly, looking at her mother. Lisa’s eyes were round, wide with worry. She had been through so many crises with Amanda that she was not going to be reassured by anything MacKenzie said, especially since MacKenzie would only be guessing anyway. MacKenzie bit her tongue to keep from assuring her mother that Amanda would be alright and picked up her paperback. She wasn’t going to read anything else. Not with Amanda breathing so heavily, now on oxygen, with the doctor being paged. They all knew that Amanda’s condition could turn on a dime.

11

Amanda's breathing seemed to be growing faster and more labored. The doctor had not yet put in an appearance, but the nurse had been checking in on her regularly, her mouth a straight, uncommunicative line.

MacKenzie stood up. She didn't know what to do, but she felt like she should be doing something. Lisa apparently felt the same way. She shook Amanda's shoulder to wake her up.

"Amanda? I want you to talk to me, sweetie. Can you tell me if it's hurting? Amanda? Wake up for just a minute, sweetie."

Amanda's eyes opened. Not just slits this time, but wide with alarm. Her gasps became even more panicked. She reached for the oxygen cannula. Lisa grasped her hand so that she couldn't pull the oxygen out.

"They're giving you oxygen, sweetie. It's okay. Just leave it be. They'll make sure you're getting enough air."

Amanda gave a couple of deeper breaths. "Can't... breathe..." Another wrenching breath. "Mommy... can't..."

Lisa smoothed Amanda's hair, trying to quiet her. MacKenzie hurried back out to the nursing station. "Please. She's really bad. She needs help."

This time, the nurse's movements were swift. She came at a run.

She didn't put on her stethoscope, but immediately adjusted the flow of the oxygen. Her fingers went to Amanda's pulse.

"Calm down, Amanda. I want you to try to take long, slow breaths for me. I know you're scared, but it's going to be okay. Let me hear a nice deep breath."

Amanda wasn't able to calm her stentorious breathing. The nurse hovered over her for a moment, trying to calm her. She readjusted the bed, raising the head. It gave MacKenzie a better view of Amanda's panicked expression, which she really didn't want. She tried to look at Amanda calmly rather than turning away and giving away how worried she was.

"Let's get you turned over," the nurse told Amanda, repositioning her arms and legs. "I'm just going to roll you to your front. You might find it easier to breathe that way." Once she got Amanda settled into the new position, without much change in her breathing, she hurried out of the room, calling to other nurses and giving instructions.

In a minute or two, she was back, filling in a young doctor who looked like he'd just been pulled from a nap. He blinked at Amanda, checked her pulse and listened to her breathing, and nodded at what the nurse had done to make her more comfortable. A couple of other nurses wheeled in a gurney, forcing MacKenzie and her parents to abandon their chairs and move out of the way.

"Mom and Dad, we're going to take Amanda to ICU where we can help her with her breathing. Once we've got her stable, we'll bring you up to speed."

Lisa opened her mouth to ask a question, but the doctor wasn't stopping to chat. Amanda was moved to the gurney for transport, and in a minute he and one of the nurses were wheeling her out of the room.

"What's happening?" Lisa demanded. "Somebody tell me what's going on."

The nurses who had stayed behind tried to calm her down. "They're just going to make sure she's getting enough oxygen. They'll take good care of her. Once she's stabilized, you'll be able to see her again."

"But why is she having such trouble breathing? Is it a cold?"

"We can't answer that, ma'am," the other nurse said. "The doctor will talk to you when he can."

The hardest thing was waiting. They had done it many times before with Amanda and her illness, but MacKenzie found it the hardest part. Waiting to find out what she had. Waiting to find out if they could do anything about it. Waiting for a donor. For the transplant. Waiting to see if it would take. Waiting to see if the malaria treatment would work. MacKenzie liked to be in control of things. She hated not being able to direct or predict the outcome.

But Amanda had always pulled through. She was a fighter, and she had always managed to rally and get through whatever life had thrown at her. She wasn't going to be kept down by a chest cold.

MacKenzie tried to focus on her book, but was not getting anywhere. She kept turning pages forward and back and could not pick up the thread of the story. Her mind kept going back to how pale and listless Amanda had been lately. Like something was gone out of her.

It was just the malaria. Once they got her over that, their dynamic, cheerful Amanda would be back again. She'd get the energy and the will to fight off whatever other viruses or infections got to her. She'd be able to keep her new kidney for another ten years. She'd be able to live the life that she had been—a darling of the socialites, her mother's favorite, Daddy's little girl, and MacKenzie's beloved baby. Even if MacKenzie had only been six at the time, she had fed and changed Amanda and considered Amanda to be her own, as much as if she'd been MacKenzie's daughter. She'd always sort of resented the fact that as Amanda's real mother, Lisa had the say in Amanda's medical care and how she was raised. She felt like she should at least have an equal say.

MacKenzie closed her book and held it between her hands, head bowed low, mentally urging Amanda to get better and the doctors to come talk to them and tell them she was okay.

They were shunted from one waiting area to another without

being told why. Without being told how Amanda was doing or when they would be able to see her.

Then, at long last, Dr. Brady was there. He pulled up a chair and sat close to them. He spoke in a careful, measured voice about something called acute respiratory distress syndrome. "It does sometimes occur in malaria cases, even after the malaria has been treated and the infection is reduced or eliminated. It isn't because anybody did anything wrong."

"What is the treatment for this respiratory distress syndrome?" Walter demanded.

"As you saw, giving Amanda oxygen, repositioning her, admitting her to ICU so that she could be put on a ventilator to help her to breathe. Doing everything we could to help her lungs oxygenate her blood."

MacKenzie swallowed. There was a lump in her throat. 'Doing everything they could' made it sound like they were no longer helping Amanda. Like the life-giving measures had failed and been abandoned.

"Is she stable now?" Lisa asked.

Dr. Brady looked at his hands. He took a couple of breaths and then looked at their faces, meeting each of their eyes. Connecting with them like he had been taught to do when delivering bad news.

"We did everything we could for Amanda. But in the end, our best wasn't good enough. I'm sorry to have to inform you that Amanda has passed."

MacKenzie choked. Her eyes burned with tears and a rushing sound filled her ears. She felt like she couldn't breathe herself, like Dr. Brady had just pulled all of the air from the room.

"What?" Lisa said in disbelief, her voice breaking. She looked at Walter. "What? No!"

He put out both arms and enfolded his ex-wife, almost pulling her out of her chair.

"No," Lisa repeated. "It isn't true. He didn't say that. Amanda is going to get better."

Walter held her close and rubbed her back. MacKenzie thought he was sobbing, but that couldn't be true, because her father never cried. Never.

She sat there, beside them and yet separate from them, her stunned brain still trying to take it in and to believe that what the doctor said was true.

12

The rest of the day was lost from MacKenzie's memory. As were many hours and days afterward. She had only spotty recollections of helping Lisa with the obituary and arrangements for the funeral.

Her sister's funeral. Her baby's funeral. They'd had so many close calls with Amanda in the past and she had always pulled through. While MacKenzie had always feared the worst, she had never really believed that Amanda was going to die and she would be left an only child, helping her mother choose the food to serve at the reception following the funeral.

They had to pick out the clothes to dress Amanda in, discussing which were her favorites and which would look best for the open casket viewing. MacKenzie excused herself and went into the bathroom to cry, holding a cold cloth over her eyes afterward to take down the swelling, as if it were important to maintain the fiction that she was strong and holding it all together even with her mother.

Poems on the funeral program. Pallbearers. Seating plans. It was a nightmarish mix of all of the event planning they had done in the past, cruelly twisted into a celebration of what could never be celebrated.

She went home at night alone, wrung out and exhausted, only to cry into her pillow and be unable to sleep for hours. She remembered how irritated she'd been at Roger crying himself to sleep and wished she could take it back. She could have been more compassionate than that.

Her brain was far away from her body during the funeral, graveside, and reception. There was no way she could face all of the sympathetic faces and words if she had to be present and feel her feelings. So she nodded and smiled sad little smiles and shook hands and hugged and received kisses on the cheeks from old, powdered ladies, and pretended that she was accepting their comfort. That it was meaningful for her and made her feel better.

And when it was all done and she again went home alone, she stared at her computer and wanted to know why.

Her parents had been too secretive about the transplant. MacKenzie knew that there was no such thing as a black-market transplant. That there were no organized crime gangs stealing people's organs. That everything was tightly regulated and required highly-trained surgeons and an illegal organ trade was impossible. Everybody said so. All of the authorities.

Then what were her parents hiding?

She started searching for more information. If the industry was tightly regulated, then that meant that there were people breaking the regulations. There would be no rules or laws about how organ donations could be handled if there were not people who were trying to profit from them. And not just the surgeons who were performing the transplants and being paid for their services.

To begin with, all she could find were *those* stories. The urban legends that the regulators talked about. Businessmen in Vegas waking up to find out that they'd been roofied by hookers and had their organs removed while they were unconscious. Full of dramatic details about waking up in a tub full of ice with a note taped to them. Responses from the regulators saying how ridiculous the stories were and how people should not believe or be concerned about them.

But then there were other stories, ones that appeared in small columns in the news. A mother whose son had died in a tragic accident who discovered that some of her son's organs had been removed after he was declared dead, the body cavity repacked with newspaper. Bodies in dumpsters or washed up on the beach that were mysteriously missing organs, attributed to some cannibalistic serial killer. They were harder to find and were always responded to by the authorities who said that people were letting their imaginations get away from them, but MacKenzie made note of them and wondered. The more the regulators objected, the more she wondered what they had to hide. If the stories were ridiculous, then why did they find it necessary to make any defense at all?

She went back to her emails from Amanda and Lisa during the time that they were preparing for Amanda's surgery and scoured them for any details. She had been completely oblivious at the time to the secret they were keeping from her, but now that she knew, she re-examined every word and every sentence for details that they might have let slip or that were intended to hide something.

She wanted to know the truth.

MacKenzie called Dr. Proctor and made an appointment to see him. She tried to make it clear that it wasn't a medical appointment and wasn't a date, but she needed to talk to someone about Amanda, and she wasn't sure who else to call. He'd been kind to her and had put up with her questions in the past. He'd talked to her in the middle of the night about malaria without treating her like she was a child or criticizing her for disturbing her sleep. She felt like she could trust him to help her to separate the lies from the truth.

At first, she made a reservation at her favorite restaurant in Burlington, but then decided she might not want to be seen talking with Dr. Proctor or have friends interrupt her or overhear what she was talking about. It wasn't exactly polite dinner conversation, and she didn't want it getting back to her parents. They had been through enough already, without thinking that she was questioning their decision to take Amanda out of the country for a new kidney.

So instead she arranged to meet with Dr. Proctor at an out-of-the-way sandwich shop. Not a high-end place, not somewhere she had ever been before. Not an up-and-coming new kid on the block that she or her friends thought was going to become the next Starbucks. There were no reservations required, she just made sure that she was there before Dr. Proctor to get them a table so that he wouldn't have to stand around waiting for her.

She waved at him as he stood in the doorway. Not that she was hard to find. There were only a few other patrons there, most of them eating alone while reading the newspaper or a paperback they had brought with them for the purpose. MacKenzie looked around at them, speculating on why they were alone and what kind of quiet lives of desperation they were living. Did any of them have friends or relatives who had been through an organ transplant? They were all working people and she didn't think they would be able to afford the money it took to get such a procedure. Organs were supposed to be free, but like any other medical service in the USA, the procedure and stay at the hospital were not. And the working class certainly wouldn't have the resources to go to some island in the South Pacific to get a kidney from some donor flown in from Germany.

"MacKenzie, how are you doing?" Dr. Proctor held her hand for a few seconds longer after shaking it, looking into her face and inquiring in a tone that imparted that he really did want to know how she was handling Amanda's loss; he wasn't just looking for a social "fine, thanks."

She gave his hand a squeeze back, then pulled away. "I don't know. It's difficult. In spite of how sick she always was, I wasn't really prepared to lose her."

Dr. Proctor nodded sympathetically, and they both drifted up to the sandwich counter to place their orders. They sat back down at MacKenzie's table.

"And how are your parents? I have been worried about Lisa. So much of her life was about Amanda and taking care of her, I'm worried about what she'll do now with all of that extra time on her hands."

"She's been doing surprisingly well," MacKenzie admitted. Maybe that was part of what was bothering her. Seeing her mother throw herself into charities work and busy herself with other people's causes so soon after the funeral felt wrong to her. What did MacKenzie expect? Did she expect Lisa to lock herself at home in mourning and to wear black for five years? Lisa had always been social, had always been involved in charitable causes. She needed something to fill the void, and it hadn't taken her long to find it. MacKenzie, meanwhile, didn't feel like going out to any of the events she had previously committed to, let alone anything new. She didn't want to hear about anyone else's suffering and the ills and injustices of the world. She just wanted to think about Amanda. And she didn't want to think about Amanda. "I think she'll be okay. As long as she has something to do, it seems like she'll be happy. I mean, not happy happy, but… okay. Able to go on."

Dr. Proctor nodded. He was an older man. When MacKenzie had been little, she had thought him old, but looking at him with the eyes of an adult, she realized that he wasn't as ancient as she had once thought. Yes, he was balding, with only a tonsure of white hair left, and he wore wire frame glasses when he was reading or doing close work, but he probably wasn't older than sixty, which meant that when she was a child and he used to come to the house to see one of her parents or look in on Amanda, he would only have been in his forties. That didn't seem quite as old to her as it once had. Where would she be when she was forty? Would she have finally decided what it was that she wanted to do with her life? Would she be a clone of Lisa, working with her charities? Would she be political like her father, trying to right the wrongs of the world, or at least the state? Or would she have her own passion, something completely different that she wasn't even aware of yet?

"Lisa is a strong woman. She can be driven. As long as she is still working with her causes… I imagine she'll be able to hold it together."

MacKenzie took a drink of her water. She noticed that Dr.

Proctor didn't ask about her father. Was that just because he was a man, and men were supposed to stuff their feelings, expected to go on with and bury themselves in their work, even if they had just lost a daughter? It was expected that he wouldn't feel it as keenly as Lisa, who had been by Amanda's side daily?

"I guess you're probably wondering why I wanted to meet with you today."

He studied her. "I did wonder… I thought maybe you wanted some advice on school. What program to pursue."

MacKenzie was surprised. She was done with school. School had always bored her, and she hadn't found anything she was interested enough in to pursue for another year, let alone another degree.

"No, actually. I wanted to talk to you about Amanda."

"She wasn't my patient. I talked to your mother sometimes when she was wondering about whether to take Amanda to the hospital or to pursue one course of treatment or another, but I was just a sounding-board. Not her physician."

"That's okay. You might be able to help me out more that way anyway. If she was your patient, you wouldn't be able to talk about her, would you?"

He smiled and nodded. "You're right about that. As a friend of the family, I'm not bound to any kind of confidentiality. If she was my patient… well, I'd love to help you, but there are standards of confidentiality that even I have to follow."

"How would I get her records? I mean, I don't know if I qualify as next of kin, and if I'd be able to get anything if I asked. Could I?"

"That would probably fall to your parents. What is it you're looking for?"

"I don't know." MacKenzie studied a chip in one of her nails, hiding from his gaze. A woman behind the counter brought their sandwiches around to them, and she and Dr. Proctor took a few initial bites, exclaiming on how fresh the ingredients were and how the shop was a diamond in the rough, just waiting to be discovered.

"I want to know more about Amanda's transplant," MacKenzie explained. "I want to know what happened. If something went wrong."

He raised his brows. "Well, you were there, my dear. You were part of all of that."

"No, not that transplant. The one a year ago."

He stopped with his mouth open, about to take another bite. Then he put his sandwich down on the plate and looked at her, frowning. "Her transplant a year ago?"

"You didn't know?"

He shook his head. He ate a slice of pickle, considering. "Like I said, I wasn't her physician. There's no reason for them to tell me about a second transplant."

"They didn't tell me about it either."

He frowned. For a few minutes, they ate in silence. MacKenzie watched Dr. Proctor covertly, trying to be patient and not look like she was hovering over him, waiting for his answer. Even though she was.

"How could they keep a transplant from you? You would have known she was in the hospital. It's a pretty big thing. A complicated procedure with a lot of hospital time. I'm sure you would have been there, waiting to know the outcome. Weren't you? Was that when you were in Europe?"

"No. I was home. They told me that she was having surgery to try to improve her kidney function. Some new procedure. They never told me it was a transplant."

"Why would that be a secret?"

"That's what I want to know. I think… I know that there's not really a black market for organ procurement, but I wonder whether it was something… a little bit shady." She grimaced. "I don't even want to say that. It all sounds so dramatic, and I'm sure everything was just routine, but…"

Dr. Proctor didn't say anything. Most notably, he didn't deny that there was a black-market trade in organs. He waited for MacKenzie to go on.

"Can you think of any reason they would keep it quiet?" MacKenzie asked.

Maybe it was a new trend. Reducing stress on the patient by not telling the public that they were going through a transplant. Maybe transplantation was getting some kind of social stigma, some ghoulish, Frankenstein's monster reputation. Multiple organ donations could be seen as something cannibalistic. Or it could be something to do with social standing, something that only the ultra-privileged could take part in, and Lisa and Walter had wanted to keep it quiet so that their friends or Amanda's friends wouldn't think that she was being greedy or taking more than her share.

"I'm afraid I would have the same concerns as you," Dr. Proctor admitted. "I would want to know whether everything was aboveboard. It seems very odd that they would keep it quiet, at a time when Amanda needed extra support."

"Yeah." MacKenzie picked at the crust of her sandwich. Should she have asked for them to cut the crust off? Was that something that only a diva would do? Or was it socially acceptable in a specialty sandwich shop? "I would have been there, if they had let me. I could have gone with everybody to this clinic, wherever it was. But they said that they were supposed to limit Amanda's exposure to possible pathogens, that they didn't want anyone extra around. Even Mother and Daddy had to stay in a separate housing facility. They weren't allowed to stay with her in her room, like they do here."

"Someone whose immunity is suppressed is very susceptible to every little thing."

"Right. So that could have been legitimate. Or... it might have just been an excuse to keep me out of it. But why would they want to keep me out of it? I was family. I was Amanda's sister. Even if they didn't want a whole lot of people visiting and possibly infecting her, I wasn't a whole lot of people... just one. Just one more person. They could have at least let me visit her. Or wave at her through the glass. Something..."

"You're searching for answers, but there may not be any logical answers. We do what seems best at the time, and sometimes we make wrong decisions, based on fear or someone's advice at the time."

"I guess." MacKenzie motioned to one of the sandwich shop workers, indicating her glass, and the man drifted over to refill it from a glass jug, then walked away again.

"Can I ask... I didn't hear the details of what it actually was that

Amanda died from," Dr. Proctor said slowly. "Did she reject the kidney?"

MacKenzie shook her head. She was happy to discuss the medical details she knew rather than why her parents had kept the transplant a secret.

"She did have malaria. They did the tests like you said and found it, and they put her on the anti-malaria drugs, but she got something called acute respiratory distress syndrome."

Dr. Proctor nodded his understanding. "Nasty thing, ARDS. Very dangerous, very difficult to reverse once it has started."

"They did everything they could, I guess, but she still couldn't get enough oxygen."

"Even when they are able to save the patient, it is very damaging. She probably would never have been off of supplemental oxygen again."

MacKenzie pictured Amanda having to lug an oxygen canister everywhere she went.

Her lively, vibrant sister would not have liked that.

13

Mother, could I help you by going through Amanda's things?" MacKenzie asked, segueing from the discussion of upcoming events over lobster bisque at the house. "I could sort through what should be donated and what we want to keep, go through her papers to see what the accountants need for her final tax filing, that kind of thing."

Lisa scratched at an invisible mark on her spoon. "I can do that, dear. You really don't need to do that. I'll get to it."

"I'd like to help, and that's something I could do."

"I don't like the thought of you doing it by yourself. We could do it together," there was a moment of hesitation, "when I'm ready."

MacKenzie was glad to see that she was correct and that it was something her mother did not really want to do. "I can do it," she repeated. "I want to. And I can do it while you're out doing something else, so you don't have to be around and thinking about it."

Lisa stirred her bisque. "You don't want to do that all by yourself. It's a big job."

"What else do I have to do?"

"There's the big cancer fundraiser at the Main Street Landing. You said that you would help out with it." This had already been repeated several times over the previous few days, and MacKenzie had already made it clear that she was not going.

"I can't do that right now. I told you that. And I already called them to beg off. They didn't mind. They know about Amanda, so they were very understanding."

"You know I don't like you not following through on your obligations like that. That's not the way you were raised."

"Would you be understanding if one of your volunteers had just lost a family member and said she was not up to doing an event?"

"Of course, but that's not the point."

"You want to lose yourself in good works. I understand that. But I don't feel the same way. I want to think about Amanda. I want to do something for her, and for you."

Lisa nodded slowly and finally had another spoonful of her bisque. "You are so like your father."

MacKenzie was surprised. "Like Daddy?"

Walter had already gone back to his apartment in Montpelier. MacKenzie thought that, like Lisa, he just wanted to get on with his life and block out the pain.

"He's a much more passionate person than I am," Lisa explained. "He feels things so much more deeply. I know he is hurting. And he wants to do something in Amanda's memory. Something that will show what she meant to him."

"Like what?"

"I don't know. He doesn't have much to say. But I know him. When you've been married to someone for thirty years—" she stopped herself, "—even if you've been divorced for a couple of years —you understand each other on another level. One that doesn't always require words. I know him inside. What he doesn't say."

Someday, maybe MacKenzie would have a relationship like that. Someone that she could get to know on a deeper level, not just the superficial relationships she had with the men in her life so far. Someone who had passions, and wasn't just a playboy, looking for the next opportunity for a good time or to get his hands on her trust fund. She needed to get to know a man who, like her father, had a passion for the causes he was involved with.

"So, when would be a good time for me to work on Amanda's things? Are you out tomorrow?"

"For the half-marathon. Yes. They start quite early," she advised, giving MacKenzie an amused look, "And then I'll be booked up at least until six o'clock. There is a lot to go through, but if you make an early start, you might be able to get most of it done by then."

An early morning. Not just early for MacKenzie, forever sleeping the morning away, but early even for regular people. The kind of people who got up before dawn to run in the cold. MacKenzie shuddered.

"Okay. I'll plan to be up with the birds tomorrow."

It wasn't very ladylike to snort at one's daughter, but that didn't stop Lisa.

MacKenzie didn't manage to get to the family home quite as early as she had planned, but she was still there before the staff, which was quite good for her. She went up the stairs to Amanda's room. It was the house she had grown up in, so she felt perfectly comfortable there, not like she was intruding on someone else's privacy.

But she wasn't prepared for the flood of emotions and memories to hit her when she opened Amanda's door. It was the room that Amanda had had when she and MacKenzie were growing up. The room that she had started in as a baby lying in a crib that was hard for MacKenzie to reach into, because she was still a child herself and the sides were tall.

She could remember what the room had looked like then, blue with fluffy white clouds painted on the walls, white furniture, colorful mobiles and pictures, and a rocking chair in the corner where she could sit and give her baby a bottle and rock her just like a grown up.

Over the years, the decorations and the furniture had changed. A toddler bed and then a grown-up bed. Playing on the floor with Amanda and her dolls, having tea parties and fundraising events and whatever else the two of them had done to mimic their own mother's life.

It was the same bedroom as had been the sick room when Amanda was doing poorly, trapped by her disease and not able to go out to the dances and dates and other things that the kids her age were doing. The room where they had exchanged stories and secrets and grown closer and closer together as sisters.

And then Amanda as an adult. But just barely. She had been hardly more than a child and she was taken away from them. It was unfair that she wasn't allowed to get older and marry and have babies and a family of her own. She should have been allowed to have her own family. She had wanted them so much. Even when they were little, she had talked about being a mommy. She had always planned to have a dozen children and to spoil them rotten and raise them to become doctors and presidents. MacKenzie's chest hurt as she looked around the little room. Amanda would never return there. They would never share secrets and girl talk there again.

MacKenzie had thought that going through Amanda's things would be pretty easy. She had collected a lot over the year, hanging on to possessions when her grip on life itself was so tenuous. She had tried to live out her whole life in those few short years, trying everything, living life fully. MacKenzie had pictured herself sorting everything efficiently into boxes. These one for charity, these ones for keepsakes. These ones just junk to be disposed of. But it wasn't going to be that easy. Not by a long shot.

She sat down on the end of Amanda's bed and closed her eyes. She felt the room around her. Amanda was everywhere. Her smell and sense of style permeated the room. The memories and the grief were almost overwhelming.

She allowed herself thirty breaths. Thirty breaths to feel the grief and to move on and get herself under control. It wasn't long. Then she forced herself to get to her feet and go to Amanda's closet.

The rod was jammed with clothes of every color and description. MacKenzie looked over them with an unemotional eye. She picked out a few of Amanda's favorite things and laid them on the bed, smoothing out the wrinkles and tidying them up. The rest of the clothes could go. She descended to the storerooms and looked around for boxes. There were a few that seemed to be made for the job, so she carried them back upstairs and set them on the floor and removed all of the clothing that remained in the closet. It looked very empty, but it was easier to focus on what else needed to be organized.

Most of Amanda's old toys had been packed away in boxes. Amanda didn't want to let anything go and had insisted that she might want them for her own children. MacKenzie just piled the boxes to the side. The ones that had really been precious to Amanda were already out on her shelves. MacKenzie left them there.

The thing that she had really wanted to do was to look at Amanda's papers. There were a few journals and art portfolios in the closet. There were files in the drawer of her writing desk. And there was a computer.

MacKenzie sat down to go through them.

14

She felt like she was invading Amanda's privacy by opening up the journals. But Amanda was gone, and who were the journals for now that she was gone? She didn't have any children to pass them on to. MacKenzie was her family. MacKenzie was her sister, and that was who Amanda would have wanted to have the journals. Still, she felt like a peeper opening them up.

She skimmed through the entries, looking at the dates and trying to find the pages that covered the time when Amanda had her last transplant. She was sure that Amanda would not have gone on a trip without bringing a journal along with her. She always had a book near her side to make notes in when she didn't have the energy to do anything else.

She tried not to look for her own name. She didn't want to hear that Amanda had been disappointed with her or that she'd held bitter feelings toward her able-bodied sister. The one who could do whatever she wanted without ever being slowed down by a body that was constantly sick and tired. Amanda had spent so much time in the hospital and MacKenzie had continued to go to parties and events and to volunteer for fundraisers that her sister was too sick to attend even as an honored guest.

MacKenzie found a series of entries leading up to the secret transplant. Amanda was excited and scared, hoping that things would turn out alright but terrified of what conditions she would find and whether she would catch an infection or reject the stranger's organ. They had been given glossy brochures showing pictures of the spotless, shining hospital. White floors and mint green walls, and windows that looked out onto a gleaming white beach and azure blue sea.

"I can't believe that I'm going there for a kidney," Amanda's voice spoke to her from the pages. "It looks like a spa as much as a hospital. Somewhere you go on vacation and relax where everybody dotes on you and spoils you with massages and five-star meals. It is a beautiful place. I really couldn't ask for more."

Amanda had read the profile of her kidney donor that her mother had mentioned, the young woman who was coming from Germany (not Sweden) to give Amanda the gift of life. She was a young person with an amazing giving heart. "Or a giving kidney." Amanda's words brought a giggle from MacKenzie's lips. There was a margin doodle of a kidney, fat and red and healthy looking. Amanda's new kidney, to replace the one that MacKenzie had given her, which had failed before it should have. MacKenzie had been so wrapped up in her own life that she hadn't even known how poorly Amanda had been doing. MacKenzie should have known. She should have been aware that her baby sister was again sitting for hours in the hospital beside a machine, just so she could survive from one week to the next.

Her eyes were caught by her own name on the page. "It's so hard not to talk about it with MacKenzie. But Mother says she would worry too much, and that it's best to just let her live her own life. She doesn't need to know that the graft failed. Pretty soon I'll have a brand-new kidney and she'll never know the difference. But I do wish she could come. It won't be the same without her there."

MacKenzie closed her eyes and let herself remember when they had been in the hospital before, recovering from the donation. MacKenzie couldn't believe how sore she was. It looked so simple on the videos and in the written descriptions. Just open her up, gently remove the kidney, pass it to the team working on Amanda, suture the dead-end vessels, and sew MacKenzie up again. The work done on Amanda's side was much more complicated, making sure that all of the vessels and ducts were connected together so that she would have good blood flow and the kidney could do its job.

But MacKenzie had felt like they had thrown her down the stairs. She was convinced the first few days that they must have dropped her when transferring her from the gurney to her bed. Every movement hurt. The anesthesia had made her throw up and every time she retched, it hurt like someone was trying to rip the missing kidney from her body with their bare hands. Or claws. Amanda had seemed to recover from it more quickly than MacKenzie, in spite of all of the drugs they had to give her to make sure she didn't reject the organ.

"We'll get Mother to read to us when she comes," Amanda promised, when MacKenzie was bored to tears, but too sore and scatterbrained to do anything about it. Even television seemed too difficult, her brain sluggish after the procedure, either because of the anesthesia or because her body was in shock and trying to heal, stealing blood and life force from her brain. "Only we'll get her to read Cosmo instead of Trixie Belden."

MacKenzie remembered cuddling with Amanda at bedtime while Lisa read to them, trying to find books that would entertain them both in spite of the six-year gap in their ages. The adventures of the girl sleuth Trixie Belden had been a good choice. MacKenzie liked her better than Nancy Drew, but could never seem to solve the mystery before the solution was presented.

After the transplant, Lisa had read to them, sitting between their two beds and first holding MacKenzie's hand and stroking her hair while she read, and then switching to Amanda.

"My two sweet girls. I'm so proud of both of you."

MacKenzie put Amanda's journals to the side and went to her desk. She opened the file drawer and looked through the file folders neatly labeled in Amanda's careful, round printing. It would be easy to pull out what the accountant would need for Amanda's terminal tax return. There was also a file labeled "Will" and it took only a glance to see that it was, in fact, Amanda's last will and testament. MacKenzie didn't take it out to look at it. She knew that Amanda didn't have any of her own wealth. She had been supported by a trust fund, like Amanda, but that trust had ended when she died and wasn't hers to give to anyone else. The only thing that Amanda had to divide up were her personal effects. She didn't even have her own car. MacKenzie promised herself that she would look at the will before throwing anything out. She didn't want to get rid of any personal items that Amanda had meant for someone else.

She continued to look through the files, and she found a series of thin folders that appeared to pertain to Amanda's medical care. She drew them out and laid them on the desk.

Forsberg Transplant Care Clinic.

MacKenzie opened the folder and saw the glossy brochure that Amanda had referred to. Thick, shiny pages showing the beautiful, spa-like hospital where Amanda would get her new kidney. It did look like paradise. Somewhere that MacKenzie might consider taking a vacation if she wanted to pamper herself rather than getting away from all of the suffocating attention she already faced in her day-to-day life. MacKenzie's eyes skimmed over the flowery description of the transplant hospital. She turned the pages, looking for information on the doctors and the owners of the clinic. There was an office in New Jersey. The names she did find were unfamiliar to her.

Eventually, she turned the advertising brochure over to look at the other documents in the folder. Instructions on the logistics of going to the island. Travel documents needed, what to pack, what procedure to follow once Amanda got there. Everything was very detailed and orderly, reassuring the reader that they knew what they were doing and were professional and cared about the patient's health. She had at first pictured a third-world shack with flies buzzing around, lines of people waiting, and an inexperienced backwoods doctor butchering the patients, but the brochure and other documents were reassuring. It was a professionally-run organization, not just a fly-by-night scam job.

She leafed through the other documents in the folder and found a page about the donor.

Her name was given as Katrina. No last name, because the organ donation industry didn't give identifying information for donors. Apparently not even foreign transplants that took place on remote tropical islands. There was a handwritten form filled in with her answers to questions about her background, family, and why she wanted to donate an organ to a stranger she would never meet. Clipped to the front of it was a photograph. A beautiful blond young woman smiling at the camera. She exuded health and vitality and the unselfish love she had for the recipient of her organ donation.

On one hand, MacKenzie could understand why the woman would do what she had done. After all, MacKenzie had done the same thing herself. But on the other, MacKenzie hadn't been donating to a stranger. She had been giving life to her sister. It wasn't unselfish. It wasn't anonymous. She didn't travel halfway around the world to a third-world country to give up a piece of herself. The recovery from donation had not been easy or without complications, and she was sure that Katrina must have been given the same warnings about the hazards as MacKenzie had. It could fail. She could get an infection. She could react to the anesthesia. There was a risk that she would die while trying to give life to her sister, and there was the possibility that it wouldn't even take, but instead Amanda's body would simply reject it as a foreign object and refuse to support it.

It had all worked out in the end, as had Amanda's second transplant. And they owed it all to a stranger named Katrina.

15

MacKenzie decided to takethe files on the transplant home with her. She could examine them in more detail there, and look up the various doctors and contacts that she could find associated with the clinic on Google. No one would miss the papers. They weren't needed for anything else now that Amanda was gone. She poked through the other files for anything else that might be helpful. Then there was Amanda's computer.

It was a laptop, the only thing that was practical for Amanda, since she spent so much time in bed and in the hospital. With a laptop computer, she could entertain herself wherever she was.

MacKenzie booted it up. She typed her own name into the password box and the Windows desktop arranged itself on the screen. Colorful icons for a number of games were arranged in neat columns. Amanda had a lot of time to while away, and she didn't always have the energy to put into anything requiring brainpower. MacKenzie opened the File Explorer and looked through the folders. Some more journal entries, little bits of poetry, notes that Amanda had written to remind herself of upcoming events. Lists of things to do when she got home or things that she wanted Lisa to buy for her or bring her from home when she was in the hospital.

A little slice of her life.

When MacKenzie left for the day, everything was neatly arranged and awaiting Lisa's return. Boxes were labeled. The files that were needed for Amanda's estate were laid out on the desk. Amanda's favorite things were still on the shelves and in the closet, but ninety-five percent of her possessions were ready to be donated or otherwise disposed of. Lisa could decide what she wanted to do with the rest in due time.

MacKenzie took the files with her. And Amanda's computer. Her mother wasn't going to use it, after all. No one had any use for it, and it was not mentioned in Amanda's will. So MacKenzie might as well take it and get some use out of it. She could play solitaire in bed and remember Amanda.

She said goodbye to the kitchen and cleaning staff that she passed on her way out of the house and drove herself back to her apartment.

It seemed cold and lonely after being in the warm, bustling house that she had grown up in. She needed some company, and she didn't really care who it was.

Well, not Roger. Other than that, pretty much anyone would do.

MacKenzie awoke to her ringing phone. At first, she was thrown back to the period of time before Amanda's death, back before the malaria attacks, and for a blissful instant she didn't remember what had happened since. But never again would it be her mother calling to let her know that they were on their way to the hospital, or asking whether MacKenzie would have time to meet with Amanda at the park or some other place where she could visit and get some time outside the house without it being too taxing on her system. MacKenzie had always said yes.

At least she had that. She didn't have to face the guilt of having turned Amanda away and pursued other occupations, interests, or relationships. She had always come to the call to support Amanda.

She had always been there when Amanda asked for her, and many times when she hadn't.

At least she had that.

MacKenzie lay there for a minute without moving, trying to get back that instant of comfortable innocence before she had remembered Amanda's death. She reached over to her bedside table and found the phone handset resting in the base where it belonged. She picked it up and pressed the button to answer it.

"Hello?"

"MacKenzie." Her mother. Who else would be calling her so early in the morning? All of her friends knew she didn't get up before noon if she could help it. There was a note of worry in Lisa's voice. A little bit of panic that MacKenzie didn't quite understand. Amanda was dead, after all. Lisa couldn't be worrying about her. And any concerns over Amanda's estate could wait. She didn't need to rush into anything. "I wanted to thank you for doing all of that work in cleaning out Amanda's room."

For that, Lisa needed to wake her up? But MacKenzie knew that wasn't the reason. This was just the small talk. The real request would come after. When they were both comfortable.

"You're welcome. I'm just glad there was something I could do for you."

"It was a big help."

"Good, I'm glad."

"There's just one thing, MacKenzie. There were some files missing…"

"Files?"

"Some medical files. Did you take those with you?"

MacKenzie considered her answer. Her brain was still groggy with sleep, but she sensed the worry behind Lisa's words. Almost panic. Why would she be panicking about MacKenzie taking Amanda's medical files?

"I picked some stuff up," she admitted slowly, feeling her way through the explanation. "Just some stuff about the clinic that she went to. For the second transplant. I wanted to learn a little bit more about them. We really should consider making a donation to them in Amanda's name, don't you think?"

"What? Yes, of course, that's certainly something to consider. I need you to bring those files back, MacKenzie. That's personal medical information of Amanda's and it really shouldn't be out of our hands."

"Why not? It isn't like she needs it anymore. I just wanted to learn more about what happened. I don't understand why you kept it a secret from me."

"It wasn't a secret; we just didn't want to upset you."

"Then why won't you talk about it now?"

"We thought it would give her another ten years. Now it seems like... what was the point? If you're right and she was bitten by a mosquito because we took her to that clinic... I just can't talk about it, MacKenzie. It's too upsetting. But I need those files back."

"Why? Why do you need them?"

"There is information in there that the accountant will need. Those expenses need to be documented. We put a lot of money into that trip and the surgery. He needs all of those files to justify it."

MacKenzie sighed. She was too tired and full of grief to find any argument. She hadn't thought that anyone would miss the files. But in truth, she didn't have any right to them and if her parents needed them, she had no excuse not to give them back. "Okay. I'll drop them by later today."

"I need them right away."

"I need a few more hours of sleep. Then I'll bring them by."

There were a few seconds of silence from Lisa. "Fine. Please make sure you bring them today. Don't forget."

MacKenzie grunted. "Love you, Mother. I'll see you later."

She ended the call. Beside her, the covers stirred as the man next to her shifted his weight and turned toward her.

"MacKenzie."

"What?"

Christopher Marsh cleared a raspy throat. "Everything okay?"

MacKenzie put the handset into the base and turned to cuddle up against his warm body. "Yeah. It's fine."

"That Lady Cole-Kirsch?"

"Yes. Just need to take her some papers later today."

"You don't need to do it now?"

"No."

"Good." He pulled her closer, and she snuggled her face against the warm smooth skin in the hollow of his neck. He'd been a lot more fun than Roger Milford. Considerate too. A winning combination. She closed her eyes and breathed in his scent, seeking the return of sleep.

It was late when she woke up, and she knew it. She had planned to be up by noon, but without having an alarm set, and warm and cozy in bed with Christopher, she had just kept sleeping. She could still get the files back before Lisa got home from her regular spa appointment, but MacKenzie had wanted to copy them before she returned them. It was the best of both worlds. Lisa could have the files back right away for her accountant, but MacKenzie could still review them at her leisure and refer back to anything she needed to later on down the line as her research progressed.

"Where can I get something photocopied quickly?" she asked Christopher as he sat down on the couch to tie his shoes.

"Library is always a possibility. There's one not too far away from here."

MacKenzie remembered the dim library she had used while in high school and the monstrous old photocopiers there. She shook her head. She'd be there all day if she were forced to use one of those persnickety old machines. She'd end up with the librarian breathing down her back and people waiting for her, and some of her copies were bound to get jammed up in the machine, which became a privacy risk if she needed someone to help her to clear them or if she threw them in the garbage there.

"No?" Christopher considered. "What about a business services store? Kinko's, UPS, something like that."

"Yeah. They'd be quick and have state-of-the-art equipment, wouldn't they? In and out of there in a few minutes…"

"Sure. They want to get people through as quickly as they can, they've always got top-line machines."

"That's what I'll do, then." MacKenzie hauled out the Yellow Pages directory and flipped through the ads for the business services stores, looking for one that was close to her, or at least between her apartment and the family home.

She paused for a moment as she thought about the family home. The only person who was left there was Lisa, bouncing around the empty house like she was in a pinball machine. Walter was no longer there. Amanda was gone. MacKenzie had moved out early on. So now it was just Lisa and the staff in that big, empty house. Did Lisa mind? She must feel the loneliness of it. Or maybe if she worked hard enough, it would eat up the time and she would just go to bed exhausted at the end of the day, unable to worry about anything because she passed out as soon as her head hit the pillow.

"Do you think she's lonely?" she asked Christopher.

"Who?"

"My mother."

He pulled his winter coat on thoughtfully. "Well… I would imagine so. With your dad out of town so much…"

"He's not living there anymore."

"Not at all?" Christopher considered it. "Sounds like it might be a good time for her to start seeing someone."

"A therapist?"

"No… a date." He gave her a knowing smile. "Having a man around can be very comforting when you are lonely, you know."

She gave him a little swat as he headed toward the door. He turned to pull her into a bear hug, lifted her off her feet for a moment, then gave her a vigorous kiss.

"Give me a call next time you're feeling lonely, Mistress Kirsch."

He gave her another quick squeeze, and then he was gone. MacKenzie stood there with a stupid, sloppy grin on her face for a minute, still feeling the tingle of his touch, then gathered together the files to take back to Lisa.

16

MacKenzie left her copy of Amanda's files in her car and took the originals into the house to give to her mother. She had not managed to beat Lisa back to the house after her spa appointment, and Lisa was apparently watching for her arrival. She was at the door to let MacKenzie in even before she got up the front walkway.

She didn't look well and relaxed after her spa treatment. She was usually pink and happy after an appointment, but she didn't look like any of that. Her face seemed dry and mapped with lines that hadn't been there before. She was pale, almost ashen in appearance. MacKenzie hadn't seen her look so bad since Amanda's death. She'd always looked presentable and healthy and as if she were in control of everything. Maybe it was just because she had been wearing makeup before, but it had been cleaned off during her spa treatment and she hadn't yet reapplied it, letting her pores breathe for a while. Maybe this was what she had looked like under the layers of makeup ever since Amanda had gone back into the hospital.

"Mother." MacKenzie put one arm around her, the one that was not holding a stack of file folders. "Are you okay?" She bussed Lisa's cheek. "You look like… you've had a rough day."

Lisa looked at her for a minute as if she didn't know what to say at first. Then she shook her head. "No, it's been fine. I just wanted to make sure that you got everything back to me today."

"You look worried. Did you really think that I wouldn't?"

Lisa used both hands to pull the files from MacKenzie's grasp. "Thank goodness. I'll just go put these away."

She turned and walked away from MacKenzie, hurrying across the front hall and up the grand staircase toward the bedrooms. MacKenzie stood watching her, stunned by Lisa's brusque manner. It would appear that she had, in fact, believed that MacKenzie would not bring the files back. Why? Was she so concerned about whatever deductions the accountant would be able to claim on the terminal tax return? Was she worried about having to pay? There was plenty of money left in the trust account. So why was Lisa so concerned about the money?

Lisa returned a few minutes later, running her hands down the front of her skirt. MacKenzie wasn't sure whether her was smoothing out wrinkles in the skirt or wiping something off of her hands. Lisa still seemed stressed, but she made an attempt at natural conversation.

"Are you able to stay for a visit? Not off to anything right away?"

MacKenzie looked back toward her car. She actually wanted to spend some more time going through the copies of Amanda's files. Lisa's behavior was making her more curious about what exactly had happened.

"Why don't we have a drink?" she suggested, motioning to the sitting room off of the hall, where there was a well-stocked sideboard.

Lisa wasn't much of a drinker, but she acquiesced. "Yes, certainly."

It wasn't yet five o'clock, the generally accepted hour for drinking to begin. And Lisa always observed the five o'clock rule. MacKenzie made no comment on this. It would be rude to point it out, especially when it was so obvious that Lisa was worried about something. They sat down in the sitting room after pouring out their preferred drinks.

They didn't talk about Amanda or the files.

MacKenzie did not tell her mother that she was flying to New Jersey to check out the transplant clinic. After seeing her nearly melt down over the files, she wasn't about to tempt fate by offering the information that she was digging deeper into the clinic to satisfy herself that everything was being done honestly and aboveboard. If they were everything they appeared to be on the surface, maybe she could put it to bed and stop worrying about it. But until she saw it for herself, she just wasn't sure that she was going to be able to sleep at night. She kept seeing Amanda in her mind, gasping for breath, so pale and exhausted from the recurring fevers. Could they have avoided that? Were there warning signs that Lisa and Walter should have seen and not jumped into the foreign transplant with both feet? They had wanted Amanda to be better and to have good quality of life, but had they moved too quickly and been too eager to take what appeared to be a good solution? They could afford to throw whatever money they needed to at the problem, jumping ahead of those who were patiently waiting in line in the US. Unethical, maybe, but they obviously hadn't believed it to be illegal or dangerous.

A year later, Amanda was dead, when she should have had more time.

But who could predict what twists and turns her health would take? It wasn't like her path had ever been particularly straight and predictable.

It was a ninety-minute flight, which gave her time to look through the files to get everything cemented into her memory. She needed to be able to talk like she had been aware of everything that was going on at the time it had happened, not like she was a latecomer, just catching up on it now.

She was good at social talk. She was sure she could pull it off.

She realized looking at the time that she wasn't going to be able to get to the clinic before it closed, so she was going to have to find a hotel and the sundries that she needed for an overnight stay, and then visit the clinic the next day when there was plenty of time to talk to the bigwigs, get a tour, and whatever else she could convince them to do. She was going to be a big fish, and she was sure that they were not above being persuaded by the promise of a large endowment.

Not knowing a lot of people in New Jersey, she was going to have a lonely night. She couldn't think of anyone she could call on the spur of the moment like she could in Burlington. And however much she didn't want to have to face the darkness alone, she wasn't going to stoop to picking up strangers in a strange town.

She went to bed early, got very little sleep, and rose at a decent hour to get herself ready for her appearance. She was going to use every devious trick she knew to get their attention and convince them that she was the answer to their fundraising prayers. Even if they didn't know that they needed any more funding, she was going to convince them that they did.

She pulled up in front of the clinic in a shiny black town car with a uniformed chauffeur. They didn't have any way of knowing that he was just an hourly hire rather than her own personal driver. She waited while he walked around the car to open the door for her. MacKenzie slid gracefully out of the big car and minced her way toward the big front doors of the Forsberg clinic. It was a nice place, but she could make it better. Classier. Serving an even more prestigious clientele. She fixed these goals in her mind and stopped at the door, waiting for either her chauffeur or one of the clinic's staff to jump in and open it for her. A receptionist stared at her for a moment in consternation, then jumped up and trotted around her desk to get to the front doors and open them for MacKenzie. MacKenzie deigned to nod and smile at her. She swept the waiting room with a glance and did not choose to sit down. Instead, she stood stiffly a few feet from the reception desk, waiting for the receptionist to sit back down and serve her.

"Welcome to the Forsberg Transplant Care Clinic," the young lady said brightly. "How can we help you today?"

MacKenzie was wearing white gloves. She pulled each of the fingertips in turn to inch the gloves off of her fingers. "I would like to speak to the Executive Director."

"I don't know if Dr. Dutton is going to be in this morning. Did you have an appointment?"

"I do not," MacKenzie said succinctly, as if that had no bearing on the situation and they should have known that she was going to show up and been ready for her anyway.

"I see… can I get your name, ma'am? I'll see what I can do."

"Miss MacKenzie Kirsch."

The receptionist wrote it down and looked nervously up at MacKenzie, wondering if it was a name that she should know. She swallowed strenuously. "And will Dr. Dutton know you? Are you a friend or a patient?"

"My sister was one of his patients. I am considering a substantial endowment for the clinic in her name. I assume he'll want to hear what I have to say about that."

"I'm sure she will," the receptionist agreed quickly. "Could I… get you a coffee and… show you to a conference room, where you'll be more comfortable?"

MacKenzie gave an imperious nod and was shown to a somber boardroom furnished with heavy dark wood furnishings. She sank into one of the well-padded chairs and indicated that the receptionist should place her coffee *there*.

The little receptionist must have been working frantically once MacKenzie was out of the way. It was only half an hour later that a tall, blond woman knocked lightly on the door of the boardroom and glided in to talk to her.

"Miss Kirsch, I can't tell you how delighted I am to see you. I am Dr. Mildred Dutton and I'm the Executive Director of the Forsberg Clinic."

MacKenzie didn't stand up to greet her. And she didn't shake Dr. Dutton's hand, but merely held out a limp hand as if she expected Dr. Dutton to kiss it. Dr. Mildred Dutton gave it an awkward squeeze and let it go. She seated herself at the end of the table, at an angle to MacKenzie rather than across from her in a position that might be taken as adversarial.

"Do tell me how Amanda is doing," Dr. Dutton encouraged, giving MacKenzie a brilliant smile.

MacKenzie didn't say anything. She let the silence draw out uncomfortably long. She readjusted the position of her white gloves and then finally answered.

"Amanda recently passed away."

Dr. Dutton's face expressed shock. She covered her hand. "Oh, dear! I'm so sorry, I had no idea. Please accept my deepest condolences."

MacKenzie gave a single nod.

"I am considering giving the clinic an endowment in Amanda's name. A rather sizable endowment, if everything seems to be in order. I believe that the clinic can do great things, if only they are well-funded. Our organ donation system here in the US is sadly lacking and in terrible need of reform. In the meantime, I believe that only by making foreign donations available to more people can we get rid of the bottleneck here in the States and make surgery a viable option for everybody who needs it."

"Yes, yes," Dr. Dutton agreed enthusiastically. "That is exactly what we believe here at the Forsberg Clinic. You can't know how much a donation like that would mean to us. There are so many people who are in need of a transplant."

"It is an untenable situation," MacKenzie agreed with a slight shudder.

"How can I help you? You must have questions for me. I don't know how involved you were at the time that Amanda received her… uh… kidney?"

"Kidney," MacKenzie agreed with a stern nod. "This was her second one. Of course, the waiting list here was three or four years, and there was no way that we could wait for that long."

"Oh, of course, I understand. No one who has the means should have to sit around waiting to be called up from a list when there are organs available from all over the world right now. It is vital that we reach as many people as we can."

"I was out of the country myself for much of the time that Amanda was in the hospital and going through these challenges,"

MacKenzie, said, fudging the dates of her time in Europe to cover any ignorance she showed of the situation. "But Amanda told me so much by email and on the phone. I can't tell you how excited she was to visit your overseas clinic. She was so impressed by the presentations she was shown, the pictures of your hospital, and by the donor she was matched with. It was a very exciting time for her."

Dr. Dutton nodded, smiling widely. "I'm so glad. We try to take very good care of our patients. It's important to us that they are treated in a clean, modern facility and that there is no extra stress brought on by facing the unknown. We want them to know what is going to happen along every step of the way so that they feel fully prepared."

"Yes," MacKenzie gave another regal nod, enjoying her role. "Would it be at all possible to have a tour of this facility? It would allow me to see how the money would be best put to use, and what the opportunities are for memorializing Amanda and her story."

"Of course. I would be happy to take you around myself."

Without further conversation, MacKenzie stood up. She held herself ramrod straight and waited for Dr. Dutton to stand and begin the tour. The director looked startled and uncertain for just a moment, but then moved immediately toward the door. She led MacKenzie out the door, and then they walked side by side for the tour. Dr. Dutton led her down a hallway filled with portraits of various doctors and donors who had set up the clinic or contributed to it in some big way.

All men, MacKenzie noted. The new director was a woman, but she was obviously working in a man's world. They could use some female faces on the walls.

Dr. Dutton led her through corridors to family meeting rooms, examination rooms, offices with computers and big screens, a library full of thick, heavy tomes, and eventually back to the boardroom where they had begun.

17

MacKenzie looked around the boardroom at various pictures of happy, healthy organ recipients with their stories on plaques, the gold- and platinum-level donors to the clinic, and a couple of abstract shapes that she assumed were supposed to be awards for all that the clinic was doing in the donation industry. She took a thin folder out of her attache and placed it on the table in front of her, closed, the contents out of sight. Dr. Dutton sat down, leaning toward her like they were friends gossiping over luncheon.

"What other information can I give you today, Ms. Kirsch? Do you have questions?"

"Of course." MacKenzie gave a curt nod. "I would like to see the curricula vitae of each of your directors, senior officers, and top surgeons. I would like to see your five- and ten-year business plans and hear about what projects and expansions you are considering and what kind of funding they will need. I would like to talk to some of your other donors," she nodded to the donors wall, "and also some of your organ recipients." She saw the concern in Dr. Dutton's eyes, and went on smoothly. "Of course, I understand that not every donor or organ recipient will want to talk to me. I'm sure you have some who would endorse your clinic and share their thoughts with me."

Dr. Dutton sat back, nodding, her lips pressed tightly together. "Of course. It will take me a little while to get that information together for you."

MacKenzie looked significantly at the promotional material on the walls. Clearly, they already had lists of donors and of transplant recipients who were willing to brag up the clinic. And the curricula vitae and business plans should be things that were already prepared and on hand for donors and investors.

"Really. How much time will you need?" MacKenzie looked at her watch as if considering her busy schedule.

"Umm…" Dr. Dutton didn't like being put to the test. She obviously wanted to put MacKenzie off with vague promises and to have the time to discuss MacKenzie with her associates and get together a package that was tailored to her. She didn't like being rushed into anything, but MacKenzie had swept in and demanded her time and attention. She probably wanted to step back and take a breath and to consider MacKenzie's requests and promises at her leisure. But that wasn't going to get MacKenzie closer to finding out everything she could about the clinic. She wanted Dr. Dutton to feel rushed. She wanted her to be a little anxious and feel like she had to pull the materials together immediately or she might lose a big donation.

"I would like at least a few hours to make sure I have everything together in a presentable format and that the people whose names I give you have agreed to talk to you and have been given a heads-up that you may call them…"

MacKenzie shook her head. "That's not acceptable. Why don't you give me a copy of your usual investor package?"

Dr. Dutton nodded. "Of course. I can get that for your right away, and then I can get back to you on these other requests…"

"You really should have this information on hand for when donors have questions."

"Of course, and we do, but they are going through some changes right now, and I wouldn't want to give you a product that was half-baked or was going to change tomorrow. I'm sure you want the most reliable, up-to-date information, and for that I need to touch base with our staff and see where we are on it…"

MacKenzie looked at her watch again. "You can get the rest to me this afternoon?"

Dr. Dutton hesitated. Her eyes darted around the room, checking in at the donor wall and at the transplant recipient endorsements. Calculating how much time it would take to call people to warn them about the big donor who might be calling them. "Yes. Of course. That shouldn't be a problem. Where should I send this information? To the address we have on file for your sister?"

"No. Do *not* send it there," MacKenzie said firmly. "I do not live in my mother's home and it will not get to me if you send it there. You can send me an email with the information, and then send me the hard copy…" MacKenzie picked up her purse and found a pad of sticky notes to write her information on. Maybe she should have had business cards ready to give the woman. Her mother had cards, more calling cards than business cards, but MacKenzie had never seen the point in ordering any. She went to functions that she had been invited to, so the people there already knew who she was and how to reach her. Why do extra work?

She wrote slowly and deliberately to make sure that everything was legible so that Dr. Dutton wouldn't have any excuse for not getting her what she had asked for. And to increase the tension that Dr. Dutton was already feeling. She pulled off the sticky note and handed it to Dr. Dutton.

"I will get the investor package from you now, and then you'll have the rest to me this afternoon," she verified.

"Uh—yes, of course. I'll pull that together as quickly as I can. Let me just get our usual package…" She got up and hurried out the boardroom door, leaving MacKenzie sitting by herself again. She went over to the donor wall and took a couple of pictures to collect all of the names of the donors. She went along the transplant recipient wall, taking a picture of each of the transplant recipients with their plaques. It would be interesting to see what information she got from Dr. Dutton and how it correlated with what was on display.

MacKenzie left the clinic with the package that Dr. Dutton had provided her tucked into her file folder and attache. She saw the same brochure that had been in Amanda's files, but there was additional information that she hadn't seen before. The clinic's financials, Board of Directors' bios, and so on. Not quite what she had asked for, but it was a start and Dr. Dutton promised her that they would provide pretty much whatever she asked for. They obviously knew the reputation of the Kirsch family and had no doubt that if MacKenzie said that a donation was forthcoming, it would be provided, assuming she was satisfied with the information she received.

She went back to the hotel. She had taken Amanda's laptop computer with her on the flight in the hopes that she would find something interesting on the hard drive, but then she had done other things on the flight and before bed. If she could get an internet connection at the hotel's business center, she could conduct some of the research she needed to do without having to go home to her own computer. Mobile technology was a wonderful thing.

Once there, she started plugging the names of the various doctors, managers, and directors at the clinic into Google to see what background information she could find on them. Most of what she came across was promotional material put out by the clinic, but there were, at least, a few news articles that had obviously not been paid for by the Forsberg Clinic.

MacKenzie tapped her pen on the computer, thinking about it. What she really needed to do was to find out what kind of reputation they had in the medical community. For that, she might be able to bend Dr. Proctor's ear again, if he wasn't tired of her questions.

When she had exhausted her internet research strategies, she closed the browser and again started going through the files on Amanda's laptop. She clicked on the Pictures folder and saw a long list of automatically named photographs. Probably taken with Amanda's digital camera or phone and then imported so she could see them on her desktop to view them and rename them. But she had apparently never gotten around to renaming them. MacKenzie started opening them one at a time. There was probably a better way to look through them quickly, but she wasn't very computer savvy, and she had the time to browse. She assumed that Dr. Dutton's additional package of information wouldn't arrive until late afternoon or early evening, the very latest Dr. Dutton could get away with and still claim to have met the imposed deadline.

There were random pictures of family and friends at different events. A number of them were obviously taken from the hospital, and MacKenzie looked at the dates, knowing it was going to be the interval before Amanda's transplant. She had obviously been much more ill than she had ever let on to MacKenzie. A cloud of sadness settled over her as she looked through the pictures, full of smiles and encouragement. People who had visited her at the hospital, showing up with flowers, cookies, pizza, and whatever else they thought would help to cheer Amanda up. MacKenzie knew that much of the time, Amanda had the nurses take her gifts to other units, especially pediatric, to help cheer up the patients who didn't have anything. That was just the kind of person she was.

Then there were pictures of the interior of the airport, out the window of what was obviously a privately chartered plane, pictures of Lisa and Walter sleeping while Amanda sat up, too excited and jittery or feeling too ill to sleep. MacKenzie looked at the pictures of her sleeping parents, shaking her head. Why hadn't they told her? Why hadn't she been there? She could have been, would have been if they had only told her what was going on.

A few pictures of white beaches and blue water, just like in the brochure. Then the interior of a building. MacKenzie leaned closer to the screen to examine it. It was not the pristine hospital that was shown in the glossy brochure. She tried to analyze it. The rooms appeared to be built from boards that had been painted white, not any kind of drywall, wallboard, cinderblock, or even cement building that MacKenzie had ever seen. She thought that there was glass in the windows, but she couldn't be sure. Even if all of the windows were covered, it obviously was not up to the same standards as first world construction, and MacKenzie imagined that insects could move in and out pretty freely. It wasn't quite the spotlessly hygienic environment that Walter had implied when he said that there was no way that Amanda could have been bitten by a malaria-infected mosquito.

But it didn't appear to be the hospital. Just somewhere they had stayed while preparing for the surgery. Mattresses on single, low bed frames. At least they were not rush mats on a dirt floor. MacKenzie imagined that most of the population of the tropical island probably lived in hand-built shelters with few modern amenities.

Her parents looked reasonably happy in the pictures, and one or two had been taken by Lisa or Walter, because Amanda was in the picture as well, looking pale and anxious, but smiling brightly. Getting ready for her transplant. The time was creeping closer and, having been through one transplant before, Amanda had some idea of what to expect and how she was going to feel after it was done.

There were a couple of dark, difficult-to-make-out photos, and then more outdoor and airplane pictures, apparently on their way back to the United States.

MacKenzie went back to the dark photos. She double-clicked the first one to open it in a photo editor, and then clicked on the brightness slider to try to make it a little more clear.

She stared at the dark, grainy photo, trying to process what she saw.

18

Back in Vermont, Dr. Proctor Insisted that this time he would choose the place they were to meet and would pay for the dinner. It wasn't any sandwich shop this time. But in spite of the fact that Dr. Proctor had chosen dinner at one of the higher-class restaurants, he was heartily professional with MacKenzie and didn't act like he thought it was just an excuse to have a date with her. They sat at one of the tables in the center of the restaurant, not a booth in the corner, and he didn't lean toward her or use an intimate tone when he spoke to her. MacKenzie relaxed and stopped worrying that he was going to think that she had a crush on him and was just using her sister's death as an excuse to see him.

They chatted about safe, social topics for the first little while. MacKenzie didn't really expect anything else different. He inquired after Lisa and asked how MacKenzie was doing and actually pressed for an answer instead of just accepting a social, 'oh, I'm fine.'

"Nobody is fine after their sister dies, MacKenzie. Don't blow me off. Are you okay? Is there anything I can do to help you?"

"You already are. Or you're going to tonight. I don't know… I think I'm handling it okay. I don't want to be alone, because then I start thinking about her and crying, and I don't want to spend all my nights crying. Makes for a terrible headache when I get up."

He smiled gently, nodded his understanding.

"And then this stuff with the clinic and the transplant... I don't know. I suppose it might not be the healthiest pursuit. I want to know what happened and what went wrong and why everybody is being so hush-hush about it. I mean... they always did try to give Amanda her privacy and dignity, letting her decide what she wanted to tell people and what she didn't. Not like a lot of parents who think they can just broadcast everything they want to about someone without their say-so. So, on one hand I get it, but..."

"But this is different," Proctor suggested.

"Yes. It is. I read some of what Amanda wrote in her journal, and she wasn't the one who decided not to tell me anything. It wasn't her trying to keep me from worrying. It was Mom and Dad. Why? I don't think there is something inherently bad about going out of the country for a transplant, do you?"

Dr. Proctor tipped his head slightly, maybe considering what he thought about it and maybe a sort of a shrug. "That's not an easy question to answer."

"You think there is something wrong with going out of the country?"

"It isn't exactly ethical to work around the system, jumping ahead of people who have been waiting longer than you have, using money to get what you want. Transplants are very difficult for the working poor to afford as it is, so they're already out of the running. So, the wealthier individuals are the ones who are on the list. The ones who are very wealthy and savvy know that they can buy their way onto waiting lists all around the country, increasing their odds, especially if they research what areas don't have a lot of people waiting for transplants ahead of them. And then the ones who have the kind of wealth your family does..."

"More money than sense," MacKenzie contributed.

"Not necessarily," Proctor said with a chuckle. "Well, those who are extremely wealthy can afford to go to private clinics overseas. They pay a huge premium to get what they want. They jump ahead of everyone else who is waiting."

"But on the other hand, it means that they're not competing for the same organs. They're not jumping ahead of the other people who are waiting, they're jumping right out of the pool."

Dr. Proctor nodded. "True. But the next problem is, how ethical are the practices that are being used in those other countries? Are they paying poor people to donate what organs and tissues they can in order to have a better chance of survival? Here, you can't actually pay someone for their organs, but in other countries, they don't have the same bias against paying donors."

"But it's a free market... They'll pay what the market will support... and if it helps poor families to get somewhere in life, is that a bad thing? If it's a way for them to climb up out of the slums..."

He nodded. "There are many different ways of looking at it. Different people have different perspectives. But we shouldn't leave it up to the people who need the organs. Because they are not going to have the same ethical standards as someone who doesn't have skin in the game, so to speak."

MacKenzie nodded and had a sip of her wine.

"But we know that's not the case here anyway. The donor came from Germany. They didn't pay her, they just paid for her expenses to get there and her medical care for the procedure. She did it out of the goodness of her heart, because she wanted to give something back, to give people like Amanda a chance at life that they wouldn't have had otherwise."

"I'm sure that helped them in making the decision to proceed. I would expect your father to take some of those things into consideration... if he was able to look at the situation dispassionately."

MacKenzie sighed. She wasn't sure what to think on that point. Her father was known as a 'white hat' lobbyist, meaning that the people he represented and the causes that he lobbied for at the senate were charities and not-for-profits. He spoke out against the 'black hats,' who were working for the corporations, sometimes mega-corporations, and were perceived as only being in it for the money. Walter could say that he was working for the good guys and trying to make the world a better place. But she also knew him to be a shrewd man, one who didn't forget his own needs or those of his family.

He didn't forget himself in service. He always remembered himself. He was number one. And his family fell somewhere behind that; MacKenzie wasn't sure what order they came in, but he was a devoted family man. Knowing that Amanda needed a kidney, and that throwing some money at the problem would make it go away, would he really have considered the ethics of the situation? Or would he just have taken the opportunity when it came up?

"MacKenzie?" Dr. Proctor said, watching her carefully. She shook off her uncertainty and smiled.

"Yes, I'm sure you're right. Daddy wouldn't have pursued it if he thought it was unethical."

Dr. Proctor buttered a roll for himself. "But you are still determined to dig deeper and make sure that they… what? That the clinic was ethical? That they didn't put Amanda at any unnecessary risk?"

"Yeah, I guess. I just want… to understand why they did what they did, why they did it the way that they did. Did Amanda really need a new kidney right away? She could have survived on dialysis, couldn't she? She could have waited for a year or two until her name came up and they found a match for her? She didn't need to put herself at risk for picking up malaria or some other tropical disease."

"I'm not sure she could have," he admitted. "I spoke with your mother frequently about Amanda's care and any changes in her case, and there were concerns that she was not going to last for very long on dialysis. As much as we try to mimic what mother nature can do, we knew we were losing ground. The machine doesn't replace a functioning kidney. Not completely. And the longer she waited, the more likely it was that she would come up with another infection or disease. Not malaria, maybe, but influenza. A resistant staph infection. Something else unexpected."

"Poor Amanda. I wish she had talked to me about it. She must have felt so alone."

Proctor wisely said nothing about that. MacKenzie looked around for their waiter, wondering how much longer it would be before their main courses arrived. He caught her eye from the other side of the room and raised one finger to her in a familiar gesture that MacKenzie recognized as meaning that it would be there shortly. One minute. Or just one more order before yours. MacKenzie rubbed at a smudge on her fork.

"I have collected the names of the directors and surgeons at the Forsberg Clinic," she announced. "I was wondering if you could look at them… let me know if you recognize them or know anything about their reputations."

"I know a couple of names off the top of my head. As far as I know, there haven't been any rumors of anything untoward associated with the clinic. I would have warned your parents if I had been aware of anything."

MacKenzie thought about that. It was strange, in view of the ethical concerns he had already mentioned, that he hadn't warned them against pursuing a foreign transplant through the Forsberg Clinic.

"So you didn't have any problem with them doing a foreign transplant?"

"I understand how desperately they wanted her to get a new kidney. How important it was for them. Who am I to step in the way of the one real solution they could find? Who am I to say that I have more scruples than they do? I have been friends with your family for a long time. I couldn't tell them not to get a transplant."

MacKenzie nodded. That made sense. She hadn't come into the picture until after the transplant was done, and it was easy to judge them for what they had done. It would have been different if she had known ahead of time. She would undoubtedly have agreed that they should go ahead with the one option they had. She wouldn't have dared to tell them that some high-ranking official's ethical concerns were more important than Amanda's surgery and survival. The pie-in-the-sky arguments went out the window when faced with the actual choice. Go ahead and get the kidney that Amanda needed and let others ponder the ethics of the situation. If it was legal, then why not? It didn't have to follow the same rules as the United States regulators had put into place. There were plenty of laws that changed from country to country and even from state to state.

The waiter greeted them in a soft, respectful voice as he approached them with a couple of steaming plates. Amanda waited for him to put the chicken in front of her, and she and Dr. Proctor both unfolded their napkins and prepared to eat.

MacKenzie looked over at Dr. Proctor's rare steak, and had a moment of nausea. She saw Amanda under the knife, the surgeon's scalpel separating the raw flesh, carefully preparing to graft in the new kidney.

"Are you alright?" Dr. Proctor questioned in concern.

"Yes… I'm fine. I just…"

He followed her gaze down to his bloody steak. "Oh… I'm sorry, does this bother you? I can have them cook it more…"

"No, no." MacKenzie shook her head. "That's always the way that Daddy has it. He could never understand anyone preferring it any other way. It doesn't bother me. Or… usually it doesn't. It's probably just low blood sugar." She gave a little laugh. "I'll be fine after I've had something to eat."

He sliced into the steak, looking back up at her after, weighing whether she was telling him the truth or not. "At least it's not steak and kidney pie," he offered.

"Oh!" MacKenzie shook her head at the mental picture and gave an unsteady laugh. "I'm glad you didn't. I think that might just be a little bit too much."

19

Dr. Proctor looked at the list of people MacKenzie handed to him. He gave a frown of concentration. He didn't say anything initially, and MacKenzie waited to see what he would say. After a minute, he looked up, shaking his head.

"I don't know most of these names," he said. "I know they're not local, but I did expect to see a few more names that I recognized. I know most of the big players in transplants, and I thought they would have some of them in advisory positions on the board..."

MacKenzie nodded. "Most of the surgeons seem to be from other countries. I don't think any of the doctors who actually do the transplants are from the US."

"I suppose that would put them in a conflicted position ethically. They can't very well claim to be following the regulations that the US regulators have laid down if they are going out of the country to perform transplants that they can't perform here. So, they would have to hire people from countries that had different regulations. Or emigrate from the US for good."

"Yeah. Now from what I understand, or what I've heard, there are not a lot of surgeons around the world who are trained in or experienced in organ transplants. It's a specialty and needs very rigorous training."

"Here in the US, yes. You wouldn't find a transplant surgeon practicing general medicine. They would only be doing transplants. Because there is a limited supply of organs for transplantation, there is a cap on the number of surgeons who can be performing transplants. So only the cream of the crop can actually get jobs as transplant surgeons."

"But in other parts of the world? You don't think they're as well-trained?"

"I'm sure they must be well-trained. I'm just not sure that they would be *quite* as well-trained or specialized. These are very complicated surgeries that can take many hours. It's delicate work, and if you miss connecting some duct or blood vessel, it could mean the patient's life. You want someone who does a lot of these and has perfected their technique. Not someone who dabbles or has only read about it in books or watched training videos."

"I'm having a hard time finding anything out about any of these doctors. I have their bios, but they are short on details. I've asked for detailed curricula vitae..." MacKenzie looked at her watch. "They should have been emailed to me yesterday, but I haven't seen them yet. I'm hoping that you can tell from those whether these guys are properly trained or not."

"To make that judgment, we would have to know that the information they provide is true. It may not be verifiable. We would have to rely on them being truthful on their faces... which is a poor way to judge someone's experience. You know how often resumes are padded with information that, at best is a stretch, and at worst is an outright lie."

"Do you have colleagues in other countries who would be able to look into it?"

Dr. Proctor scratched his chin. "Is that really going to give you the information you want to know? I'm not sure it would be worth our time to chase that information down. You could hire a private detective to look into their backgrounds. Someone who is trained to do this kind of thing and can get you the information you are looking for quickly. I don't think I can do it. I don't have the time to be wasting on a fruitless investigation."

MacKenzie was surprised by this. She had been working on the assumption that he would answer any of her questions and be completely onside with finding out the rest of the information she was searching for. So far, he had been willing to answer her calls in the middle of the night and to take time out of his day to talk to her. He hadn't made any complaint or told her mother that she needed to rein MacKenzie in.

But apparently there were limits to what he was willing to do.

"Oh. Okay."

"I'm sorry, MacKenzie." He put his fork down and touched her hand briefly. "I don't like to disappoint you. But you know this is a wild goose chase. You're looking to assign blame to someone… and if you want to pin it on the foreign donation and the Forsberg clinic, you have every right to do so. But I can't waste my time checking into people's backgrounds. Especially when these people don't even live in the US. Get an investigator who is experienced in international investigations. Maybe he'll be able to find something. But don't involve me in this."

"No, I'm sorry. You're right. I know your time is valuable, and you've already spent a lot of time with me answering my questions and giving me advice. You've been more than generous with your time."

"Are you sure? I feel bad about it, but I do need to be aware of how I spend my time. I need to enforce some boundaries. I love you and your family, and I want to help… but there's only so much that I can do."

"Of course. You're right. I'll look into it further myself, or hire someone to look at these guys." She hesitated. "I do think there is something to it, though. You may not think so, but… I just don't get a good feeling about it. I think that at least some of the information that the Forsberg Clinic is giving is false and misleading. I don't think that they're quite as professional as their front in New Jersey suggests."

Dr. Proctor looked thoughtful as he cut pieces off of his steak and ate. MacKenzie turned her attention back to her own food, realizing that she had barely even touched her chicken since it had been placed before her. It was beautifully plated and MacKenzie was sure that it was delicious, but she couldn't even taste it. Everything just seemed to turn to sand in her mouth.

20

MacKenzie knew the name of the big private investigation firm that her father sometimes hired to look into backgrounds and dig up information for his lobbying efforts. He never referred to it as 'dirt,' but MacKenzie suspected that was exactly what it was. Walter would fight the other lobbyists and politicians with whatever means he could, and that included smearing reputations.

Using Walter's name, she got past the phone gatekeeper and was put through immediately to the senior manager of investigations. She wasn't sure whether he was actually the top of the organization or whether it was just a title intended to inspire confidence. But it didn't really matter. She knew that they would do their best to track down the information she was looking for, and if a lower-level investigator were not able to get it, then her name would be enough to get them to transfer it to a more senior investigator. MacKenzie had rarely traded on her name before. She had used it to get into functions that she wanted to attend, but usually people were calling her with invitations for her to attend rather than her having to ask a favor. She had been pleased with the way that the Forsberg Clinic and Dr. Dutton had responded, and the investigations firm seemed to be eager to jump at her command as well.

"Lance," MacKenzie was quick to use Lance Reacher's name to establish a more personal relationship between them. "I'm so glad you were available to take my call. You know that Mountain Investigations is always my father's first choice when he has a problem."

"Of course," Lance agreed. "We've been very happy with our relationship with Mr. Kirsch, and I hope you will be as well. Is this regarding one of his efforts, or…"

"No. Nothing to do with Walter's work. This is… a very personal matter."

"Oh, I see," his voice immediately dropped to a more intimate level. He was probably thinking that she wanted the background of a boyfriend checked. "Well, why don't you tell me how we can help you today?"

MacKenzie explained to him about her desire to donate to the clinic that had helped her sister get the lifesaving organ transplant, even though it had only given her another year, but that she wanted to check out everyone associated with the clinic and the transplants they did first to make sure there wasn't any bad PR that was going to come back as a result.

"Yes, of course," Lance agreed. "That's very wise of you. Especially if you're considering a large donation. If you become known as a supporter of this clinic, you wouldn't want to be associated with anything unfavorable."

"Right. Now, most of these doctors are international, so my doctor friends here in the States aren't of much help to me. And I'm not finding very much on Google when I try to look them up."

"Don't waste your time on your own investigations. That's exactly what we're here for. And we have associated firms all over the world, so we can look them up locally. We have all of the resources in place so that you don't have to worry about doing the legwork yourself."

"Okay, good. I asked the clinic for curricula vitae, but the bios I got back are… They're just press packages. All of the stuff that sounds good and nothing about who they really are and their education or jobs over the years. Just the very high-level, pumped up stuff."

"They should have at least given you a proper resume. No worries. We'll be able to trace work history, see whether they've had any complaints filed against them in the past, any malpractice issues or ethical violations. Do you want to get into their personal lives as well, or just professional?"

MacKenzie considered. She hadn't thought about that. How much did she need? Just enough to show that they were competent surgeons and not GP's who were doing their first transplant surgeries? Or was she looking for any dirt?

"I think…" MacKenzie blew her breath through her teeth, anxious about giving the wrong answer. "I don't think I need anything personal, unless it relates to… financial matters. I don't care if a doctor is cheating on his wife. But if he's deep in gambling debt, he could be doing transplants that he's not qualified to just for a big pay-off."

She could hear Lance's computer keys tapping away. "Uh-huh. Makes sense," he agreed. "How about addictions? If the guy's a drunk or if he needs a line of coke to keep him awake during the surgery…"

"Uh, yeah. Better be on the lookout for that too."

"No problem."

"Good. Great. Thank you for looking into this for me. I'll email you the names and the bios that I have."

"Perfect. We'll get started on it right away."

MacKenzie hesitated, unsure what else to say to him. She hesitated to reveal that she was worried that the clinic itself might be a scam and have contributed to Amanda's death. She didn't have any proof of it yet—and wouldn't telling Lance they might have been responsible for Amanda's death be slanderous? It was probably best if she kept that to herself until she was sure. Besides, Lance might be talking to Walter about another investigation and happen to casually drop a bombshell. Walter would not be happy to hear that she thought there were issues with the clinic.

"Was there something else, Miss Kirsch?"

"No. No, that's it. Thanks. I'll send you this email. Get back to me once you've had a chance to check them out."

"Will do, Miss Kirsch. Thank you for your business."

MacKenzie hung up the phone thinking about her father and

how she was going to tell Walter and Lisa that she knew more about the clinic than they had been willing to tell her.

The next step in MacKenzie's plan of attack was to talk to other people who had been to the island for transplant surgery. Dr. Dutton had sent her the list of people who had agreed to talk to her. She compared it to the photos she had taken of the pictures and plaques on the wall of the boardroom. Why would anyone who'd had a successful organ transplant with the clinic, as evidenced by their photo on the wall, refuse to talk to someone who wanted to make a donation to the clinic?

So rather than calling the people she'd been told to, MacKenzie wrote down the names of the transplant recipients who had apparently not given their consent to be contacted. They had allowed their photos and stories to be posted on the boardroom wall, so what was it they had to hide?

The first name on the list was a Magnus Benjamin Phelps. MacKenzie looked up his name in the White Pages directory and dialed his number. It rang a few times before it was answered by a woman with a Hispanic accent, who MacKenzie immediately assumed was a maid or other household servant.

"I'm looking for Mr. Phelps. Is he in?"

"No, Mr. Leslie Phelps is out of town at the moment. Would you like to talk to someone else? His wife or his personal secretary?"

"Oh, Not Leslie Phelps," MacKenzie corrected. "I was looking for Magnus…?"

There was silenced from the maid. MacKenzie looked again at her notes to make sure she had gotten the name right and hadn't crossed up two different records.

"Is Mr. Magnus Benjamin Phelps there?" she asked, once she was sure of her information. Maybe the other Mr. Phelps went by Benjamin rather than Magnus, tipping the maid off that she didn't actually know the man she was calling.

"Are you a personal friend?"

"Well, no," MacKenzie admitted. "He knew my sister, though." She didn't have any idea whether this was true. "They both had transplants done at the same clinic."

"Ah. Is your sister there? Are you with her?"

MacKenzie swallowed. She was going to have to get used to saying the words. People who hadn't heard of Amanda's passing were going to ask her how she was or were going to invite her to events.

"No… my sister passed away recently. I was hoping to be able to talk to Magnus about… his transplant experience."

"I'm so sorry… Mr. Magnus has also passed."

MacKenzie sat there with the phone to her ear, feeling numb. That was not what she had expected to hear. How stupid she had been. Why would someone who'd had a transplant through the Forsberg Clinic not be on the list Dr. Dutton had given her? Because they had since passed away. How stupid and clumsy she had been, assuming that a name missing from Dr. Dutton's list was something suspicious.

"Oh… I'm so sorry to hear that. I apologize for disturbing you."

"Would you like to talk to Mr. Magnus's mother?"

MacKenzie considered. The maid had made the offer without prompting, so Mrs. Phelps must be willing to talk to people about her son. She must have talked to others or the maid wouldn't have offered.

"I don't know. I don't want to upset her. Do you think it would be good for me to talk to her, or just to leave it alone?"

"Oh…" The woman drew the word out, thinking about it. "I don't think it bothers Mrs. Phelps to talk to people about Magnus. And with your sister having passed as well… I think she would like to talk to you. It's good to have someone who understands your grief."

MacKenzie upgraded her assumptions about the woman who had answered the phone. Maybe not a maid. Not even a house manager. Someone who knew Mrs. Phelps well, and had been with her long enough to understand her feelings and reactions. A personal secretary? Old nanny? Not the maid.

"I… well, yes, I guess if you think she'd be interested in talking to me, and it wouldn't upset her… you could ask her if she wanted to take my call. But please, there's no obligation. She's not expecting my call and I don't want to be a bother."

"Let me check with her."

MacKenzie was put on hold while the woman went to talk to Mrs. Phelps. When the phone was picked up again, she was expecting to hear the Hispanic accent once more, but the voice that answered was more cultured, with a recognizable Boston twang.

"Hello, this is Geraldine Phelps."

MacKenzie swallowed her anxiety and let her extensive social training take over, speaking the words without really thinking about them, while her brain struggled to catch up with the moment. "Mrs. Phelps, I'm so sorry to hear about your son, Magnus. Are you sure I'm not intruding?"

"Of course not," Mrs. Phelps said graciously. "I'm always happy to talk to anyone who will listen about Magnus. We're at that stage where people no longer want to mention him, in case it is upsetting, but I can't go on as if he didn't exist and I'm not missing him. I want to talk about him, but people feel too awkward about grief."

MacKenzie let out her breath, nodding. "Yes, that makes sense," she agreed. It was surprising how quickly one reached that stage. People had already said that they were sorry about Amanda, and then they didn't know how to treat her the next time they talked. Mention Amanda again? Avoid the topic? Pretend that life just went on as normal after a loved one's death? "I hope I didn't mislead you; I didn't actually know Magnus. He had a transplant through the same clinic as my sister, Amanda, and I saw Magnus's picture and story on the wall. I wanted to…" she decided she didn't want to give Mrs. Phelps the story about considering a donation to Forsberg. "I wanted to learn more about the transplants that Forsberg is doing. For personal reasons. So I thought I would call some of the transplant recipients. I didn't know that Magnus had passed away."

"You want to know about the transplant?" Mrs. Phelps sounded confused. "What about it?"

"My family has been very quiet about the surgery… to be honest, I didn't even know she'd had a second transplant. But when she recently got sick, I had reason to believe that she might have gotten sick as a result of going out of the country for a transplant."

"Why? How do you think it was related?"

"My sister contracted malaria. That's not something you get in the United States. Only through foreign travel to tropical climates. I think she must have been bitten by an infected mosquito when she was there for the transplant. Nobody knew she'd been bitten at the time, not until she got sick a couple of weeks ago."

"I see. But that doesn't mean that the clinic did something wrong."

"No. I'm not throwing any accusations around. I'm just trying to… I don't know… follow Amanda's footsteps over the last year. Look at what happened and understand why…"

"You couldn't have prevented her death," Mrs. Phelps said compassionately. "Don't take yourself down that pathway… you mustn't. Your family did everything they could to help Amanda, it was just what was supposed to happen."

MacKenzie shifted uncomfortably. *What was supposed to happen?* She wasn't a believer in God or fate. She didn't believe that there had been no other pathway for Amanda. If they had made different decisions, then the outcome would have been different. If they had left her in the United States, on dialysis, until a new kidney became available, then she would not have contracted malaria and she would not be dead. That was the way it played out in MacKenzie's head. There wasn't any greater power directing matters on earth, pointing the finger at Amanda and dictating that she must die.

"If she hadn't gone to the island, she would not have gotten malaria. What happened with your son? What did Magnus die from?"

"His body rejected the graft. He received a lobe of liver. He had profuse internal bleeding… it was very quick."

"I'm so sorry." On one hand, it must have been a big shock for Mrs. Phelps. But on the other hand, maybe a quick demise would have been easier than to watch Amanda struggling and falling back into that cycle of fevers over and over again. Fighting and seeming to get better, only to be struck down yet again. Then at the end, when her breathing became so strained. MacKenzie would never forget the panic in Amanda's eyes as they took her away to intensive care, struggling to get enough oxygen.

"It is one of the potential outcomes of the transplant. We thought… their success rates were so high. We understood that there were risks, of course, but they had given us such assurances, we didn't think it would happen. I wish we had weighed the risks more carefully. If I had known then… maybe we would have at least put off the transplant… until it became more urgent."

"But then he would have been weaker," MacKenzie pointed out. "He might not have been able to travel, or to survive the surgery."

"Yes. You're right, of course. We made the best decision we could based on the information we had at the time."

"Looking back now… you don't think they were lying about anything, do you? The cleanliness of the facility? The training of their surgeons? The risk calculations?"

"I have often wondered. But what good is second-guessing going to do? It won't bring Magnus or Amanda back. It won't change anything."

"But if they are operating in a way that is dangerous… lying to people… then shouldn't we raise the alarm? So that other people can avoid having the same thing happen to them?"

There was a long silence from Mrs. Phelps. "Do you know something?" she asked finally. "I don't have any evidence that they lied about anything."

"I don't have proof. Just… well, some things that are bothering me. And maybe it's nothing. I'm just being paranoid and trying to make sense of why my sister died. I can't answer that yet… which is why I'm trying to talk to others about their experiences. Trying to reassure myself… or to discover the truth."

"We went to the clinic in New Jersey. It was very professional, very clean. They had a lot of information for us. Everything seems completely aboveboard. I realize that some people might not think it is right for us to go out of the country to do what the regulators wouldn't allow here… but no one is complaining. The people who were waiting in the US are still waiting. We didn't take anything from them, except maybe to reduce the demand to make way for someone else to get an organ that Magnus would have taken otherwise. I don't see anything wrong with that."

"Did you go with him to the island?"

"No. You sound like a very young woman, so I assume your sister was quite young. My son was in his forties. He took his companion with him, not his mother. Did you go with Amanda?"

"My parents did. They didn't tell me what was happening."

"I'm sure they didn't want to bother you. It's very stressful. But you and I are in the same position, we are looking at something that happened overseas… we weren't there. We didn't see any wrongdoing."

"No… but… my sister took pictures."

21

The feeling of being wrung-out emotionally was becoming familiar to MacKenzie. She sincerely hoped that wasn't the way she could expect to feel for the rest of her life. Sooner or later, the stress and the grief had to lessen. Had to become more livable. People had family members die all the time. They didn't become walking zombies like MacKenzie felt she had. She wanted to go to bed and not have to think anymore. But she didn't want to be alone. She wanted company without having to be company. Everything she did seemed to take more energy than usual.

The phone rang and she ignored it. She wasn't prepared to deal with anybody else's needs. Not even a telemarketer's. She needed to just let her heart and her brain recover.

After the landline stopped ringing, her cellphone started up. MacKenzie looked at it, frowning. It wouldn't be her mother; Lisa was still resistant to calling the cell phone, feeling like it was an intrusion on MacKenzie's privacy. Cell phones were for emergencies, not conversations. Some of her friends did have both numbers, but calling each in sequence meant that it was urgent, and none of her friends had any urgent business with her.

Her father. She knew even before she picked up her cell phone and looked at the number that it was Walter. As much as she wanted to just rest and relax, she knew she needed to talk to him. With a knot in her stomach, she answered the call.

"Hi, Daddy."

"I want to know what you think you're doing!"

He was never so cross with her. MacKenzie gasped at his sharp answer, taking a physical step back as if that would distance her from his anger.

"Daddy? What's wrong? I don't understand."

"First, I hear from your mother that you have taken it upon yourself to take Amanda's private medical files from the house. Then I hear that you're showing up at the Forsberg clinic asking questions. I want to know what the hell you think you're doing."

"I'm... trying to satisfy myself about what happened to Amanda. I think her death could have been prevented, and I'm worried about the clinic continuing to operate, maybe putting additional lives in danger."

"That's ridiculous. What have you gotten into your head? The clinic saved her life. It isn't their fault that she got sick a year later. That's just one of those things. Cruel fate. It wasn't something that could have been prevented or foreseen."

"She wouldn't have gotten malaria if she hadn't gone to that island."

"She wouldn't have survived if she hadn't gotten the transplant."

"She would have for a while. Maybe long enough to get a transplant here, locally."

"You're wrong. You don't know, you didn't know how sick she was."

"No. And I don't understand why you kept it from me. Shouldn't I have known? I could have spent more time with Amanda. I could have been involved in the decision to get the transplant. Or not get the transplant. I would have liked to have known."

"That's what all of this is about. You want to punish us for not involving you in the decision. We didn't exclude you to make you feel bad, MacKenzie. None of us would have wanted you to feel bad. But we wanted as few moving parts as possible. No extra variables. No one else who could have given her a virus, or talked her out of the transplant, or made her more stressed because she was trying to pretend to be happy and healthy when she was not."

"Did you see the clinic?"

"Of course. We went on a tour of it before we went overseas."

"No, I meant on the island. Did you see the hospital there? The place they would actually be getting her surgery."

"We had the pictures. I can show you the brochures, but I'm sure you already saw all of that when you visited the New Jersey clinic. How could you go there without even talking to me about it first?"

"I didn't think I needed your permission to talk to them."

"Well you don't," he admitted, disgruntled. "Are you really considering giving them a donation in Amanda's memory?"

"I may," MacKenzie lied. "I want to know more about their operation before I make that decision."

"You don't need to know anything else. She had the transplant. It was successful. It has nothing to do with getting sick later."

"Except that she wouldn't have contracted malaria if she had stayed here."

"You keep saying that. But it's a fallacy. She would not have survived if she hadn't gotten a transplant. She could not get a transplant here. She couldn't get one anywhere else. This was our only option. And it gave her another year that she wouldn't have had. I still don't believe all this about malaria. I think the doctors here made a mistake. It was another parasite. Or a bacterial infection. It wasn't malaria."

"There was something wrong with the clinic on the island," MacKenzie said.

"Something wrong? What do you mean?"

"Amanda took pictures while she was there. I have pictures of the place you stayed in while you were there. It was no Hilton."

There was silence from Walter that stretched out uncomfortably. MacKenzie waited, knowing that he would defend them.

"It was no Hilton," Walter agreed, blustering. "But would you expect it to be? We weren't there for our own comfort. We were there so that Amanda could get her surgery. The hospital was different. It was a fully modern facility."

"I don't think it was."

"I saw the pictures. They had all of the amenities, all of the technology they needed to perform state-of-the-art surgery."

"You didn't go there."

"No. Patients were isolated. To prevent them from picking up viruses or infections while they were in such a susceptible state. Just by implementing that one control, they were able to reduce the risks of infection by thirty percent. Would you want to put Amanda's life at risk by insisting on being there with her? You would accept an increased risk of thirty percent? You'd risk her death just to be able to sit by her bed as she recovered?"

MacKenzie thought of the last few days of Amanda's life. The last few minutes. It was an immeasurable comfort that she had been able to be there with her sister to the end. She didn't know if she could have obeyed the stricture that she couldn't be with Amanda after the surgery. Even understanding that it put her life at risk, MacKenzie didn't know if she would have been able to stay away.

So maybe it was a good thing she hadn't been told about it. She would have insisted on staying with Amanda, putting her life at risk. She couldn't imagine having to make that choice.

"You two were close," Walter said, "and I understand you feeling betrayed that we didn't tell you what was going on at the time. But we were protecting Amanda's health. Giving her the best chance we could at surviving and recovering."

"I want you to see the pictures."

He hesitated. "Amanda never said anything about taking any pictures at the hospital. She was asleep most of the time she was there. They kept her unconscious in order to give her the best chance to heal and recover."

"She never said anything to you about the conditions there?"

"She said it was like a spa. That she felt like she was on vacation instead of being sick."

MacKenzie didn't know what to say to that. Had Amanda been afraid to tell him the truth? Was her brain scrambled by whatever they had put her on to keep her unconscious and she didn't even remember it? Anesthesia could do strange things to the memory.

When she had downloaded the pictures from her phone, had she even looked at them? Or maybe just a few of them? Maybe she didn't bother trying to correct the ones that were too dark.

"What was in these pictures?" Walter demanded. "I think you must have misunderstood things. Maybe they are more pictures of where your mother and I stayed."

MacKenzie suppressed a shudder. "No. I don't think so. I think you should see them."

"Send them to me, then. They're digital?"

"I don't want to send them to you by email. When are you coming back to Burlington next?"

MacKenzie was more careful with the next transplant recipient on her list. She searched for any obituaries or other press first, to make sure that John Hopewell had not passed away since his transplant. She didn't want to bumble into another surviving family's life. There weren't any obvious signs that he had died, so she looked up his contact information and called his number, crossing her fingers and hoping for the best.

"Hello?" It was a man's voice. Not quite brusque, but definitely giving the impression of impatience. Better not be a telemarketer, or he would hang up when the first two words were out of her mouth.

"Mr. Hopewell? You don't know me, but my sister Amanda had a transplant through the Forsberg Clinic," she said quickly, hoping to catch his attention before he decided that she was too much of a bother and hung up. He didn't immediately hang up, so that was a good sign.

"Yes?" he asked eventually. "What's your name?"

"MacKenzie Kirsch. My sister was Amanda Kirsch."

"I never met her."

"Yeah, I didn't suppose you probably had. I just… was hoping to talk to some of the people who have had transplants done through Forsberg, get a feeling for what the company is all about."

"Why?"

MacKenzie shifted uncomfortably in her seat, glad that he wasn't there to see her discomfort. "It's sort of hard to explain. Amanda recently passed away."

"Oh," his voice dropped to an appropriately somber tone "I'm very sorry to hear that, Miss Kirsch."

"Thank you. The thing is, it looks like she died because of her transplant, and I just wanted to know… whether anyone else had experienced similar problems."

"How did you get my name?"

"Your picture and plaque in the Forsberg boardroom."

"I see. I should call and ask them to take it down."

"You weren't happy with their services, then? You'd rather not be associated with them?"

Hopewell made a clicking sound with his tongue. MacKenzie waited out his silence. Finally, he spoke again. "They did what they said they were going to do. I got a new kidney. But certain things about the experience were… unsettling. And I've had a number of health issues since my return. I don't know whether I picked something up at the clinic, or if I'm just more susceptible with the drugs I'm on."

"What kind of health issues?" MacKenzie asked eagerly.

"I don't feel particularly comfortable discussing this over the phone."

He was shutting her down. He didn't want to share the details with her. And why would he? She was a complete stranger to him.

"Perhaps we could meet face-to-face?" Hopewell suggested.

"Certainly," MacKenzie agreed immediately, relieved. "I would be happy to meet with you at your convenience. Is there a particular time that would work for you?"

"Where are you? Are you in New Jersey?"

"No. Vermont. But I can make it there if you like. It's just a plane ride away."

"Actually, Vermont is better. I'm in New Hampshire. How close are you to Manchester?"

"I can get there," MacKenzie said, not telling him how many hours she would have to drive to meet with him. He was doing her a favor by answering her questions. The least she could do was to go to his house to show her face and let him suss her out in person. "Is tomorrow good? What's your address?"

"I could do this evening, if it isn't a bother for you. We could have supper. A public place is always better for a first meeting with someone you don't know."

"Sure. I have a couple of things that I need to do first… would an eight-thirty dinner be too late?"

"That would be perfect. I'll make a reservation for us at the Hampshire House. You can find it?"

"No problem."

"I will see you then."

22

MacKenzie had to hurry to get herself ready for supper. It was a three-hour drive to get to Hopewell, so if she wanted to make it on time, she had to leave within half an hour. But she'd gotten herself dolled up for a date in less time than that. She needed a dress that she could sit in for a number of hours without it seeming rumpled, so she looked through her closet quickly to find a black cocktail dress that had done well for her on other occasions. She threw a toothbrush and a few other items in an overnight bag, figuring she wouldn't be making the three-hour drive back after supper concluded at ten-thirty or later. Then she hopped into her car and was on her way.

At first, she drove with the radio on, but after a while it began to bother her. She was trying to think through what she knew about the Forsberg Clinic, to marshal all of the arguments that what they were doing was unethical and crossed the line against the arguments that the service they were providing saved lives both abroad and domestic, and that if people were prepared to pay the rates that were being discussed, there shouldn't be any impediment to their seeking the services overseas and leaving US kidneys in the US for domestic transplant. Was the clinic operating in a gray area? That much seemed clear. But she wasn't sure how dark that gray was, and if they had crossed into black, harming the transplant recipients they were supposed to be saving. Or if the pictures were what they appeared to be.

She reached the Hampshire House in good time. She introduced herself to the maître d', and he escorted her to her table. John Hopewell was already there ahead of her. He jumped to his feet and gave a little bow as the maître d' pulled out MacKenzie's chair for her.

"Miss Kirsch. It was very gracious of you to join me like this. I know making a trip like this on a whim isn't easy, but I appreciate your willingness."

"Of course."

She studied him as she sat down. He was skinny and pale. While a young man, his hair appeared to be thinning. It was hard to tell in the dimly lit dining room, she thought that his skin seemed yellowish. She put him at perhaps twenty-five years of age, yet at a quick glance he easily looked forty.

They discussed the weather and the menu. Hopewell ordered wine and then wouldn't touch it himself. "I have to be careful," he said obliquely, not offering any real explanation. MacKenzie felt awkward drinking without him, so she barely touched the wine herself, and the bottle sat there, getting gradually warmer as the evening wore on.

"I was hoping that you could tell me some details about your transplant surgery," MacKenzie said after a while. "I have run into a few… irregularities in my review of the Forsberg Clinic and I wanted to know if what happened to Amanda was related to her surgery, if it could have been prevented if they had followed proper procedures… or if she could have survived if they had just waited here until a kidney became available. I'm just… trying to make sense of it all, I guess."

"Trying to make sense of something that doesn't make any sense," Hopewell said. "Good luck with trying to justify who gets sick and dies and who doesn't." He shook his head. "I remember thinking as a kid that if I made all of the right choices, everything would turn out wonderful. If I ate healthy, I would be healthy. If I studied and did my homework, I'd be at the top of my class. If I followed the right path in dating and my relationships, then I would get married, become a father, and be able to have it all. I was very pragmatic. Just do this subset of things, and your reward will be…"

MacKenzie smiled. It was a bit simplistic, but she recognized similar magical thinking in herself as a child, and even as an adult, believing that if she did the right things, then that, combined with a little luck, would lead to a happy and satisfying life.

"I guess I can understand that."

"But then I got sick. Very sick, and in a few months, I was diagnosed with kidney disease, and soon after that, any plans and expectations that I had… I found out that I was going to be sick for the rest of my life. That I didn't have any control over the matter, over my body deciding to be sick when I had been doing all of the right things. Some of the things we do might prevent some of the disease subsets—reduce your risk of cancer, diabetes, heart disease—but you can't do anything about kidney disease. It isn't one of those things you can avoid the risk factors for. And once you've got it, you've got it. You're like a ticking time bomb. You never know when your time is going to be up, but it isn't ever going to get better."

"No," MacKenzie said quietly. Even though it hadn't happened to her, she still felt the same way. She had felt the same way since Amanda had been diagnosed. They had all been traumatized by it, discovering suddenly that life was not something they could control, but that this disease could sneak into their lives without warning and ruin all of their plans. Amanda would never be free of kidney disease; it would always be hiding in the wings.

Until it took her.

Hopewell gave MacKenzie a little smile and patted her hand. He didn't try any useless words of comfort. Just patted her hand and gave a little grimace of understanding.

"I'm sorry," MacKenzie said. "That really sucks. I wish it hadn't happened to you."

"Thanks."

"When were you diagnosed?"

"I was a teenager. Was on dialysis for six years. My tissue type seems to be difficult to match." He gave a shrug. "They didn't know when it would be that they'd be able to find me a kidney. Things were starting to look pretty grim. I knew I couldn't stay on dialysis forever, and that my health was starting to fail. I needed to get a new kidney, and I needed one pretty quickly."

"Did you already know about the Forsberg Clinic, or did someone tell you about them?"

"I started making some inquiries. I figured there had to be other pathways to getting a transplant, even if they were…" Hopewell hesitated. "Even if they were not approved methods here in the States. There had to be a way for me to get the surgery."

"So then you found Forsberg."

"They were mentioned to me by a friend and I followed up. I checked them out, saw the success they were having. They said that they were sure they could find me even if I was a hard subtype to match. They were sure they could get me a transplant within a year." Hopewell blew out his breath. "Funny how a year can seem so long and so short at the same time."

MacKenzie nodded.

"It was a godsend. I knew that I probably wasn't going to survive more than a year without a transplant. The system here in the States couldn't promise anything. Just that they would keep looking and they'd let me know if a kidney fell into their laps that was a match that they could use. And who knows how many people were on the transplant list before me. There was no guarantee that if they got a kidney it would be for me, even though things were getting pretty dire."

MacKenzie nodded with interest, encouraging him to go on. She took a sip of her wine, though she still felt weird about drinking when he was not. But Hopewell seemed to take no notice of it.

"So, how could Forsberg find you a match? I mean, if they couldn't find one in the US system, how could this little private clinic find you one?"

"There wasn't ever really any question of it. They said that they had a lot of potential live donors in their system. It was all on the computer so that they could search for certain combinations. They had recruiters. I don't think that's something you're allowed to do in the US, but maybe in some other places around the world… they actually have people who are in charge of signing up people who may be interested in donating an organ or tissue to someone in need. They weren't just waiting until people died and entered the system. For a number of organs and tissues, they can use live donors now."

MacKenzie nodded. "I know. I was Amanda's donor the first time. Gave her one of my kidneys."

Hopewell gave her a smile. "Good for you. I didn't have any siblings; nobody close to me was a close match. They can sometimes do media appeals, asking people if they would get tested to see if they are a match. It works with little kids, because people feel so bad, they feel driven to jump in and give a child the gift of life. An adult like me, not so much. There was no point in trying to get more donors through any kind of commercial effort for me." He shook his head, grinning. MacKenzie thought he had a very nice smile. He could say that an appeal to the public would never produce the organ he needed, but he couldn't know that. MacKenzie could just imagine the line of women signing up to see if they could possibly be a tissue match for the handsome young man who had appeared in the news.

"So you went to Forsberg, and they told you what a wonderful program they have. They said they probably had something in the system that they could help you with, because they have all of these people signed up."

"Yeah. It was pretty amazing to walk into the place and have them saying yes, they could find me a kidney, and they could have the transplant done within a year, so I could get off of dialysis and get healthy again. It was a lifesaver, literally. I would have done anything to get that kidney."

Anything? MacKenzie took a deep breath and let it out again.

"So you agreed to go with them, and they told you that they had found a match?"

"Yes. Almost immediately."

"Who did you deal with at the clinic?"

"A Dr. Dutton. Not the friendliest woman, but she seemed

competent, and she was getting me what I wanted, so I wasn't really concerned about personalities."

"I met her when I showed up at the clinic and asked for a tour," MacKenzie said. "I don't know if there is actually anyone else operating out of the New Jersey center."

"Maybe not," Hopewell agreed. "It was always pretty quiet whenever I went over there."

MacKenzie thought about her tour through the clinic. It had been pretty quiet. She hadn't run into any other staff in the hallways or as they looked around the clinic. But it was just an administrative center. The actual surgeries were not done there. The surgeons listed in their pamphlets or on the list that Dr. Dutton had given her were from other countries. There were probably management meetings, directors' meetings, and others at that building at strategic times, but that didn't mean they had to keep any amount of staff there full time.

"Where was your donor from?"

"Germany."

"They must have done a lot of recruiting there. That's where Amanda's donor was from too."

Hopewell nodded. "I don't know how many countries it is legal to do that; I haven't really looked into any of the international transplant law. But I got the feeling that a lot of stuff ran through Germany and Iran."

"Did you get to meet her? I know in the US, they have this policy where they keep it a secret and won't tell you the identity of donors. But those are dead donors. I don't know if the same thing applies to living donors."

"I didn't meet her, but they gave me a profile. Details about her."

"Yeah. I saw Amanda's. I thought that was pretty cool."

"It helped me to know where the kidney came from. That it wasn't coming from some impoverished third-world country. That even though I was paying for her to be flown to the clinic, she was donating out of the goodness of her heart, not because she was getting paid off."

MacKenzie nodded. "Exactly. I know Amanda was glad to know who her kidney was coming from too."

"I'd like to meet Sarah Hartwell someday. I'd really like to be able to thank her. I know it isn't done, but I'd like to be able to."

MacKenzie stared at him. "Who?"

"Sarah Hartwell. The woman who donated my kidney."

MacKenzie stared at him, mouth open.

23

MacKenzie was reluctant, for once, to step onto the sidewalk that led to the front door of her family home. Her brain was muddled with all of the facts and she wasn't sure how to present them to her father. Walter was not going to be pleased. But she didn't know how he was going to react. Outraged at what was going on? Defensive? The Forsberg clinic had given Amanda another year. Her parents kept repeating that and saying that MacKenzie shouldn't look any further into the surgery. Was that because they suspected?

Were they blind to what was going on? John Hopewell had told her that the transplant recipient and his family were required to sign confidentiality agreements with respect to the clinic. He and the others were not allowed to talk about the details of the clinic's operations. MacKenzie knew that meant that Amanda and her parents had also signed the confidentiality and non-disclosure agreement. That would be one of the reasons they were being so secretive about what had happened overseas. They had said they wouldn't tell.

But MacKenzie was family, not a member of the public. That was different. And there had to be exceptions to confidentiality agreements. Cases where one was required by law to reveal what they knew, whether there was an agreement in place or not.

She entered the house and closed the door behind her. She just stood there in the hall, wondering where Walter would be. She tried his office, but he wasn't there, and the room gave the impression of not having been used in a long time. It was just a front, to make MacKenzie and anyone else think that Walter was really living there, not in a separate residence.

MacKenzie followed her nose to the kitchen, where Walter had a row of bread slices arranged across the counter as he put together some sandwiches.

"Hi, Daddy."

"MacKenzie." He gave her a smile, but it was reserved. Like he was required to smile at her, but didn't really have anything to say to her. MacKenzie sat on one of the stools on the opposite side of the island from Walter.

"So," Walter said slowly, his voice full of disapproval. "Have you come to your senses and decided that it's time to let this nonsense go? You need to accept Amanda's death and move on. She wouldn't want you to be wasting all of your time trying to find out what happened. Whatever events led up to her death, you need to just accept it and go on with your own life."

"But what about the other people?"

He frowned at her, eyebrows drawing down. "What other people?"

"The other people who get transplants through that clinic."

"Just let them live their lives. Who are you to tell them what they can or can't do? It's ridiculous, MacKenzie. You need to just move on."

He slapped cold cuts onto the bread. MacKenzie watched him add some lettuce to each and then close them. She wasn't hungry. In fact, the sight and smell of the meat was making her nauseated.

"What if what they are doing is dangerous or illegal?"

"Organ transplant carries risks. But Amanda was well taken care of. They never put her at risk. And as far as legal goes..." he gave a shrug. "Laws change. You know that. I've made a career out of lobbying for change. And you can believe that I'm lobbying to get changes made to the transplant laws. It's ridiculous to have such barbaric laws in place putting limits on who can get an organ when they need one."

"You think it should just be free market?"

He considered. "Why not? What harm is there in allowing people to pay for what they need? It benefits the donor as well as the recipient, so why not?"

"I think you should look at these pictures *before* you eat."

He snorted. "You really think I have that weak of a stomach? I've seen plenty of transplant pictures. Even watched movies of transplant surgery. I know what it looks like."

"I don't think you know everything."

He just looked at her. MacKenzie put her attache on the counter in front of her and took out the envelope the pictures were in. They were brightened and blown up, so they were grainy, but they were clear enough to make out. Walter picked up one of the pictures and looked at it, frowning.

She wondered if he saw the same thing as she did at first. A family asleep in the same kind of knocked-together shelter as Lisa and Walter had stayed at during their stay. Bodies of varying sizes lying side by side on a bare concrete floor with a sheet pulled over them.

She remembered the dawning feeling of horror as she looked at them, gradually understanding that they were not sleeping, but dead. Corpses lined up on the floor with a sheet pulled over them to hide the gruesome sight. A few feet poked out the bottom of the sheet. Dark-skinned feet.

Walter looked over the picture at MacKenzie. "Where did you get these?"

"Amanda took them. They were on her computer. Between the pictures of the place you stayed and the flight home."

The crease between his eyebrows deepened. "I don't know what this is, but she never said anything to us."

MacKenzie nodded. "She didn't say anything to me either. I don't know how she could see this and not talk about it to anyone. Maybe the anesthesia made her forget what she had seen. Or maybe she felt so guilty that she didn't want to admit what was going on. Or maybe because she'd signed a confidentiality agreement, she didn't think she could."

"What do you think you're seeing here? You're making assumptions. We don't know what this is."

MacKenzie scowled at him. "These are corpses. These are the organ donors."

"You don't know that. It's a medical clinic. They could have died of anything. Typhoid. Influenza."

"It wasn't a medical clinic. It was a transplant hospital. They didn't do anything else there, did they?"

"How could we know? They could have a community medicine program as well. Something to compensate the islanders who let them build there. Modern medicine for development permission."

"Do you remember the donor profile for Amanda's donor? Sarah Hartwell from Germany?"

"Yes, of course."

"Last night I had dinner with a man who also received her donor profile for his transplant."

"Maybe… she donated other tissues."

"He received a kidney."

Walter opened his mouth to argue with MacKenzie, then closed his mouth. A single donor could make multiple tissue donations. But a living donor could not give two kidneys, one to Amanda and one to John.

"A simple paper mix-up," Walter said finally. "They accidentally gave the same profile to both of them. One of them should have received a different profile."

That's what MacKenzie had been trying to tell herself. But coupling the identical donor profiles with the pictures of the bodies weakened the argument.

"Daddy. These are not a paper mix-up," she tapped one of the photos of the bodies. "People are dying at this clinic."

"I'm sure there's a logical explanation. You're jumping to conclusions based on very limited information. We have dealt with the people at this clinic. We've met them face-to-face and talked to them. We've been there, on the island. Believe me, if they were killing natives to harvest their body parts, it would be discovered very quickly." He gave a chuckle. "People disappearing from a little place like this, it would be noticed."

"But this many people dying of influenza wouldn't be unusual?" MacKenzie countered, looking at the picture of the bodies again. She pointed to the floor a few feet away from the bodies, where black-looking liquid pooled. "And what is this?"

Walter squinted at it. He looked through the pictures slowly. "I don't know, MacKenzie, and neither do you. It could be oil. It could be anything. You can't look at those pictures and tell me you can be sure *what* liquid is pooled in the room."

"It's blood."

"You can't tell from a picture. Certainly not one with this kind of lighting and resolution. I understand you are concerned. I understand you want to find someone to blame for Amanda's death. You want an explanation." He held his hands palm-up in a pleading gesture. "So do we. But the answer is simple. She had kidney disease. We did everything we possibly could for her, but in the end, her body simply couldn't deal with it."

"I don't believe that. I know she had kidney disease, but she didn't die from that. She died from malaria."

"She died from ARDS."

"Which was caused by malaria. Which was caused by her going to this tropical island to get a transplant from an organization that is… is…" She struggled to find the words, "…is engaged in questionable practices. And I want some answers."

He shook his head impatiently. "You need to get your head out of the sand. You're making up stories to suit yourself. You're looking for someone else to blame."

"And this doesn't bother you." MacKenzie nodded at the pictures. "They showed you pictures of a big, modern, clean facility. One where, as you say, she couldn't possibly have been bitten by a mosquito and contracted malaria. And instead, you find out that she was being operated on in some dirty shack where they're piling bodies up like cordwood. That doesn't make you question everything else they told you? Everything they showed you, from the glossy brochure down to the handwritten donor profile was fake."

"Yes, it is concerning," he agreed. He stopped, looking at MacKenzie and waiting for her to take this in and be ready for the next thing he said. "But there is a bigger picture." He lowered his voice, as if they were out in public and someone might overhear his words to her. "I am lobbying for substantive changes to the organ transplant business. I can't have you running around, looking underneath rocks, stirring everything up. You need to leave it alone. Trust me, I will look into it, and I will deal with it if they have been lying to us. But do not mess this up for everyone else. People need this system. They need these reforms. Or more people will die."

MacKenzie stared at her father, floored. "You're willing to let them get away with this? With killing your daughter?"

"That's overstating. I said I would look into it. I will take care of it. But if you are going to start spouting off about how the system needs more regulation instead of less, you are going to be the cause of the deaths of hundreds, even thousands of people who could be saved with these reforms. We're not just talking about one life," he said fiercely. "There are thousands of people waiting for organ transplants who will die before they get it. And thousands more who can't even get onto the waiting list because they are too sick. Think about that for a minute. The regulators say they are too sick to get a transplant, the only thing that could make them better. But because they don't have enough organs to go around, they have to eliminate people somehow. So those who are too sick, they lose out. Along with a lot of other people they have found a way to exclude."

MacKenzie covered her eyes, trying to wrap her mind around his argument. "You think it's okay, what this clinic is doing."

He held up a finger. "I think that what this clinic *claims* to be doing is okay. Obviously, or I would not have taken Amanda there. What they are supposed to be doing is providing a way for us to get around all of the over-regulation of the industry to get that transplant. If they are doing something else…" he looked down at the photos and shook his head. "I never said that was okay."

MacKenzie didn't know where to go with that. Walter put

together several sandwiches. He put a single one on a plate and pushed it in her direction and put a couple more on a plate for himself. He stood eating, saying nothing more, while MacKenzie stared at the sandwich, not hungry and not sure how to even talk to her father.

"Daddy…"

"You need to leave it alone, MacKenzie. You leave it to me."

24

She declined her father's invitation to stay at the family house for the night. She didn't want to be in the same house as he was. She needed to get away and be able to think things through. Somehow, she needed to clear her head and figure out what was going on.

She hadn't expected him to argue with her once he saw the pictures. She thought that he would have the same reaction to them as she did—that they were proof of nefarious goings-on at the Forsberg clinic. Proof that they were not just providing a workaround for people who were willing to pay more for a transplant. Those bodies lying on the floor haunted her. She tried to make out the relative sizes of each. Were they a family? Were the smaller ones children? Women?

It hadn't occurred to her that they could be anything but the organ donors. She had immediately jumped to that conclusion, as Walter had observed. He'd been right about that, at least. As far as she knew, Forsberg wasn't offering general medical services to the natives. They were only doing transplants. But she didn't *know* that. They could be. The dark pool of liquid, though, she was sure it was blood. And why would there be blood pooled in the room, except if that was where they were performing surgery? Walter couldn't be right about the people having died of influenza or some other virus. They wouldn't have been left in a surgical room if that were the case.

MacKenzie wasn't sure she wanted to go home. But she didn't want to have anyone over, either. It was getting to be tiresome to have to deal with anyone else. When she invited men over, they wanted to be entertained. They wanted her attention. They didn't want to just keep her company, watching TV or doing something undemanding. That was the problem with not having a steady boyfriend. She didn't have anyone she could just let down her hair with and kick back to enjoy a quiet evening. Everything had to be an event.

Christopher had not been too bad. But she'd enjoyed her time with John Hopewell more than Christopher. What did that say about her? She would rather have dinner with a sick man than a night with a virile man like Christopher Marsh? She'd never been a Florence Nightingale, attracted to men who needed to be cared for. She'd always thought that kind of woman weak.

For a while, she just took random turns.

The phone rang and MacKenzie picked it up as she drove. She didn't see the number before she flipped it open.

"Hello?"

"Is this MacKenzie?"

"Yeah."

"It's Lance."

It took MacKenzie a minute for MacKenzie to remember who Lance was. The private investigator at Mountain Investigations. The guy who was supposed to be looking up the principals on the clinic's board to see what he could find out about their backgrounds.

"Oh, hey Lance. Good to hear from you. What've you got?"

"It sounds like you're driving."

"Yeah, I am."

"Why don't we meet somewhere. I don't like giving reports over the phone, that much less so when the other party is driving. I don't want you having an accident, and you can't really absorb everything if your attention is on the road."

"Just go ahead, I'll get it. There isn't much traffic and I'm just... driving around aimlessly."

"Do you know where the Fox and Hound is?"

"Sure." It wasn't somewhere MacKenzie frequented, but it was a popular pub and she knew where it was. More the kind of place that would suit Walter, which was probably what made Lance suggest it. He had probably taken Walter there at some point.

"Fine. I'll meet you there," she agreed.

"I'll be there in about ten minutes. See you whenever you get there."

MacKenzie hung up the phone. She turned the car around and headed toward the pub. It took her about fifteen minutes. There were hardly any spaces left in the parking lot when she got there, and she drove up and down the aisles for a few minutes before finding one that she could squeeze her little car into, beside a jeep that was taking up more than its allotted space. She grabbed her purse and attache, climbed out, and locked the doors.

She had seen Lance before, but she didn't really know him and wasn't sure she would recognize his face. But he was watching for her.

"MacKenzie."

She startled at the voice in her ear, turning to him quickly.

"Sorry," Lance apologized, putting up his hands, "didn't mean to scare you. It's Lance."

He was taller than she, in his late thirties, blond, with broad shoulders but not a heavy build. A handsome face, but marred on one side by what MacKenzie thought were burn scars.

She let out her breath. "Of course. Nice to meet you, Lance. Well, officially, I mean."

He nodded and smiled and motioned for her to go with him to a table that he'd managed to corner despite the busyness of the place. "Here we go, have a seat."

MacKenzie looked around. "I had no idea that this was such a popular spot. I mean, I know that Daddy came here, but I always pictured it as a pretty quiet place."

Lance shook his head. "No, it's almost always full during regular hours. You want to get it quiet and you need to get a private booking."

"I don't imagine that comes cheap."

"No, it doesn't. But it's effective if you want somewhere private to meet away from offices and homes."

MacKenzie nodded. He was younger than she had expected him to be. She had expected him to be Walter's age. Much closer to MacKenzie in age than she ever would have thought. It was funny how differently she perceived people's ages as she got older.

He had some fine lines on his face, most of them pleasant and reaching upward rather than downward. Someone who smiled more than he scowled. Which was something she hadn't expected in a private detective. They saw the seamier side of life, didn't they? She would have expected him to be more grim.

"Drinks?" Lance offered.

"I'm going to be driving, so… no more than a glass."

He motioned for a waiter and got the attention of one of them immediately. The waiter hovered as they placed their drink orders, then moved away to give them some privacy once more.

"So, how has it been going?" MacKenzie asked. "The investigation, I mean. Was everything what we expected it to be?"

He cocked an eyebrow. "That depends on what you were expecting."

"I don't know… everybody well-respected. Not too perfect, but nothing scandalous… nobody charged with manslaughter for killing a patient on the table, or something like that."

Lance smiled. "Well, no one was charged with manslaughter. So you got that part right."

"Good." MacKenzie nodded. If Forsberg were hiring unscrupulous surgeons, people who weren't' properly trained or board certified, then she would have expected there to be some charges. Somebody who said that they should never have been practicing medicine in the first place. "No… malpractice or anything?"

"Well, malpractice is another story."

Their drinks were delivered, and each sipped theirs for a moment before going back to the conversation.

"They've been sued for malpractice?"

"Hard to find an eminent surgeon these days who hasn't been. Seems like a lot more of them have been than not. But I think a lot of that is just our litigious society. You didn't like the outcome of your elderly mother's surgery? Sue them. So that in itself really isn't a red flag. Unless someone has a larger number of malpractice suits than you would expect. Or has actually been convicted of malpractice or lost his license."

"And was there anyone like that?"

"Well, you're rushing ahead a little bit. Why don't you let me give you my report, and then if you have questions after that, you can let me know?"

MacKenzie shrugged and smiled. "Daddy was just getting after me for jumping to conclusions. I seem to be doing a lot of that."

Lance took another sip of his drink and put it to the side to make room for the file he placed on the table. "Okay. Let's go over the directors first. Most of them are domestic, so they weren't hard to find or to trace their careers and other details."

MacKenzie listened carefully while he gave her a brief summary of each of the directors. He had a written report on each director, so she didn't have to make notes, but just listened to what he had found. They were the kinds of men that she would have expected. High-powered doctors or businessmen with a history of political involvement.

"None of them have been convicted of anything that would be of concern," Lance said slowly. "But on the other hand, none of them exactly has clean hands, either. Some issues with the SEC, sanctions from the medical board... just warnings to stay on the right side of the law and not to play it fast and loose. The kind of things that high-powered investors get involved in when they decide to see just how far they can push the envelope."

MacKenzie nodded. Her father was, she suspected, in the same boat. He wasn't a criminal, and he was known in the lobbyist circles as a white hat, but that didn't stop him from playing the stock market or making a business investment in a less-savory company. She didn't know whether he had ever been officially investigated or sanctioned by any regulator, but she could remember hearing more than once over the years how he was dealing with one board or government agency or another as they tried to sort out his affairs and he tried to answer their questions without giving the game away. He strove to remain on the right side of the law, but that didn't mean he didn't have the occasional reach over to the dark side.

"Okay, that all sounds pretty much what I expected," she said, taking a stack of reports from him so that she could look at them more carefully later. She'd had a long day and while the wine was soothing, it wasn't exactly conducive to studying research reports. She squared the pages and set them in front of her. "And what about the rest of them? The woman who is running the clinic, the surgeons they have overseas..."

"We'll come back to Mildred Dutton. But let's go overseas and take a look at the doctors that they have operating the clinic."

MacKenzie remembered the lined-up bodies and the pool of blood. She had a steadying drink and nodded at him to go on.

"First of all... most of them don't exist."

MacKenzie had to think about that one. "They don't exist?"

"Yeah. I told you, we have partner firms all over the world, so we have the best local access to information. It isn't just that they don't show up when you search them on Google. It's far deeper than that. These men are ghosts. If they do exist, they're just your run-of-the-mill GP's or general surgeons. Not transplant experts."

"Could someone like that be performing transplants?"

"Quite possibly, yes. Just because a doctor doesn't have a reputation as a great surgeon, that doesn't mean that he hasn't taken the necessary training or had someone to show him the ropes so that he can do it on his own. But these are not men who would be operating as transplant surgeons if they were in the US. Not out in the open, anyway. They may be perfectly competent. But they may also be hacks. They didn't really exist until they started working for the clinic."

MacKenzie shook her head. "I don't really know what that means."

"We're still investigating, so I can't tell you for sure what it means either. They may be doctors who have operated in other countries who changed their names or who we can't be sure of because they changed their practice area. When you have a John Smith operating in England as a gynecologist, and then later a John Smith operating in some tiny island as a transplant surgeon, how do you know whether it is the same one? We have to get access to social security numbers, birthdates, photos, something that will tie the two of them together. They might have been trained in their own country but never passed the boards. Or they may have been trained in a country that doesn't really regulate their medical profession. It all depends on how far you want us to look. How deep do you want us to go?"

MacKenzie nodded slowly. "For now… maybe we'd better back off a bit. Daddy is on a rampage about me screwing things up for him. If I told him about all of this… he might have an aneurysm. I didn't tell him that I was actually investigating them. He only knows that I looked at Amanda's files and went to the Forsberg Clinic in New Jersey. You didn't tell him about this, did you…?"

"You are my client in this matter, not your father. I wouldn't tell him without your permission."

"And you don't have any kind of conflict of interest in looking this kind of thing up? When he would be against it?"

"I'll let you know if I see a conflict. Right now, no. He hasn't retained us to investigate anything in connection with the clinic or the transplant industry."

"He might. He says it's something he's lobbying on right now, so he could come to you and ask you to look something up."

"We'll cross that bridge when we come to it."

"Yeah, just let me know… I don't want to get in Daddy's way, but I do want to know what happened to Amanda."

He sat back, studying her.

MacKenzie raised her brows. "What?"

"Why don't you tell me the backstory here?"

"What backstory?"

"When you retained me, you told me that you just wanted to look into this clinic before making a donation, to avoid tarnishing your reputation. But you're not surprised that some of the principals are... risk takers and that the doctors may not be trained to American standards. So tell me, what *did* happen to Amanda?"

MacKenzie had forgotten the ruse she had used in hiring him. Her cheeks warmed.

"Oh."

"You obviously suspect them of some wrongdoing. This isn't just a background check to make sure there are no red flags for publicity."

MacKenzie nodded slowly. "You're right. Amanda's death... may have been related to her transplant overseas at the Forsberg clinic."

"You think they made a mistake? Malpractice?"

"At first, I thought it was just a fluke, that she got malaria because she had her transplant done overseas instead of stateside. But there have been other issues... a lot of secrecy around the transplant, like it's something they wanted to hide... I came across some disturbing pictures on Amanda's computer... and it looks like all of their brochures and literature are lies. So, hearing this from you... it isn't that surprising. I think what's they're doing is... dangerous."

"Knowing your father and something about the transplant industry, I expect there is a lot of money involved here. And people trying to protect their money can be dangerous too. I don't think that the transplant recipients are the only ones who have reason to be concerned. If you are putting their livelihood in jeopardy, you could attract attention of the wrong sort."

MacKenzie gave a little laugh and shook her head. "That's a little melodramatic. I'm not doing anything to put anyone's livelihood in danger. I haven't tried to stop them from doing what they're doing, I'm just trying to find out... exactly what it is."

"One will lead to the other. Are you telling me that if you discover it is a criminal enterprise and Amanda died because they were unconcerned about the conditions the transplants were done in, you wouldn't blow the whistle on them and try to get them shut down? Put them in prison? I realize that I don't know you personally, but I know your father and I know the way he talks about you. You're not going to let this go."

MacKenzie rolled her eyes at that. She had not been a particularly rebellious child growing up, and she had never been a fighter, but Walter frequently made comments about her being a spitfire. She suspected he just wished that she was more like he was. Wishful thinking.

But she couldn't argue with what Lance said. It was true—if the Forsberg Clinic were responsible for Amanda's death, she wouldn't be able to back down and let it alone. She was already feeling anxious about the pictures of the transplant hospital and her father's reaction to her poking around. She couldn't ignore the way that those bodies had been lined up on the floor. Not if it meant what she thought it did. She wanted to do what her father said, but she couldn't just ignore those bodies, and Amanda's death. She needed to know more. She needed to know the truth.

Lance was watching her, as if he could read the thoughts running through her mind. MacKenzie shifted uncomfortably. She tapped the attache enclosing her papers and the photos.

"Does your firm do any kind of… photo analysis?"

"What kind of analysis? Forensic? There are some specialists we could engage. Gets pricey, though."

MacKenzie raised an eyebrow. "I'm not concerned about price."

He laughed. "I guess not," he agreed. "You have them with you?"

"I took them to show to Walter. He… didn't react the way I'd hoped." MacKenzie hesitated, then opened the attache and pulled them out. She placed them on the table in front of Lance.

25

Lance examined the top photo with a casual air, then his eyes narrowed, and he looked at it more closely. His eyes moved from one part of the photo to another. He looked at MacKenzie.

"Where did you get these?"

"They were on Amanda's computer. By the date codes, this is the hospital where she received her transplant."

"Hospital?" His laugh was a sharp bark. "This looks more like a slaughterhouse. Tell me what you think you're looking at here."

MacKenzie looked down at the table, suddenly tongue-tied. She was getting the reaction from him that she had hoped to get from her father. She had wanted him to be outraged. To swear that he would find out what had happened to Amanda in that place and see that it didn't happen to anyone else ever again. But instead, his reaction had been to stop MacKenzie. To tell her to back off. Was it because he was concerned about her? Or about his own projects? She didn't want to think that money overrode his love for his daughters. She had always thought herself a cherished part of his life.

"Kenzie..."

She looked up from the table, into Lance's deep blue concerned eyes. Amanda was the only one who called her Kenzie. And Amanda was gone forever. He put his hand on her arm.

"Kenzie, look at me. I need you to stay with me here. You might think this is something you can keep quiet, but it isn't. The police should be notified. The feds. Interpol. We're not talking about malpractice here. This… this is something you can't ignore. This isn't a little fraud or trying to work around regulation."

"Daddy said it could have been typhoid or influenza. They could be operating a public medical clinic, and there was an epidemic."

"Of course that's a possibility…" His eyes returned to the photo. "But with all of the blood… Maybe a hemorrhagic fever, but still… this just doesn't look right. If a first-world clinic was offering their services in a place like this, I would still expect to see beds, body bags, medical equipment. Not just… bodies lined up on the floor."

"In an epidemic, they might have run out of beds and body bags."

"And they still had your sister and others into the hospital to do transplant surgeries? With an epidemic like that raging? You wouldn't bring someone with a suppressed immune system into an epidemic."

MacKenzie lowered her eyes. "No," she admitted. "They made a big deal about how they avoided exposing the transplant patients to infections. Family members were not allowed to stay with them at the hospital. They were put up somewhere else and the transplant patients were taken to the hospital without them."

"What did Amanda tell you about the conditions there? Did she verify these?" He indicated the pictures again.

"She didn't talk to me about it at all. I found the pictures after she had died."

"If these were the conditions at the hospital where she got her transplant," Lance gazed at the boards nailed together haphazardly and the concrete floor, the bodies piled along the wall and covered with a sheet, and the pooled blood. "Why would she not tell you about it? Why wouldn't she tell your parents? They were there on the island with her. If she got there and discovered these kinds of conditions, wouldn't she just turn around and say that she wasn't going to go through with it?"

MacKenzie shook her head. "I don't know. I don't understand

what happened. It's like they were all brainwashed. They didn't tell me what was going on at the time, said she was just going to have a surgery to improve her kidney function. And she didn't say anything when she came back. I thought… maybe the anesthesia made her forget this, and anything else she saw there. Maybe there was another hospital where she recovered, and everything looked like it should."

"If they had a real hospital, then what was this?"

"I don't know."

He pondered, looking down at the pictures. The crowds around them were noisy, everybody having a good time. It was a strange place to be discussing something so nightmarish.

"I think you should talk to the police about it."

"And say what? I found these pictures on my sister's computer. She saw something horrific but she never told me about them. I think it was the Forsberg Clinic's transplant hospital, but I don't know for sure. I think they were… organ donors, but I don't know, that's just a guess. It's all just wild speculation."

"Maybe you could find some of the other transplant patients. Talk to them about it. See if anyone else saw anything like this, knows where it might be."

"I've been trying. Some of them are just following the clinic's party line, so I haven't bothered to talk to them. The ones that Forsberg didn't tell me I could talk to, I'm trying to get in contact with."

He nodded. "Good idea."

"Some of them have died."

"Ouch. I suppose so."

MacKenzie remembered her dinner with John Hopewell in New Hampshire. "Everybody who was involved, both the transplant recipients and their families, signed confidentiality agreements. They're not supposed to talk about it with anyone."

Lance looked into her eyes. "But…?"

"I met with someone… he's having a lot of the same symptoms as my sister. His doctors keep telling him he's just susceptible to whatever viruses are going around. I told him that they should test him for malaria."

"What could he tell you about the hospital where he got the transplant?"

"I didn't show him the pictures. I just asked if it was like the pictures of the hospital in the brochure."

"And…?"

"He said 'more or less,' and wouldn't commit to anything. He said that there were things going on that disturbed him, but he also said that he was drugged up a lot of the time, and he didn't know how much of it was real, and how much was nightmares."

"So he's a dead end, unless he decides he's willing to tell you more."

MacKenzie shrugged. "I guess so, yeah."

Lance walked MacKenzie to her car, though she really had no concerns about running into any bad characters in the parking lot at night. It was a brightly-lit lot, there was lots of activity, and there were security guards patrolling it on and off throughout the night.

"We want to keep you safe," Lance said lightly. "If your father thought I let anything happen to you…"

But she didn't think he was really concerned about people lurking in the shadows either. He just wanted to walk with her.

They stopped at her car. "This is me," MacKenzie said, gesturing to it.

He looked at the sedate little compact. "You should have something with a little more… power."

"I'm just buzzing around town. It gets me from point A to point B."

"I just think you should have something more interesting. Something… sexier. Like you." He chuckled. "Did that sound as cheesy to you as it did to me?"

MacKenzie grinned. "Pretty much."

"Then I apologize." He started to say something else, then shook his head. "Okay, no more comments about the car. It's all going to come out sounding lame."

"What do *you* think I should be driving? What do you picture me in?"

"Maybe a little red convertible. Something fun and powerful. You have the money. You could splurge on something that made you feel good instead of something that just got you from point A to point B."

MacKenzie nodded, looking at it. "Not exactly practical for Vermont."

"Exactly my point."

MacKenzie laughed. She turned away from him to get in. His hand was on her arm, stopping her.

"Kenzie."

The way he said it made goosebumps stand up on her arms. She stopped, looking at him. "Yes?"

"Just be careful. These guys have a lot at risk. They'll want to protect their investment. Don't talk about it to anyone."

MacKenzie nodded. "Okay." She thought about all of the people she had already talked to and felt guilty. But she was sure he was overreacting. Nothing was going to happen to her.

26

MacKenzie's mind was whirling as she drove home and parked in the parking garage. Not just with the new information about the clinic, but also with Lance's apparent romantic interest. She was used to men being interested in her due to her social standing and family wealth. But she got the feeling that Lance was interested in more than that. He was concerned about her welfare, which was sweet. He definitely knew about her father and that he wouldn't be an easy man to get along with if he became aware MacKenzie was seeing the investigator. Lance was not their social class and Walter would not be impressed.

As intrigued as MacKenzie was by Lance's advances, her mind fell quickly back to thoughts of Amanda. Had the doctors who performed her surgery even been properly trained? Was she operated on in some slapped-together shack rather than the big, modern facility that the brochures showed? What had she been thinking the last year as she had kept her experiences a secret? Had she wanted to tell MacKenzie about it but been worried about the confidentiality agreement she had signed?

How many others had died like Magnus Phelps or were currently sick, fighting bizarre tropical diseases that their doctors didn't know to look for? If they'd only caught Amanda's malaria a little sooner, would it have been enough to save her? If John Hopewell had the same thing, would treatment spare him the same death as Amanda?

MacKenzie reached out to fit her key into the lock at the apartment door, but it swung open at her touch, not latched properly.

MacKenzie looked at it, bewildered, as her mind ran through possible scenarios. Had she not pulled it shut behind her? Had she already unlocked it, but been so distracted by her thoughts about Amanda that she had just forgotten it? Had the doorman come up to deliver something for her and forgotten to shut it? Or maybe he was still in there?

MacKenzie rested her hand on the doorknob. "Hello? Is there someone here?"

There was only stillness in response. No answering voice or movement.

"Hello?"

MacKenzie pushed the door open. There were no packages in her front entryway. She pushed the door shut behind her, but it didn't latch. She looked at it to see what had blocked it, and saw the splintered frame. The door had been kicked in, busted through the doorframe. MacKenzie's heart was pounding hard, her breath caught in her throat.

"Hello? Is there someone here?"

She was afraid to walk through the entryway of her apartment into the large front room to see if there were anyone still there. She forced herself to look anyway, like when she was a little kid afraid of monsters under the bed or in the closet. If she just looked, then she would know that there was nothing to worry about.

There was no sound. She walked through to the front room. Nobody there.

But someone had been.

MacKenzie backed away, back through her entryway and the door out to the elevator. She waited impatiently for the elevator to make it back up to her floor, heart pounding like a train engine. When it finally got there, she jumped in and stared at the floor buttons blankly for a moment, freezing up. It seemed like an eternity before she remembered that the L button was the one she wanted, and she pushed it. The elevator lurched, descending back to the main floor. No one else got on to interrupt its descent. When it stopped and the doors opened, she tripped over the space between the floor of the elevator and the floor of the lobby, stumbling unceremoniously into the big, echoing lobby.

"Miss Kirsch? Is something wrong?" Eddie, the night doorman, was quickly at her side, taking her arm to steady her and looking into her face with concern. MacKenzie held on to him, trying to steady herself and get the words out.

"Someone in my apartment," she gasped out. "Someone was there."

"There is someone in your apartment?" He escorted her over to the little grouping of chairs and couches to sit her down. "Who? An intruder?"

MacKenzie breathed heavily, nodding. "Not anymore—or I didn't go all the way in to check—door is broken. They..."

His eyes widened with alarm. "You just wait right here, Miss Kirsch. I'm just going to get security and the police."

He hurried over to the phone at the desk and placed a couple of quick calls. MacKenzie sat there, looking around at the lobby like she'd never seen it before in her life, trying to sort out what was happening. Eddie returned to her in a few minutes.

"Somebody is going to check on it right now, and the police are on their way. Are you okay? Can I get you anything? A drink?"

MacKenzie clutched her purse to her, feeling the need to hold on to something and to ensure that her property was safe. She couldn't believe that someone had broken into her apartment. Why would anyone target her? She had money, but so did everyone else who lived in the building. Was it just because her suite had been unoccupied? Had anyone else been targeted?

"Miss Kirsch? What can I do for you?"

"That's good, that's fine," MacKenzie babbled. "I don't know why..."

"The police will find out what happened. Don't you worry about that. I'm going to get you a coffee, would you like that? Or tea?"

"Tea," MacKenzie said faintly. She didn't want something that was going to keep her up all night. "Thank you."

Her mother would want her to remember her manners, even if her personal space had been violated. A lady always remembered her manners. MacKenzie looked around for her mother. She wasn't there. Should MacKenzie call her? Tell her what had happened? Lisa would be concerned. She would want to know.

But it could wait until after the police had come and could tell her something.

"You just rest here for a minute, and I'll get you something soothing," Eddie promised.

She was aware of people coming and going, walking by her with curious looks, Eddie pressing a cup of herbal tea into her hand and encouraging her to have a sip. It seemed like forever before a couple of police cars pulled up in front of the building and the officers made their way into the lobby.

"It's the top floor," Eddie told them. "Penthouse. A couple of security guards are up there to secure the scene, they said that no one is there anymore."

One of the police officers took charge, a big man with a florid red face. "You're sure that someone has broken into the apartment? This wasn't just..." he glanced at MacKenzie, "a misunderstanding? Someone forgot to lock up or let themselves in with a key...?"

"No one has a key," MacKenzie protested. She followed Walter's advice to never give anyone a key to her apartment, no matter how good she felt about them. A policy that applied to everyone, so she didn't have to make a judgment call.

"The door was broken," Eddie advised, repeating what he'd heard from the security guards, since MacKenzie hadn't given him any such details. "It was definitely a break-in."

"We'll go take a look. Why don't you stay with her," the cop said to the one female officer who had come with them, "get her statement. Find out if we have any suspects."

The female cop nodded and sat down with MacKenzie while the others went up to have a look.

"You must be very upset about this," the cop said, moving as close as she could to MacKenzie without crowding her. "Why don't you tell me, from the beginning, what happened when you went up to your suite?"

MacKenzie rubbed her eyes. She wasn't sure why tears were leaking out the corners of her eyes. She was afraid they made her look weak or hysterical. She blinked, trying to clear her vision, and looked at the officer's name bar. Ferris.

"I just went up to my apartment… nothing different than usual… but when I got there, the door was open. Broken through the frame. I only went a few steps inside… but there was stuff scattered everywhere. Like someone had *tossed* my apartment." She shook her head in disbelief. "I don't understand it. Who would do something like that?"

Ferris nodded sympathetically. "It's hard to make sense of it all, isn't it? You poor girl. Is there someone we can call to sit with you? You want to have someone to keep you company?"

"No… I don't know… maybe later. What are they doing up there? Whoever it was, they've left."

"They're just investigating. Seeing what was done and gathering any evidence as to who might have done it. Don't you worry about that."

"I don't understand."

"No. It doesn't make much sense, does it? Have you had any problems before?"

"No. I've never had a break-in."

"Do you have any valuables in your apartment…? You must…"

"I don't know…" MacKenzie thought about the contents of her apartment. Yes, it was nicely decorated, and she had some jewelry and art that were worth a pretty price tag, but she would never have expected anyone to break in to steal them. What kind of person did that? "I have… I have nice things."

"Yes, I'm sure you must. Is there anything new? Or anything anyone has particularly admired lately?"

"No… I don't think so."

Ferris nodded. "It might have just been a crime of opportunity. This is a nice building, and it makes sense that the penthouse suite would contain valuables… it might not be anyone who actually knows you."

MacKenzie blinked. Someone who knew her. Would someone who knew her have done something like that? Broken into her apartment and messed things up?

"Someone I know?"

"Have you had any arguments lately? Anyone who might have resented or targeted you for some reason? Sometimes the silliest little things can set people off. Someone that you brushed off, or who thought you should have invited them up to your room? Or maybe an ex who was jealous over a new boyfriend…?"

At MacKenzie's blank stare, she amended. "Or girlfriend?"

The suggestion made MacKenzie laugh, breaking through some of the inertia she was feeling. "No, definitely boyfriend," she said.

Ferris held pencil poised over her notepad. "Was there anyone who you can think of who might have wanted to get back at you for something? Or who maybe admired your jewelry just a bit too much…?"

"No… I don't know. There was Liam Jackson… he was irritated when I wouldn't let him stay in my apartment alone. I had to go see my sister, who was in hospital sick, and he was kind of pouting about it."

She watched Ferris write the name down and immediately felt guilty. "But I'm sure he wouldn't do anything. Just because he wanted to have a long shower, that doesn't mean… he wouldn't have turned around and done something like that."

"You never know," Ferris gave a shrug. "At least it's a starting point. Anyone else?"

MacKenzie was reluctant to suggest any other names. "I… well… Roger… he was pretty mad about getting kicked out, I threatened to call the police… but I needed some sleep…"

"Roger…?"

MacKenzie rubbed her forehead. What if the names she disclosed to the police ended up in the paper or community gossip? The last thing she needed was a reputation as a tramp or tease, someone who invited men up to her apartment and then kicked them to the curb when she was done with them. Her mother already thought her behavior was scandalous, and she didn't know half of what MacKenzie did.

"What was Roger's last name?" Ferris prompted.

"Milford. But I'm sure it wouldn't be him. Neither one of them. They wouldn't have any reason to steal anything from me, they're both quite wealthy themselves..."

Ferris wrote it down anyway. "That doesn't rule out revenge, though. They might not have taken anything. It might have just been to scare you or get back at you for kicking them out."

MacKenzie shook her head. She really didn't want the police going after these prominent families. "Look, I really don't think that it could be either of them. It could cause me real problems if you go after them..."

"No one is going after anyone. We are just investigating. We'll be discreet."

"I don't know..."

"Is there anything else you can think of? Have you had any threats? Any strange phone calls or hang-ups?"

MacKenzie thought of Lance's warnings, which she hadn't previously connected to the break-in. What if it was someone who was connected with the clinic? What if they had gotten wind of her investigation? Suddenly dizzy with the possibilities, she picked up her cup and had another sip of the tea. They couldn't have found out about her investigation. She had been careful. Lance's firm would have been careful not to tip the clinic off. Dr. Dutton still believed that MacKenzie was interested in making a donation to the clinic.

"What is it?" Ferris asked.

"I don't know... I don't think..."

"We need to be aware of all of the possibilities. We can't investigate if you're holding back information."

"I know... I'm just... I don't think anyone could know..."

But Lance knew. Walter knew. The other donors she had

contacted knew. The pool of people who knew about her suspicions of the clinic was getting broader, which made it more difficult to keep the clinic from finding out. Someone might have said something to Dr. Dutton or someone else at the clinic by accident, or might have intentionally given them a heads-up. And Lance had warned her they could retaliate.

27

As she sat with her hands over her face, trying to sort it out, the big cop in charge came back down to the lobby to talk to her.

"Everything is secure. We'd like you to come upstairs, if you're up to it. Have a look around and let us know what, if anything, is missing."

MacKenzie looked at Ferris, who nodded encouragingly.

"Yeah, okay. I'll do that," she agreed.

It was a minute before she could convince her legs that she really did want to stand and stagger back into the elevator. The big cop looked like he was ready to catch her if she didn't make it.

"How bad is it?" she asked on the way up. "Did he destroy anything? Leave anything disgusting behind…?"

"It's pretty superficial. I don't think there is anything irreparably damaged. And nothing that seems… personal."

MacKenzie wondered how he could tell, but she was somewhat reassured by his words. Maybe just a regular burglar, someone she didn't know. He had tossed the apartment, taken whatever was quick and easy to liquidate, or maybe he even got interrupted before he was able to take anything, and had just gotten away while he could.

They got off the elevator at the top, and the big cop looked at MacKenzie. "You okay? You ready for this?"

"Yes, I think so… if it really isn't too bad…"

He nodded and led her to the door. She felt like it was foreign territory, not her own apartment. She saw everything in disjointed pictures. Saw the broken doorframe again. Heard the police officers who were still in the apartment as they talked in low voices. She went into the front room once more and looked around at the mess. The cop—she looked sideways at him to read his name—Hunt—had primed her when he said it wasn't too bad, and she was able to look at it clinically to see if he was telling the truth.

Furniture had been tipped over and throw pillows tossed around, but she didn't see any broken glass or ripped-up upholstery. She looked around at the decorative touches, looking to see what had been stolen. The paintings had been torn from the walls and thrown around but were still there. Some vases and other bits of pottery and glass was scattered but seemed to be accounted for. She moved slowly into the room. The other policemen quieted and watched her for her reaction. MacKenzie nodded at them politely but didn't say anything. She looked around the kitchen and again found that a lot had been dumped and thrown around, but aside from a few broken dishes that were not priceless china, everything seemed to be intact.

MacKenzie swallowed and went into her bedroom. That was where she expected to see the worst. All of her jewelry gone, including the brooch her grandmother had left her, something dead in the bed or threats painted on the wall in dripping red paint. She'd seen too many horror movies. But it was much like the rest of the apartment, ransacked but not destroyed. In the walk-in closet, her jewelry box had been dumped on the floor, but picking through it, she couldn't immediately identify anything that had been broken. The brooch was still there, and she picked it up and held it in her hand, warming the gold.

Hunt was following her, but keeping his distance, giving her room to look around.

"I don't see anything missing," MacKenzie said. "Not yet."

"Take your time and look around. This guy must have come for something."

MacKenzie nodded and continued to look around. Many of her clothes had been torn down from the hangers, but they were not ripped to shreds or sprayed with paint. Her lingerie drawers seemed to be untouched. MacKenzie frowned at them, opening and closing them without touching anything. She looked over at Hunt. He shrugged.

"Like I said… didn't seem to be personal."

"But if it wasn't personal, then what?"

He raised an eyebrow and waited for her to figure it out. MacKenzie left the closet and looked around again. She went through the other rooms of the apartment, and still didn't see anything that felt personal. It all felt like a violation, and she felt her anger growing at whoever had done this to her, who had dared bust down her door and enter her apartment, putting his hands on all of her stuff.

Then she turned and looked at her desk. All of her usual random papers; invitations, bills to be paid, requests for donations. And her computer.

But not Amanda's laptop.

MacKenzie hurried over to the desk, but she already knew that the laptop was not there, or anywhere on the floor around the desk. The folders of the papers she had photocopied from Amanda's files were also missing. MacKenzie pushed papers around and looked in the drawers of the desk.

"What is it?" Hunt asked.

"My computer. My sister's computer, I mean. And her papers. It's all gone."

"Those are the only things missing?"

MacKenzie nodded. She was having trouble breathing. The burglar hadn't broken in to steal her valuables or to make a statement. He had come for the documentation on the clinic.

"Could you sister have come to get them while you were gone?"

"No. She died."

"Oh, I'm sorry, miss." He looked appropriately embarrassed. "I had no idea."

"Of course you didn't." MacKenzie took a deep breath, still trying to get enough air. "This is crazy."

"Can you think of any reason your sister's things would be stolen? Was there someone else in your family who would have wanted them?"

"No..." MacKenzie thought about her mother demanding the files back and her father getting so angry about her having taken them and looking into the clinic.

Hunt could see that she was thinking of someone. He tilted his head, waiting for her to say something. MacKenzie looked around her apartment. Could Walter have done that to her? Or hired someone to do it? But how would he know that she had kept photocopies of Amanda's files?

He knew one thing, and that was that she had Amanda's computer. She'd told him that. She'd shown him the pictures and told him where she got them. MacKenzie sank to her desk chair, knees too weak to support her.

"Oh, no."

"If you think you know who might have done this, you need to give us his name so that we can follow up," Hunt said seriously.

"No. I just felt a little faint. I think this is all catching up to me."

"It's a shock," Ferris said, hovering in the doorway watching. "It has to be very unsettling to come home to something like this. And worrying about getting it all cleaned up again..."

"I don't care about that," MacKenzie said. "I can have someone in. It's just all so... I can't believe someone would actually come in here and do this..."

"Especially someone you know," Hunt said.

"I don't think I know the person who did this... it must just have been a random thing."

"A random burglar would not have made off with your sister's things. He would have taken the jewelry. And maybe the laptop. But not papers."

"They're probably here somewhere," she looked around at the items scattered over the floor. "I'll find them when I start to clean up. Whoever it was… they probably got interrupted."

He glared at her. "I'm sure you want whoever did this to be found and punished, miss. For us to do that, you have to tell us what you know or have guessed."

"I will… if I figure anything out or have any suspicions, I'll let you know."

Hunt did not look happy about this. But MacKenzie couldn't tell him that it could have been her own father. She still held the brooch clasped in her hand. He might have been angry, but he hadn't been able to bring himself to actually destroy any of her possessions and hadn't taken any of the jewelry. What kind of burglar behaved that way?

28

It wasn't until the police were leaving that MacKenzie realized she didn't have anywhere to sleep that night. The manager had been roused from sleep by Eddie, and was hovering near her front door, rubbing his hands anxiously. He licked his lips and nodded to MacKenzie when he saw her.

"I'll have your door fixed tomorrow, Miss Kirsch. It will be done right away," he assured her.

MacKenzie turned and looked at the door again. She wasn't going to be able to shut and lock the door while she slept, and after having her suite violated by an intruder, there was no way she was going to sleep without a locked door to keep her safe for the night.

"Yes, that's great," she said faintly.

"You should arm the burglar alarm when you go out," he advised. "That way, we'll be warned if something like this happens again."

MacKenzie never used the burglar alarms unless she were going away for an extended length of time. Not when she was just going out for an hour or two. If she were going out of town and going to be away for a week. That was when she wanted to make sure that her apartment didn't get broken into while she was gone without anybody knowing about it. Having dealt with one break-in, she would be more careful in the future.

"Of course," she agreed with him. "I will."

"I don't mean you're responsible for what happened," he added hurriedly. "This wasn't your fault, of course. We'll be reviewing the lobby camera security footage to see who might have gotten in here that didn't belong. I don't know how anyone got past the elevator without clearance..."

"Okay."

Where was she going to stay for the night? MacKenzie's first through was to go home to Lisa and to sleep in her old bed, but what if Walter was staying there overnight as well? That would make it extremely awkward. She couldn't sleep under the same roof as Walter if he was the one who had burgled her apartment.

He'd only had a couple of hours between meeting with her and her getting back to her apartment. Could he really have arranged to have the deed done in that short a time slot? He didn't even know that she wouldn't be going straight home. She had been planning to go home. Even she hadn't known that there would be a couple of hours' delay while she met with Lance on the subject of his investigation. So maybe it wasn't her father. Maybe it had been someone else, and they just got lucky, hitting her apartment while she was out. It could have happened earlier in the day, while she was with Walter. Then he couldn't have been the one to order it, because he didn't know about the pictures yet.

"Miss Kirsch?"

MacKenzie focused on the little building manager again. He was still wringing his hands and looking at her worriedly. "Do you have somewhere safe to go tonight? Could we put you up at a hotel for the night?"

"Uh... actually, that would help. I was just trying to figure out what I was going to do."

"Yes, of course. Why don't you get an overnight bag together, and I will call the Harbor Club and book you a room. I will have a car take you over, you shouldn't be driving after dealing with all of this."

She was going to argue that she was just fine driving herself, but then decided to let it go. Why not let him take care of her? She was still feeling shaky and she didn't have anything to prove by pretending to be unaffected by the burglary. He was right, they should have stopped the intruder before he ever got to her apartment, and since it was their fault and they had to fix her door before it was safe for her to sleep there, they could take care of her needs for the night.

"Okay," she agreed. "I'll just pull a few things together."

And so, not much later, she was at the Harbor Club in a luxury suite, feeling comfortable and safe, though a little out of sorts. She was still fuming with anger whenever she thought about her intruder. She couldn't believe that anyone would do such a thing to her, kicking down her door and putting his hands all over her stuff. She hoped it wasn't really Walter or anyone that she knew. Just a random break-in.

But even as she soaked in a hot tub full of frothy bubbles, she knew that it hadn't just been a random thing. As Hunt had said, no random burglar would have taken the files about the clinic. Only someone who didn't want her to succeed in her investigations. They didn't want her to have anything to show the police. They wanted to send her a signal to stop poking her nose into things that were none of her business, unless she wanted to face retaliation.

She tossed and turned most of the night, so when the phone rang in the morning, it didn't wake her up, but instead provided an excuse for her to get up and stop pretending to herself that she was going to get any more sleep. She flipped open her cell phone without looking at the number. She was expecting a call from the police and from the building manager, so she wasn't surprised by an early-morning call.

"Hello?"

"MacKenzie. You're up."

It was Walter's voice. MacKenzie sighed.

"I'm up now," she agreed. "What is it?"

She was aware that her tone was sharp, but she'd had enough of his advice and, right or wrong, the anger over the break-in at her apartment immediately surged back at the sound of his voice.

Water cleared his throat uncomfortably. "I talked with your

mother last night and she informed me that I was... err... being unfair to you. That I'm letting my emotions get the better of me."

That sounded just like Lisa.

"And what do *you* think?" MacKenzie asked.

"That your mother is usually right where you and I are concerned. And that means that I was in the wrong. I'm sorry."

She'd heard him say it before in haughty tones that meant he was anything but sorry, but this time it was different. His voice was low and embarrassed. A real apology. MacKenzie's anger subsided. She took a breath.

"Thank you, Daddy. Things have been pretty rough lately. I don't want to be fighting with you."

"You're right. I think we both have the same goal, and we can each be grown up about it and recognize that the other person's position has value. You aren't trying to derail my efforts and I can respect your concerns over the circumstances surrounding Amanda's transplant. Especially since you were kept out of the loop. That must be difficult for you to understand."

"I just don't want to be the kind of person who stands by when I see something going on that is wrong or puts other people in danger."

"And why should I be surprised, since that is the way you were brought up? Neither your mother nor I are known for standing by when there is a wrong to be righted."

MacKenzie smothered a laugh. Between her mother's charities and her father's lobbying, no one could accuse the Kirsches of not getting involved.

"So, are we okay?" Walter asked tentatively.

She again felt the weight of suspicion about the break-in at her apartment. Was he apologizing because he'd already gotten what he wanted? If he was the one who had broken into her suite or hired someone else to do it, then he could afford to make up with her, since he wouldn't be worried anymore about her investigating any further. Without the computer and Amanda's files, MacKenzie would have difficulty in pursuing the matter any further. She wouldn't have any evidence of wrongdoing by Forsberg.

"MacKenzie?" Walter prompted.

"Daddy… I have to go. I have some personal matters to take care of."

"Okay. Well… alright, then. I'm headed back to Montpelier before long. I'll give you a call when I'm back in town?"

"Sure."

"Good. You take care of your personal matters, and don't worry about the clinic. I'll look into any issues there through discreet channels."

She had to wonder whether that meant he would look into her concerns at all, or whether he would just brush them under the rug with her out of the way. She could hope that he meant he would contact Mountain Investigations to take a deeper look into the clinic's operations, but then would Lance tell him about her investigation and what they had already discovered?

"I'll see you when I get back, then, MacKenzie."

"Okay. Thanks, Daddy."

MacKenzie hung up the phone.

MacKenzie had said that she could just call someone in to clean her apartment up, but once she got word from the police that they had finished with it and from the building manager that her door had been repaired and it was now secure, she headed back over to pick it up herself. She found the idea of having someone else in the apartment to clean it up as uncomfortable as finding out that her space had been violated in the first place. She didn't want anyone else in there to see the mess.

As the police had pointed out, there wasn't a lot of damage. It had been made to look violent, but it almost seemed as if care had been taken to make sure that things weren't broken. Mostly, it was just a matter of righting the furniture, replacing the cushions and decorations, and sweeping or vacuuming any debris left behind. While it took a while, it wasn't that much worse than cleaning up after a party, something she'd had to do a few times before leaving home, when she didn't want her parents to discover what she'd been up to while they were away and couldn't call in a cleaning service. In fact, it was easier than cleaning up after a party in some respects. Nobody being sick in the bathroom—or out of it. No passed-out partiers to kick out in the morning. No spilled drinks or food.

She took the opportunity to cull her wardrobe before hanging everything up, deciding to donate a few outfits she wouldn't wear again to charity. She was just standing back to take a look around her bedroom to confirm that everything had been tidied up when her phone started to ring. It seemed like her whole life was ruled by a ringing phone lately. She hadn't been going out with friends or attending any of the functions she normally did, living a much more reclusive life than she was used to. But things had happened. Things had changed. In some ways, she had changed. Maybe forever.

MacKenzie shook off the ennui and picked up her wireless phone. "Hello?"

"Kenzie? It's Lance."

"Oh, hi, Lance." Had it just been the night before she had seen him? She was surprised he had anything else to report so soon. Or maybe he wasn't calling to report, but to see how she was. He'd seemed very interested in her the night before.

"Is everything okay?" Lance asked. "You sound… different."

"I'm fine. Well… as fine as you'd expect."

"Because you're still worrying about your sister's death, you mean?"

"That… and everything else." She didn't know whether to tell him everything or not. But it would be nice to have someone she could tell. Someone who would be understanding, but not jump to conclusions. Being an investigator, he wouldn't be shocked by the developments. "I had a break-in last night."

"A break-in? When?"

"When I was out with you, I guess. Sometime during the evening. I came back to a kicked-in door and my possessions all over the floor."

"You're kidding. Kenzie, I'm so sorry. Is there anything I can do?"

"I don't see what you could do. I've already cleaned up. The door is fixed. There really wasn't much damage, just… disruption."

"Was anything stolen?"

MacKenzie sighed. "Yes… Amanda's laptop and files."

"No."

"Yeah. So I guess I've stepped on some toes. Somebody wants to stop me from looking into the Forsberg clinic any further."

"It sounds like it," he admitted.

MacKenzie cocked her head at the tone of his voice. "What?"

"Hmm?" He made a questioning sound, not sure what she was asking.

"What was that? You sounded… like you just got something."

Lance cleared his throat. "I don't know. I called you today for a reason… not just to check up on you."

"What is it, then?"

"You remember how you asked about what I would do if you and your father hired us on conflicting matters?"

"Yes." MacKenzie dreaded what he was going to say next.

"Walter did call this morning."

"What did he want you to do?"

"I can't exactly tell you that, due to client confidentiality."

"If you had a conflict, then you couldn't hire him, and there is no confidentiality."

She could hear his smile in his voice. "Unfortunately, I do need to keep it confidential when someone asks us to look into a matter, even if they don't end up retaining us. Those initial inquiries can be… inflammatory."

"So what can you tell me about what my father called about? He told me that he was going to look into the clinic and to sort out whether there had been any wrongdoing. He said that I shouldn't push any further, because he was going to do it discreetly."

"That's not exactly what he wanted. In that case, I would probably just ask for a transferal of the file from you to him. Since it's on the same matter."

"So it was on something other than the clinic?"

"It was… a conflict for us," Lance said delicately.

"A conflict with my case?"

"I'm afraid… I can't be much more clear about it."

"So did you tell him that you couldn't?"

"Yes."

"I'll bet he was pretty ticked off about that."

"There are other investigative firms that could help him. We suggested a few other names."

"So you're calling to tell me that he's going to hire someone else."

"I have no idea what he's going to decide."

"He's going to hire someone else to work against me. Trying to cover up what the clinic is doing."

"I really can't say."

MacKenzie shook her head. "He called this morning to apologize," she said. "I really can't believe he would call me to try to smooth things over and say he was going to look into it, when he was really doing just the opposite. Unbelievable. Against his own daughter! When I'm trying to figure out what happened to Amanda! You would think he'd care about her, at least."

"I think he does, Kenzie. But you and he have slightly different agendas, and different ways of going about it. I think you have similar goals, but…"

"That's just what he said. That we both wanted the same thing. But that can't be. Not if he's trying to whitewash what happened to Amanda."

"I'm sorry I can't tell you more."

He really did sound regretful. MacKenzie didn't doubt his sincerity.

"Is there anything I can do?" Lance asked. "I know you said you already have everything cleared up… but anything? Do you want me to run a security check on your apartment? Review whatever measures are in place and see how we can improve things?"

"Uh… maybe. I hadn't really thought about it. The building manager just said to make sure I set my burglar alarm when I go out. I don't usually do it unless I'm going to be away for a long time."

"I would second that. Set it whenever you leave, even for a few minutes. And depending on what kind of system you have, I would set it while you're home, too, so that you're warned of any intruders, or attempted intrusions. Home invasion is a thing. People of your caliber get kidnapped and held for ransom. You really can't be too careful."

"No one is going to try to kidnap me."

"That's what they all say." He said it in a lighthearted way, but it still held an ominous ring. Of course no one ever thought they were going to get kidnapped. If they did, they would take precautions.

"Well… when you put it that way. Maybe you should come and take a look at my system. I really don't even know anything about how it works. I don't think I *can* arm it while I'm inside."

"It may have an 'occupied' mode. I'll take a look when I get there. Are you there now? Is it a good time?"

MacKenzie hesitated, looking around. Everything was cleaned up, and she was tired and thinking it was time to get something to eat. But she could order in. She acknowledged Lisa's voice in her head that she should have food in her fridge so that she could at least get herself a sandwich in a pinch. And she did have bread, for her morning toast, but she wasn't sure how much of it there was or if there was anything else that could be satisfactorily made into a sandwich. She shrugged to herself.

"Sure, if you want to come over now, that works for me. I'm about to order something to eat. You have any preferences?"

"You don't need to get me anything. I'll be there to work, not to eat."

"No reason you can't do both. I assume you have to eat just like the rest of us."

"Okay… well, then, I'm pretty easy. Whatever you like is fine with me."

"What if I like sushi?"

"Sushi is fine."

A lot of men would turn up their noses at sushi, so Lance passed the test. "Actually, I think I'll probably get Italian."

"I was practically born in Italy."

MacKenzie laughed. "Italian it is, then. Do you need the address?"

"I have it."

She couldn't remember giving it to him, but he was a private investigator, so she supposed he had plenty of databases at his disposal to find an address, even if it was unlisted.

"See you soon, then."

29

The afternoon with Lance was enjoyable and the time went by much more quickly than MacKenzie had expected. They had a fine Italian lunch and then she watched him for a while as he investigated the electronic panel for the security system on the wall and prowled around her apartment looking at the various sensors. He also examined the doorframe that the management had replaced, *tsk*-ing and shaking his head as he looked at it.

"What's wrong with it?" MacKenzie asked.

"Well, they've at least replaced the wood instead of just gluing and patching what was already broken, so that's one point in their favor. But this is no stronger than the original work and would be just as easy to kick in a second time. You really need a steel door frame. You have a solid-core door, which is good, but the door is no stronger than its weakest part, which in this case is the frame. A half-inch of wood is not going to stop any determined burglar who can just kick it or use a pry bar to force his way in."

"Will you talk to the building manager or arrange to have someone come in and replace it?"

Lance nodded absently. "Yes, of course."

He continued to putter around the apartment. MacKenzie got bored watching him and went to her computer to check for email and see what else was on her schedule that she should be calling to give her regrets on.

She was checking the gossip columns when he appeared to give her the news.

"Do you have a few minutes to go over this, Kenzie?"

MacKenzie pulled herself out of the news and looked at him, blinking.

"Yes. Of course. Let's go into the living room and you can show me what you've got."

He obligingly led the way. MacKenzie motioned to the couch, where they sat down side-by-side to look over his handwritten list.

"You don't have to do everything at once, of course, but these are the changes that I would recommend. I'll show you how to switch between occupied and unoccupied modes on the burglar alarm, and you can get used to doing that instead of just leaving it disarmed all the time. We'll get that doorframe replaced with something more secure. And here are some other recommendations..."

He went through various items, including a camera pointed at the elevator, a wide-view peep hole on her door, remote monitoring with a hardline directly to the security company, and a few other bits that MacKenzie quickly lost track of.

"Can I put you in charge of all of that?" she suggested. "You're the expert and can ensure that they are actually doing what you've suggested. I won't know how to check that they've actually done what they say they have."

"Sure. We can work out some times for me to be here to get things installed."

MacKenzie wondered whether she should give him a key to let himself in and out as he needed to. But when they were talking about security, was it a good idea for her to just give her key out to anyone? She had hired Lance, but he also had an association with her father. Could she trust him to be there by himself?

He *had* called her to let her know that her father had tried to hire them in a matter that conflicted with MacKenzie's investigation. He was on her side, not her father's.

"Just… uh… let me know when you need to be here, and we'll make arrangements," MacKenzie told him.

Lance nodded his agreement. "Now… let me acquaint you with your security system."

She was a little embarrassed to have him showing her how to use her own system, and that he knew its capabilities when she didn't, but he was the expert, so why shouldn't he?

Since MacKenzie knew that Lisa was always collecting items for one charity or another, she stopped by the house to get rid of the clothing she had decided she didn't need anymore. She knew that Walter had headed back to Montpelier, so she could avoid running into him again.

Lisa looked pleased to see MacKenzie. "I've hardly seen you since the funeral. And then with you and your father fighting, I didn't think you would come around to visit."

"He's gone home, hasn't he?"

"Yes. He's off. But I wasn't sure you'd come by…"

MacKenzie explained about the clothing donation and held up the box that she had filled.

"Oh, that's perfect." Lisa rarely gushed. She was usually pretty reserved with MacKenzie, reminding her of her responsibilities and what her parents expected of her. But maybe the recent loss of Amanda and the fight between Walter and MacKenzie had prompted a change. She didn't tell MacKenzie that she should have given more, or something different, or collected for a charity of her own choice, she just accepted it and put it to the side to be added to whatever else she had collected. "Do you have a few minutes to visit? I know you're probably getting ready for the gala tonight…"

MacKenzie realized that, distracted by her conversations with Lance, she hadn't remembered to call in her regrets.

"I don't think I'm really up to it tonight, Mother. I was going to call and cancel. I'll still send in a donation, but…"

"You haven't been to anything since Amanda passed. And tonight is special. It's the Kidney Foundation. You're a special guest not only because of Amanda, but also because you are an organ donor. People need to see you, to understand that they can do live donations and still live a full life."

MacKenzie wrinkled her nose. "I don't really want to go out to anything…"

"Please come to this one. We're to sit together. I'd really like to have one of my girls there." A tear glittered in Lisa's eye. MacKenzie rubbed her forehead.

"Mother…"

"I had hoped that Amanda would be able to go with me. But now that she's gone… I'd really like you to be there."

MacKenzie should have waited another day to deliver the clothes to Lisa. But maybe it was time for her to put in an appearance. Lisa was right, the Kidney Foundation was an important cause for both of them. Dear to their hearts after all that Amanda had been through. If any organization needed their fundraising efforts, it was them.

"Well… alright. I'll go. But I hadn't planned to, so I'm not ready." MacKenzie looked down at herself. Dusty and sweaty from cleaning up at her apartment. She needed a shower, makeup, a good dress, jewelry, and of course, her checkbook.

Lisa nodded briskly. "We'll save our visit for at the gala. You go home. I'll take care of these clothes, and you get yourself ready. I'll see you tonight."

"Okay." MacKenzie leaned forward to give her mother a quick kiss. "Love you, Mom. And… I'm sorry that Amanda couldn't be there tonight too."

Lisa nodded. "Thank you, MacKenzie. I love you too. Thank you for coming tonight."

When she got back to her apartment, MacKenzie nearly forgot to put her passcode into the security system. It was down to the last few seconds before she managed to tap it in correctly and stop the count-down. MacKenzie breathed out in relief. It was going to take a while before she was used to that routine. But she imagined that it would become second nature if she stuck to it. It was always hard to start a new habit.

Even though she knew that no one had been in her apartment because the alarm had been set, she still found herself taking a walk around on tiptoes to make sure that nothing was out of place. Everything seemed to be as she had left it, including the dirty dishes that she'd left out after the Italian lunch. So much for being grown up and responsible. At least she had put the leftovers into the fridge.

And she would eat them before they went bad this time. Probably.

She took one last look around the apartment for intruders, though she didn't go as far as to look under the bed for monsters. She stood in her bedroom looking down at the street far below as lights started to come on. Everything was as it should be. There was nothing for her to be concerned about.

MacKenzie got down to work to ready herself for the gala. She would be expected to look as polished as if she had stepped off the runway, even though she didn't have a team of artists doing her clothing and makeup for her. The fact that she was bereaved wouldn't give her any latitude with the crowd that would be at the gala.

Checking her watch and looking at her hair and makeup one last time, MacKenzie transferred everything she would need, including her checkbook, to a small clutch purse, put on her coat, and let the limo know she was on her way down. It pulled in front of the building just as MacKenzie stepped out of the elevator.

Eddie opened the door for her, smiling and nodding, and the limo driver opened the car door for her. MacKenzie slid in, careful not to mash her dress or catch her coat in the door. It would only take a few minutes to get to the ballroom.

There was a car pulled over down the block with its flashers on, and MacKenzie studied it for a moment, frowning. It wasn't usual to see cars pulled over there. But maybe he was having engine trouble. As she was watching, the little black car turned off its flashers and pulled out into traffic, sliding into the lane behind the limo a few cars back.

Not engine trouble, then.

MacKenzie turned her mind back to the gala. From what Lisa had said, MacKenzie suspected she might be called upon to say a few words to potential donors or to accept some honor on Amanda's behalf. She wanted to clear her mind and be prepared to say a few gracious words in either event. It wouldn't do to look like a deer caught in the headlights and have nothing prepared. There would be reporters there, maybe even TV news cameras, and she wanted to do the best for the Foundation, and Amanda and Lisa, that she could.

She closed her eyes and worked through a few words, polishing up what she would say if she were put on the spot. She'd been speaking at such things since she was a teenager, so it wasn't something new or scary, but she wanted to do it right.

The limo pulled up to the event center and MacKenzie waited for the driver to come around and open the door for her. She got out of the car without tripping or stumbling and nodded at him.

"I'll likely need a drive back around midnight."

He nodded. "I'll be here, miss."

MacKenzie walked up to the building and followed the signs and the music to join the gala.

30

It was good to be sitting with Lisa. MacKenzie had been at too many events alone before Amanda's death, or in need of a date to drag along for appearance's sake. It wouldn't do to appear alone at too many events. People would start to make assumptions. MacKenzie remembered Amanda's dancing eyes as she teased MacKenzie about the necessity of bringing a date, mocking their mother's frequently repeated warnings.

She wished that she were there with Amanda instead of Lisa, but either way, she was happy to be with a family member instead of a date. She wanted to get to know some of the men in her circles better, but on the other hand, if she saw someone too many times or appeared to be getting too close, the rumors of marriage would immediately start. Couldn't a girl get to know a man without their nuptials immediately being announced?

Dr. Proctor was also at the table, along with a woman who might have been his date or an executive assistant or administrator from the hospital. Their relationship was not clear. There were four other people at their table, faces that MacKenzie was sure she had seen at other events, but couldn't be bothered to recall. Everybody smiled and nodded as if they were old friends, and MacKenzie was sure many of them were. It tended to be the same people attending the gala and other similar causes one year after another.

MacKenzie mostly listened to the chatter around her and nodded and smiled as required.

"How are you ladies getting along?" Dr. Proctor asked MacKenzie and Lisa sympathetically, leaning toward them and putting his hand over Lisa's. "Such a tragedy, losing Amanda like that."

Lisa nodded and blinked at him, giving a strained smile. There was nothing worse than honest sympathy to trigger tears. MacKenzie could deal with all of the social platitudes that were offered about her sister, but one truly sincere and heartfelt condolence would reduce her to tears. Lisa was obviously having a difficult time holding it together.

"We're trying to look forward," MacKenzie said, a little too loudly. "Raising money for the Foundation and other good causes, trying to help others so that they can have all of the benefits that Amanda did. That's what Amanda would want us to do."

Lisa nodded in agreement. She withdrew her hand from Dr. Proctor and looked at MacKenzie, getting strength from her.

"Yes, MacKenzie is exactly right." Lisa looked around the table, involving everyone else in the conversation. "We all need to give generously to this cause. We need ways to treat kidney disease before it is too late and transplants are the only solution. And we need to learn why transplants succeed and why they fail, and what else we can do to improve the quality of life for those who have kidney disease. This is a malady that doesn't just affect those who are old or who have not lived a healthy lifestyle. It strikes children and teenagers and people who up until then were perfectly healthy. We need more research and we need better treatment options. Dialysis is a miracle in itself, but we can't stop there."

Around the table, everyone's heads bobbed up and down. It wouldn't be long before they would be reaching for their wallets. Which was exactly why they were at the table with Lisa and MacKenzie. If there was anyone who could squeeze blood from a stone, it was Lisa.

MacKenzie nodded at her mother and smiled encouragingly. They would focus on the donations, not on Amanda. Even though it was in Amanda's memory, there would be no tears at the gala.

Eventually, the evening wore down. The financial officer had whispered in MacKenzie's ear that the donations had been better than they had dared hope for, and MacKenzie hoped that a good deal of that was due to their efforts on Amanda's behalf. Amanda might not have been able to be there in person that night, but she was there in spirit, delighted at all they had done for her.

Lisa was looking tired and worn by the time the night was over, and MacKenzie saw her on her way home before leaving. Otherwise, who knew how long Lisa might stay there to help encourage the last few guests and help with the clean-up and take-down. She had done enough and needed to get her sleep.

MacKenzie had called for her driver to make sure he was ready, and when she got to the front of the center, she could see a couple of limos waiting to pick up guests from the gala. She walked up to one and bent down to speak to the driver and see which one was hers. Down the street, a car's blinkers went off, and an engine turned on, amplified by the still, crisp night air. MacKenzie looked in that direction for a moment, then back to the driver.

"Are you here for MacKenzie?" she inquired.

"Miss Kirsch? Wait one moment." He got hurriedly out of the car and opened the door for her. "I'm sorry. I should recognize you by sight."

"Oh, there's no reason you should. Thank you." MacKenzie slid into the seat and looked behind her at the car that was waiting to pull into traffic. Was it coincidence that another little black car had been sitting a short distance away when she got into her limo?

She sat in the middle of the seat. As they pulled out, she took a compact out of her purse. She held it up as if to check her makeup and squinted in the mirror at the lights and the shape inside the car behind them. It was too dark and the compact too small to make out any details. MacKenzie closed it and put it back into her purse. When she got back to her building, she took her time, making the driver stand there waiting for her to get out as she kept a lookout for the black car behind them. She made sure that Eddie was standing outside the building ready to hold the door for her. There was no chance of someone jumping out of another car and snatching her. Not between the driver and the doorman. She wouldn't be out of sight of either of them for even a second.

Taking one more look down the street at the car that pulled over and turned on its hazard lights, MacKenzie walked from her car to her apartment building and stepped in the door.

31

How was your evening, Miss Kirsch?" Eddie inquired pleasantly as he followed her in the door.

MacKenzie turned to him. "I think someone was following me."

He looked back toward the limo as it pulled away from the curb. "Someone was following you… at the event you went to tonight?"

"Someone was following the limo. When I left here and when I came back. There was a car waiting a block back both times, and then it pulled out and followed the limousine…"

They both watched out the window, waiting for the car to appear behind the limo. It didn't. MacKenzie let out her breath.

"They know I live here. There's no reason to follow me once I got back. Or they're still waiting out there somewhere. They wouldn't keep following the limo after it dropped me off."

"No," Eddie agreed slowly. "I guess it wouldn't. Do you want me to call the police?"

MacKenzie bit her lip, thinking about it. She was tired and she didn't really want more drama. She just wanted to finish her night at home in bed and not worry about intruders or ill-wishers. She had just spent the night raising money for an important charity. Why would someone target her when she was doing something good?

"I... don't think so. But if you would walk me up or get someone from security to walk me up. I'm just... nervous of something happening." She looked at the elevator. "It's silly, I suppose. You can see me get onto the elevator and it opens right at my door. But I want to be sure."

"Of course," he assured her. "We don't want anything else happening to you."

MacKenzie took a few deep breaths and tried to relax while he contacted the security guard patrolling the building. There was nothing to worry about. Lance had already made sure that her apartment was secure. Or it would be, once the doorframe was replaced with something stronger, and the other items that he advised her to fix. It wasn't like Eddie was going to let her into the elevator with some predator waiting in the car for her. Though someone could get in from another floor on her way up, if there were someone outside watching her to advise them of the timing.

MacKenzie looked back out through the doors but couldn't see anyone lurking in the shadows or peering in through the glass. But there were binoculars, night vision; she didn't know how they might be watching her.

Eddie hung up the phone.

"Bruce is going to check out your floor first, make sure there is no one waiting up there. Then he'll come down, and he'll ride up with you. Make sure you get in your door and are safe before he comes back down."

"Okay. Good. I know I'm being silly about this, but..."

"I don't think it's silly. Not when you already had a burglary." He raised his brows curiously. "I didn't hear... how much was stolen. Did you lose a lot?"

MacKenzie wasn't sure she should tell him any details. But she knew Eddie. He'd been a doorman at the building for several years. Since she had moved in there. He was always around, making sure that her needs were attended to, inquiring politely as she returned from evening fundraisers and other events.

"No valuables," she said. "They took my sister's computer and files."

His eyes widened. "You sister's? I thought she died. Er, passed away."

MacKenzie nodded. "Yes. She did. And someone broke in, apparently just to steal her things."

"That's weird. What kind of information was in there that they wanted to access?"

MacKenzie looked at him, frowning, as she thought about it. Up until then, she had only thought about it from the opposite viewpoint. What was in the files that someone wanted to keep quiet? What was in there that they didn't want MacKenzie to know or to follow up on? But what if it was something that someone else wanted to know? Was it possible that her father would take those papers and the computer so that he would have the information he needed to investigate the clinic?

But that didn't make any sense, because he already had access to Amanda's original files at the house, and he had tried to hire Lance to do something that conflicted with MacKenzie's investigation of the clinic, not that aligned with it.

It was just too much to think about when she was tired at the end of the day, her feelings so tender after thinking about and talking about Amanda all evening, all topped off with a few glasses of wine to get herself through the evening. She rubbed her temples and watched the elevator for Bruce.

In a couple more minutes, the security guard stepped out of the elevator. He nodded to Eddie and MacKenzie.

"Everything looks fine upstairs. Your door is still closed and locked. There's no one hanging around. I'll take the elevator up in freight mode so that no one can interrupt it with a call from another floor. Did you see anyone down here?"

He walked over to the front doors and peered out onto the street.

"I haven't seen anyone suspicious on foot," MacKenzie said. "But I'm sure someone was following my limo to the gala and back tonight."

Bruce nodded. He stared out the doors for a few minutes, making MacKenzie uncomfortable with the amount of time he was spending checking out the street. Eventually, he turned back around. "I don't see anyone else. But that doesn't mean that there isn't anyone out there. Let's get you upstairs."

He escorted MacKenzie to the elevator. He inserted his key into the panel and switched the elevator mode, then pressed the button for the penthouse suite. The door closed. MacKenzie held on to the rail as it lurched slightly. Maybe one glass of wine too many.

They were quiet as the elevator made its way to the top floor. Bruce didn't try to make small talk or to ask her about what gala she had been to.

The doors opened onto MacKenzie's floor, and Bruce indicated she should wait. He poked his head out to check the alcove and make sure for the second time that there was no one hanging around. Then he nodded and motioned her ahead. MacKenzie walked up to her door and unlocked it. It swung open silently. There was no indication of trouble. No sound from within. MacKenzie reached for the security alarm panel and punched in her code. Bruce waited outside the apartment.

"Do you want me to come in with you and have a look around? Make sure that everything is secure inside?"

When MacKenzie was little, she had known there weren't any monsters under the bed, but that didn't mean she wasn't afraid of them grabbing her ankles when she got up to the bathroom in the night. She swallowed and nodded to Bruce.

"I know there isn't anyone here, but…"

"You wait right here," he told her.

MacKenzie looked back at the elevator, but it was still locked into position where he had left it. No one else was going to be able to come up while she was waiting there. They would have to use the stairs, and the stairwell doors were locked on the inside.

Bruce went into the apartment. MacKenzie had left lights on, so he didn't have to turn on any more or stumble around the apartment in the dark. He took a couple of minutes to thoroughly check out the suite, and then returned to the door.

"Everything looks fine. There is no one here, and I don't see any sign that anyone has been here or has gotten into anything."

MacKenzie breathed a sigh of relief. "Thanks, Bruce. I really appreciate it. I know I'm being a scaredy-cat because of what happened, but..."

"You're being cautious. And you should be. You should report to the police that you think someone was following you tonight. If they were, they may not have gotten everything they wanted when they broke in. You could still be in danger of another break-in or an attack."

MacKenzie's stomach flip-flopped. Definitely too much wine. She took a steadying breath and held it for a few seconds, trying to convince herself that he was just overreacting. "I'll think about it. Thanks."

He nodded and left the apartment, pulling the door shut behind him. MacKenzie hit a button on the alarm panel and listened to the elevator doors close in the alcove outside the door.

32

Sleep did not come quickly. She wished that she had invited someone home with her, but on the other hand, the idea of having someone else in her apartment was repugnant. She didn't want anyone else there touching her things and moving things around, taking things that didn't belong to them. She knew it was ridiculous, because nobody she brought home was going to do that. It had been a break-in, not an invited date.

But she still couldn't bring herself to have anyone else there. Not for a while. Without anyone there to distract her or cuddle her as she went to sleep, it was a lot harder to find her way to dreamland. She was feeling a little nauseated after the gala, but hadn't had enough to drink to actually knock her out, and wasn't about to try. She would just end up hanging over the toilet, and that was an even less pleasant way to spend her night than tossing and turning and flipping through channels on the TV. She would have thought that with the number of channels being offered in her TV package that there would actually be something good on, but it seemed to be a hundred channels of drivel.

MacKenzie eventually fell asleep, but it still wasn't a sound sleep. She kept dreaming about intruders and danger and her father telling her to mind her own business and go back to school, and would wake up shaking and trying to remember what had really happened over the past weeks and what was real. She hated the restless dreams, but she wasn't rested enough to get up yet.

Finally, MacKenzie rolled out of bed and had a hot shower. It didn't really wake her up, nor was she able to go to sleep after, but she felt better being up than lying in bed and moving from dream to dream, so she eventually decided to stay up.

She turned on the TV, not wanting to check her computer for email or to go down to the lobby to pick up her newspaper. She just wanted to know what was going on in the world and to know that life continued without her. Her little worries were nothing, compared to what was going on in the world. There were wars and disasters and plenty of other things to be worried about. No one else was worrying about the transplant industry. No one really cared about it other than the people who were waiting for transplants, and they were such a small percentage of the population.

She watched a morning show. The hosts were perky and talked to each other in teasing, sarcastic, and snarky tones to keep the audience interested and engaged. There were serious stories mixed with cat antics and traffic fails and headlines from around the world. All separate and removed from MacKenzie's world.

The world was, in fact, going on without her. Maybe she just needed to get out of her own head and find something else to do. She had been concerned with nothing but Amanda's transplant and the events that had led up to it for weeks. But there had to be other things that were more important in her life. She still had family, and she hadn't been concentrating on those relationships. She had friends she hadn't talked to since Amanda had gotten ill. She had dates that needed to be called back before they started to wonder if she had fallen off the face of the earth. The Kidney Foundation fundraiser wasn't the only thing she was supposed to be attending and helping to raise money for. Maybe she needed to find some other causes. Something that was different from what her mother was interested in.

There was a banner across the bottom of the screen showing other stories that were in the news or coming up on the morning show. MacKenzie watched them, uninterested in the hosts' discussion of deep-fried Snickers bars. Even if she hadn't been reading it, the words that came up on the banner would probably have grabbed her attention.

Kirsch family makes memorial donation to the Forsberg Clinic.

If the world had been going on without MacKenzie, she was pretty sure that it stopped at that point. A donation to the Forsberg Clinic? She had talked to Dr. Dutton about making a donation, but she hadn't actually done so. Had the woman leaked something, hoping to pressure MacKenzie into actually making a donation to save face? It would have been a good strategy. But surely, she wouldn't have done that. Had someone else at the clinic misunderstood that MacKenzie was merely looking into making a donation?

The words scrolled off the screen and were replaced by a line about a spelling bee. Won by a homeschooler, imagine that. MacKenzie waited for the words about the donation to come back up on the screen again. Like the next time they might be different. Maybe there would be a better description, or a correction. Someone in the prompt room had just managed to get the details wrong, mixing up two stories or having a stroke and typing out random words.

But the words were the same.

Kirsch family makes memorial donation to the Forsberg Clinic.

Then the hosts of the show turned from a segue about breakfast foods and eating to prepare for the day to address the story about the donation to the clinic.

"Well-known lobbyist Walter Kirsch and his philanthropist wife, Lisa Cole Kirsch announced today that they are making a sizable donation to the Forsberg Clinic, an organ transplant clinic that specializes in overseas transplants for those who are unable to get them in the United States. The donation was made in memory of their recently-deceased daughter, Amanda Kirsch, who had succumbed to kidney disease. Amanda had two kidney transplants in her short lifetime, one of which was facilitated by the Forsberg Clinic. The family said that Amanda frequently spoke about how thankful she was for the Forsberg Clinic and the chance that they had given her to live a normal life after the failure of her first donated kidney. There will be a presentation…."

MacKenzie stared at the screen numbly. Was this how Walter looked into any potential wrongdoings by the clinic? By giving them money and good publicity?

The hosts chattered on about organ donation and the tragedy of kidney disease and the loss of someone as young as Amanda. They talked about the good that the Kirsch family did in spreading their wealth to various charities and social organizations, in working to lobby for important changes to the law, and so on. They had apparently been given plenty of talking points.

MacKenzie shut off the TV abruptly. She didn't need to hear any more drivel. She was sure she could pull up Walter's press release online, if he hadn't already sent it to her via email. Would he have an explanation for why he had made the donation, or just pretend that she would understand his reasoning for it? Would he assume that she wouldn't even hear about it and he could just maintain the fiction about how he was looking into the clinic's operations and would take care of things if there were any wrongdoing going on there?

MacKenzie ate her breakfast and got dressed in a fugue, unfocused and moving like a zombie. She decided what to do and her body obeyed, even though she hadn't thought through the steps and what she was going to do once she got there. She just knew that she had to go over and figure it out. She accepted that her father was sabotaging her efforts. That much was obvious. If it hadn't been apparent before, it certainly was now. He had arranged for her apartment to be broken into and had stolen all of Amanda's documents and her computer, so that MacKenzie couldn't investigate them any further. He had put a tail on her so that he would know where she was at all times.

He had called Mountain Investigations and had tried to get them to help him with a cover-up of the clinic's activities. When that had failed, maybe he had hired someone else. He had made a big donation to the Forsberg clinic and plastered it all over the news, so that everyone would see that he supported them and that there was nothing wrong with whatever it was they were up to. He was trying to normalize the idea of people going overseas to get transplants, like it was the most normal thing in the world. They would start a new kind of tourism. Transplant tourism. Pretty soon, everybody would be doing it. It would be as normal as going to Mexico to get your dental work done.

She pulled her purse strap up over her shoulder, grabbed her keys, and headed out the door. She remembered at the last moment to punch her code into the security system before she opened the front door to avoid setting it off. That would have been embarrassing. But she supposed she would probably set it off a few times before it became habitual. She would just have to deal with the inconvenience.

She rode the elevator down and deliberately did not check for any little black cars following her when she drove her car out of the parking garage onto the street. If her father were going to have her followed, then so be it. He was about to get a shock.

The drive to the Forsberg Clinic was a pleasant one; it was a beautiful day with mild winter temperatures and snow blanketing the ground in a clean new sheet. But MacKenzie didn't have eyes for it. She was an automaton, another part of her brain taking over the driving and other functions while she intentionally ignored the thoughts that were trying to break through, questioning her decision and the wisdom of what she was doing. She wasn't about to be dissuaded by logic or emotion. She'd made a decision and that was that.

She didn't bother to park in the parking lot of the clinic, but pulled in front of the doors, in the "loading zone only, no stopping" area beside the curb, and parked the car. What were they going to do? Ticket her? Tow her? How would that play out when it hit the media?

When MacKenzie walked into the reception area, the woman at the reception desk obviously recognized her. She jumped to her feet, all smiles, eyes wide in surprise.

"Oh, Miss Kirsch! It's so good to see you again. The clinic is just so pleased about the donation your family made..." She put out her hand to shake MacKenzie's, and then when MacKenzie reached out, she pulled back a little, suddenly uncertain whether she should be shaking hands with such a celebrity. MacKenzie ended up just grabbing her hand and giving it a little squeeze, in a sort of grandmotherly gesture.

"It's nice to see you again too," she agreed. "Is Dr. Dutton in?"

"Well, she is, but she's in a meeting right now. Did she know that you were coming over?"

MacKenzie shook her head. "No. I just came over on a whim. After seeing all the coverage this morning, I really had to be here to just talk to her again and to tell her how much I appreciate what the clinic is doing. I was just at the Kidney Foundation gala the other night, and I couldn't help thinking about how Amanda never would have gotten that kidney transplant if it weren't for the clinic, and who knows how much longer she would have had without it. I can wait until Dr. Dutton is free…?"

"Well, I don't know, she could be a while…" The receptionist was at a loss as to what to do. Should she interrupt the boss? Let the big donor sit and wait? Either way, she was going against her training.

"Maybe you could take her a note that I'm here," MacKenzie suggested. "Then she could decide for herself whether she can see me."

"Uh… sure. I could do that." The receptionist found a pad of yellow sticky notes on her desk and dashed off a note. She reconsidered, threw it away, and tried again. She went through four different drafts before she finally decided what she wanted to say and, holding it stuck to her index finger, disappeared down the hall to take it to Dr. Dutton.

MacKenzie drifted over to the receptionist's desk and looked down at the clutter of notes and documents she had spread out over the desk. She was obviously the only administrative person in the clinic, as MacKenzie had noticed in her tour, and she had documents that needed to be changed, phone logs, and notes stuck to everything. MacKenzie looked for her father's name. It was on the press releases, and there should be a check or some other memo about the donation.

MacKenzie wasn't sure what she was looking for. Maybe the day that he had called to tell them he was making the donation. Was it before or after he had talked to MacKenzie? Before or after the break-in and the apology? Not that it really mattered. How could it matter what day or time he had called? Either he had known that MacKenzie had suspicions about the clinic and had rushed to make a donation without knowing what her concerns had been, or he had waited until after he'd heard everything and seen the pictures, and then decided to smooth things over by making the donation that MacKenzie had suggested she was willing to make to the clinic.

The little receptionist hurried back down the hall toward MacKenzie. MacKenzie leaned on the desk, feigning that she was bored and tired of having to wait for the extended length of time it had taken the receptionist to run her note to Dr. Dutton and to return to the front. The receptionist made a little flurry with her hands, as if trying to contain MacKenzie's impatience.

"I'm so sorry to keep you waiting," she said. "Dr. Dutton says that she can be with you in just a few minutes. Could I get you a coffee while you're waiting? Tea? Water?"

MacKenzie looked around the reception area. It was comfortable enough if she was going to have to wait. Who knew how long it was going to be? She didn't think that the woman would want to keep her waiting. Not with the donation still so fresh in her mind. Maybe she was wondering why MacKenzie had not been there for the ceremony in which Walter and Lisa had handed over their check in Amanda's name. Maybe her parents had given some kind of excuse for her not being there. But for all the woman knew, MacKenzie had been kept out of the loop and now needed her ruffled feathers smoothed and settled. She wouldn't keep MacKenzie waiting for too long. Not unless she was in a meeting with another big donor, maybe someone spurred on by Walter's donation. Or maybe Walter himself. That would be ironic. MacKenzie had no idea what she would do if Walter was already at the clinic ahead of her. They would have to come up with some sort of act to make it look natural.

"Yes, I could do with a coffee," she agreed. She could always do with another coffee. She wasn't sure if she had even finished her first cup that morning. She had forced herself to eat before leaving, but she had no idea whether she had drained her cup or whether it was still sitting beside the coffee maker waiting for her. Her brain had just shut down. Now it was buzzing away, fully engaged, running through scenarios and trying to decide what she was going to say once Dr. Dutton came out. She had no script prepared, no plan in place.

"Certainly, I'll get you one," the receptionist said, looking relieved. "How do you take it?"

"Black is fine."

"Are you sure? We have real cream."

MacKenzie smiled at her for trying so hard. She was sure that the *real cream* worked for some of the donors. They would be impressed that the clinic went all-out to get the good stuff instead of just offering the powdered creamer that everyone else had in their kitchens.

"No, that's fine."

"Artificial sweeteners? Whatever you like?"

In a minute, she would be telling MacKenzie exactly what kind of beans they had, from what side of the mountain, and how they had been ground. MacKenzie shook her head.

"I'll just have black. Plain old black coffee. Thank you."

The little woman nodded and disappeared through another door to get MacKenzie's coffee. MacKenzie swept one more look over the contents of the desk, but she decided that what she wanted wasn't there. They weren't going to put anything incriminating on the front desk in the reception area of the clinic. What was she thinking?

She went over to one of the well-upholstered chairs and sat down, sinking into the cushions until she wasn't sure if she were going to be able to get back out of it again.

The receptionist took longer than MacKenzie had expected to just get a cup of coffee. She must have decided that whatever was sitting on the burner wasn't good enough for MacKenzie and had decided to brew a fresh pot instead. MacKenzie could smell it wafting through the air and her stomach growled in interest. Eventually, the woman returned, and handed MacKenzie a china cup of coffee with great ceremony.

"Here you go."

"Thank you." MacKenzie looked toward the hallway that led to the boardroom. She didn't think Dr. Dutton could wait much longer. She would be wondering what her big donor wanted, worrying that there was going to be a big bust-up. MacKenzie complaining that she hadn't been recognized, a withdrawal of funds, something devastating. It must be gnawing at Dr. Dutton as she tried to finish with her previous appointment.

Finally, she heard a door and voices as Dr. Dutton moved out of the boardroom and down the hall with someone else. Final, finishing-up noises as she closed the deal or reassured him about what was in store. Then they were coming out of the hallway and into view.

MacKenzie raised her eyebrows.

John Hopewell. He was shaking hands with Dr. Dutton and hadn't yet finished turning around. Hadn't yet seen MacKenzie sitting there. And Dr. Dutton had probably not told him who it was that she had to meet with after finishing up their meeting either.

What had Hopewell been there for? He had led MacKenzie to believe that he wasn't very happy with everything that had gone on overseas. He had his own doubts and concerns about the way that the transplant had played out. And he'd been plagued by symptoms similar to Amanda's since his return. MacKenzie wondered briefly whether they did have the same donor—a deceased donor, obviously—or whether they just gave everybody that same donor profile. The fictional face of the universal donor. But surely then someone would have noticed before then that everyone was getting organs from the same donor?

Eventually, John Hopewell finished the handshake and goodbye and turned around. He took two steps toward the door and then his eyes caught on MacKenzie. She watched him for his reaction, giving him a tentative smile. She wasn't sure how he would take seeing her there, or how she should take his presence. Were they on the same side? Opposite sides? She had hoped that her information that Amanda had contracted malaria during her transplant trip would help him and he would be able to regain his health with proper treatment.

But he obviously did not have warm feelings toward her for supplying that bit of information. Rather than looking grateful or greeting her warmly as someone who had helped him out in the past, he scowled at her, his face darkening with anger and distaste. If he could have punched her in the nose and gotten away with it, she was sure he would have. She had never seen such an expression of hate and disdain on someone's face. Certainly not aimed toward her.

"Uh… John….?" Even as she was saying it, he was turning away from her and continuing his egress. MacKenzie tried to get to her feet, but the soft cushions kept her from being able to jump up quickly and by the time she put her coffee down on the table and managed to rise, tugging down her skirt to make sure she didn't expose herself to the rest of the room, Hopewell was out the door, striding toward his car without a backward glance. MacKenzie blinked after him.

She knew there was no point in following him. Even if she managed to catch up with him, to keep him from getting into his car and to talk to her, she wasn't going to like what he had to say. She wasn't going to be able to convince him that whatever he was upset about wasn't true, that the clinic was still lying to him and feeding him a big story. She just let him walk away.

There was silence for a moment. Had either Dutton or the receptionist been able to see the look that Hopewell had given her? Or had they both been far enough behind them that they couldn't see anything?

"Miss Kirsch," Dr. Dutton said in a smooth voice. "It's so nice to see you again. How are you?"

MacKenzie took a deep breath, pasted a smile on her face, and turned back around. "Ah. Miss Dutton. It is good to see you again. I'm fine. And you?"

She watched Dutton struggle with whether to correct MacKenzie that it was Dr. Dutton, not Miss Dutton, but the moment passed, and Dr. Dutton just let it go. She could have tried a "Just Mildred, dear," and avoided the issue again, but she didn't. Apparently that kind of casual greeting wasn't used, even for a major donor like someone from the Kirsch family.

"What can we do for you today?" Dr. Dutton asked, her teeth bared in a smile that was more of a grimace.

"I was wondering… I wasn't able to get here when Walter and Lisa were by, so I didn't get to see the language that was going to be used for the memorial donation… I just feel a little left out of the loop, and I wonder if you could fill me in on the particulars."

That was a pretty good bluff. Dr. Dutton frowned, but nodded. "Yes, certainly, of course. I'm sure your parents could have given you a copy…"

"I haven't seen them," MacKenzie said. "This all ended up happening so quickly. I'm not sure what the hurry was, but…"

"Certainly, of course. Let me see… Why don't you come to the boardroom with me, and I'll just get everything together? You can see the whole package and how it will all work."

33

MacKenzie looked over the documents that had been signed between Walter Kirsch and the Forsberg Clinic. She recognized his signature, but couldn't make out the name of who had signed on behalf of the clinic, even though she knew the names of the directors. The signature was an illegible scribble. She paged through the details of the donation and the recognition that Walter had asked for.

She felt the tension across her forehead as she looked it over, trying to figure out what he was doing. He was giving the money for an expansion of the hospital. He wanted to name a wing after Amanda and there were details of the picture and plaque that he wanted posted about her. That all seemed pretty generic. It was a lot of money, but he gave more to other causes. Money would stretch further in a third world country where most labor could be bought at pennies a day instead of dollars an hour.

She didn't know how much it would cost to have materials shipped there, if they really used the expected standard of materials and didn't just clap together a shack like the place where Amanda had taken pictures. If they even bothered to build what they said they were going to. How hard would it be for them to send Walter a mock-up of the wing that they expected to build, to take a picture of a plaque on a wall somewhere, and provide other photographic proof that they had done as they had agreed?

But as she read further, she started to admire her father's wolf-like cunning. The terms of the donor agreement demanded that he be given a tour of the hospital both before and after the construction, and that he be allowed to bring a small group of donors there for a fundraiser to drum up further donations for the clinic, to be used as the clinic designated them. Everything was worded in such a way as to seem natural and boilerplate, but MacKenzie could see his thinking behind it.

He wouldn't actually transfer the funds to the Forsberg Clinic until after he'd had a pre-construction tour of the facility. That would put to rest the question of what conditions Amanda had been treated in and whether there really was a hospital or whether she had been operated on in some jungle shack that was full of flies and mosquitoes and bodies piled like cordwood. He would get a chance to see if there was a building that matched the photos that had been taken. He would meet some of the surgeons that did the transplants.

There was to be an organ donor display recognizing the donors who had given living or post-mortem donations to the transplant recipients. MacKenzie supposed that would give Walter and whoever his investigators were more names to look into, to see whether they really were using live donors and the materials given to both Amanda and John Hopewell on their donors had simply been a paper mix-up, or whether they were using post-mortem donations and trying to pass them off as live donations.

There were clauses about Walter auditing the financial records of the clinic. Other due diligence clauses that would allow him to look into other aspects of the operations of the clinic.

Her father was a wily one. Her fury at him gradually dissipated. He had taken what she had started with, a bluff that she wanted to give a donation in Amanda's name, and he had finagled it into a huge media event and had talked the clinic into signing an agreement that would force them to show their hand, at least in some of the matters they were concerned about.

Why hadn't he told her what he was doing? Why hadn't he given her a heads-up on the donation, even allowed her to appear with them at the media conference? She would have liked to have been part of it. But maybe he hadn't trusted her to be able to keep her cool or to keep a pleasant expression throughout it all. If she had shown her hand, it could have blown the whole deal for him. Lisa was an old pro at press conferences like that one. She didn't know whether Walter had told Lisa the real purpose for his donation to the clinic, or whether she thought it was to recognize what they had done for Amanda and to memorialize her name. Would Lisa have gone along with the deception?

Lisa had been able to keep up the fiction of Amanda's kidney surgery on the island, rather than disclosing the details to MacKenzie. She had kept from both of them the fact that she and Walter had been divorced for several years. She certainly had the ability to stay quiet and perpetuate a fraud.

"This all looks so great," MacKenzie told Dr. Dutton, when she made an appearance to see if MacKenzie had finished going through everything. "I'm amazed that you were able to pull everything together so quickly. When was Walter first in to hammer out the details?"

Dr. Dutton passed a hand over her furrowed brow. "It all came together very quickly," she said. "It's only been a couple of days. He had his lawyers draw up the papers and we only had twenty-four hours to go through things and counter anything. He's a very… persuasive man when he puts his mind to it, isn't he?"

MacKenzie laughed. "That he is," she agreed. "He's had lots of experience in talking people into things. He's the master."

"We are very appreciative of everything that you and your family are doing here. Allowing us to expand the hospital to serve more people, to allow us to increase the number of transplants that we are able to do… this will serve so many people. Save so many lives."

MacKenzie nodded. "Yes. It will make a big difference to a lot of people, won't it?"

She thought of Amanda, laboring to breathe in those last few hours, and of John Hopewell, thin and pale and battling recurring fevers.

Indeed, it could change the lives of many people.

MacKenzie had a copy of the agreement setting out the terms, and the descriptions of the plaque and memorial that had been arranged for Amanda. That was what she should want, as a donor who wanted her sister's life to be recognized. She really only wanted the agreement so she could think about it and maybe talk to Walter later, when everything had settled down and they were able to meet and discuss it confidentially. She knew that he didn't want her to investigate any further and, seeing that he was indeed taking a hand in investigating it, she decided the best course was just to let him follow the plan that he had mapped out.

She drove home feeling much calmer and more in control of herself than she had on the way to the clinic, giving Dr. Dutton a pleasant "Goodbye and thank you, Miss Dutton," to leave her fuming about the professional discourtesy. She went back home to her apartment, resolved to let Walter take the lead in investigating the clinic's claims and proving that their facility on the island actually existed and was in use.

She went to her computer and checked her email when she got home. She had neglected it for a few days and, although she didn't correspond with a lot of people through email, she did have a number of invitations to respond to, some sympathy notes, and some notes and queries about the donation her family was making to the clinic, mostly from reporters who wanted more filler or follow up to their stories.

But in between all of the formalities and expressions of sympathy, there were a couple of emails that made MacKenzie frown. She couldn't tell where they had come from, the email addresses nonsensical collections of letters and numbers. She figured that if she replied to them, the emails would just bounce back. They were just spam. Except she had to stop and wonder why any spammer would suddenly be sending her emails about organ transplants. Were the online spammers that sophisticated? That they would be able to track her interests and target her specifically? She didn't think that technology was quite to that Big Brother level yet.

But her family's name had been in the media in association with organ transplant, so maybe that had triggered more targeted spam. It was one thing to have to weed through incessant noise about male enhancements and women who wanted to make friends online with graphic pictures that she really did not want to see. It was another to have some anonymous source sending her links about the transplant industry.

She looked at the links, wondering whether she dared to click anything. Once she did, they would be sure to publish her email address as a legitimate one, increasing the amount of spam that MacKenzie received. They would likely lead to sites about women and their forbidden desires; then she would have to spend the rest of the day trying to wipe that muck from her brain.

MacKenzie opened the header of the first email, something that one of the guys she had dated a year earlier had taught her to do, to see if she could see where the email had originally come from. There wasn't as much hidden code as she usually saw in spoofed emails, and she couldn't see multiple email addresses and domains, just the one that the email purported to have come from. She looked at the link again. It appeared to be an international news site. It probably redirected. It probably didn't go to a news site after all.

MacKenzie opened a new browser window and typed the main URL in, in case it said it was going to one site but actually directed to another. She waited for the browser to redirect and take her to another site, but it did not. The graphics on the page slowly downloaded, grinding slowly away, until she could see the front page of the paper.

There was no way she could tell whether it was a legitimate paper or not, but it appeared to be. The international stories that appeared were ones that she had seen in the newspaper lately, not wild stories about celebrities or bizarre stories that were targeted to outrage or trigger curiosity. She looked at the link in the email again and typed the page name after the URL. She again waited for it to redirect to a new site, but it did not, starting to download the new page.

MacKenzie swallowed, her eyes moving over the story. She avoided the pictures, yet kept looking back at them, fascinated and horrified.

It was an investigative piece on organ donations in China. It was one of the countries with a higher transplant rate and much lower waiting list than the US. She had assumed that was because of the denser population, maybe because of some government inducement or social pressure to donate organs post-mortem for the good of society. Asian countries had a different outlook on societal good from that of Western countries. They were far more oriented to public good. So it made sense that there would be a lot more pressure for organ donation, both living and post-mortem.

But that was not what the article said. There had been rumors for some time, and the investigative journalists were starting to uncover evidence that the donations for many of the organ donations being performed in China were not coming from living donors, or at least, not the kind that were expected in Western countries. There were indications that they were coming from death-row inmates and political prisoners. There were stories, denied by the authorities, discounted by the public as urban legend and hysterical conspiracists looking for attention.

After all, everyone knew that WHO and the United Nations and anyone else who knew anything had spoken out to deny that there could be anything illegal or untoward going on in the organ transplant industry.

MacKenzie opened a new tab in her browser and typed in a search for illegal organ transplants and black-market organ trade. The headlines and snippets that popped up on her screen were the familiar, reassuring statements. Statements that there could be no illegal organ trade. That it was impossible for a criminal enterprise to be organized around organ transplants. That they wouldn't be able to find surgeons with the technical skill to perform such surgeries. That there was no way such practices could have any existence and it was all urban legend.

That was what MacKenzie had heard before. The legends that popped up in whispered stories or emails that a friend had heard from a reliable source about people waking up without their kidneys, bleeding out or shivering in a tub full of ice were so ridiculous that she was sure no one could really believe them. There was no evidence that any kind of illegal organ trade was going on, so how could there be? The thousands of surgeries that would be required for it to be a profitable enterprise could not possibly be hidden away. There would be some whisper of it in the news. Police would have active investigations, cases where they knew that illegal transplants had actually taken place, and she had heard nothing.

She switched back to the original article, worried about reading more, but galvanized against what she was going to read there. It was just a story that someone had made up, or a mistake had been made. Like MacKenzie looking at the bodies in Amanda's photos and assuming that they were organ donors, it was easy to jump to conclusions without knowing the facts.

But the more she read, the more concerned she felt and the more her stomach sank, feeling sicker and sicker. She took a few steadying breaths.

She read the account of a prison worker who talked about the political prisoners and death row inmates being removed from the prison at night under suspicious circumstances. They were not due to be released or transferred, but they were taken away to hospitals for treatment that they didn't need. There had been no medical diagnosis made, so why did they have medical transfer papers?

She read the account of a hospital worker who testified of corneal removals from patients who were not only still living, but not under sedation. The screams and butchery described were so gory as to be unbelievable. Bodies being taken to the incinerator while they were still bleeding freely.

Dead bodies don't bleed.

She clicked away from the screen and checked to see if she'd received any other email that she hadn't reviewed. Her mind just wouldn't accept and process what the investigative article claimed. How could any government look on their prisoners as mere providers of organs? And where were those organs going? Were they all being used for domestic Chinese transplants? Or were they being used for the international organ transplants? The articles that she had read clearly stated that there was no transportation of organs across borders.

That was why the donors that the Forsberg clinic had used had to fly to the island themselves. Amanda's live donor couldn't just have her kidney removed in Germany and then have it transported to a location hours away before it could be transplanted. They had to have the donors right there. The Chinese atrocities, if they really did exist, had to be confined to the borders of China. They were closer to the island than Germany was, but still, they couldn't have been transported that far, possibly held up in customs or some other queue. They had to have the donors and the recipients in the same place.

MacKenzie thought about the pictures.

A row of bodies under a sheet. All with dark-skinned feet. If Amanda's donor was from Germany, then she couldn't be one of those people. She would have been white. MacKenzie had seen the picture of her, a young blond woman. There was no one like that in the dark shack.

Her father had to be right. Those bodies that had been temporarily stored in the shack had to be the results of some other tragedy. An epidemic. Poverty. Starvation. They could not be part of the organ transplant trade. They didn't match the identities that the donors had been shown before flying overseas to have their transplants done.

MacKenzie turned back to the article and once more looked at the pictures and the descriptions, trying to maintain a neutral, skeptical eye. They could be the victims of a natural disaster. Of a war. Of a terrorist attack. There was nothing about them that said that they were transplant donors or political prisoners. Their bodies were anonymous. There were no pictures of their injuries, no sign of what had killed them. There was, in short, no proof that they were actually of what they said they were.

And major world organizations had said that such a thing was impossible.

34

Eventually, MacKenzie went to the other email from the unknown informant or spammer. Which was he? Someone who was trying to lead her astray or make her click on something that was going to take her down a rabbit hole, or someone who really wanted to inform her about what was going on in the transplant business? The first one was a news article that appeared to be legitimate, so she wondered whether the second would take her somewhere nasty, or whether it would be another article, as bad or worse than the first.

She didn't think she could face much more as far as shocking pictures and blood-soaked sheets went. She just couldn't deal with it, even knowing that it was probably just a scam. What reason would anyone have for making her think that China was doing illegal transplants, harvesting organs from unwilling donors? Was it meant to lead her away from the clinic or to them? Were they connected in some way with such a thing? Or was it to distract her from a possibly low-level concern—less sanitary conditions, some unrelated deaths, marginally unethical payments for organs—with unproven, hysterically pumped-up nonsense? Was it just a distraction? Or was it true?

She looked at the other link. Like the first, there was nothing in the URL to tell her what it might be about. It did look like it could be another news site. But legitimate or not? And what was it going to be about? Verification of the veracity of the first? Maybe they had a source who could prove what it was that was happening in China. But why did she need it to be verified? She couldn't do a thing about what the Chinese government did in the transplant industry.

As before, MacKenzie typed in the root URL before anything else. Rather than a news site, it was an electronic bulletin board. She glanced at the top list of categories, and it seemed to be mostly medical related, but covering a wide range of topics. The page that she had been pointed to was obviously going to be something about transplants. MacKenzie clicked on a couple of subcategories, drilling down deeper into discussions of disease, organ failure, and transplants. She could see that most of what was being posted was written by patients who needed or had received transplants, or by other voices in the community. Not medical professionals. Likewise, not by reporters or government personnel. Just people on the street, like she would talk to at a fundraising event. Like John Hopewell and Magnus Phelps and Amanda. She clicked on a few topics and read through them. There was stuff on kidney donation and transplant, both live donors and post-mortem donations, but she didn't see anything on transplant tourism or China. Everything seemed to be safe and straightforward. Discussions of procedures, upcoming transplants, recovery and, for some of them, rejections and relapses. It was sad to see how many transplants failed, and families were left like hers, with their loved one back on dialysis or dead.

She returned to her email and referenced it while she typed the rest of the URL into the location bar. She pressed enter and waited for it to resolve, either taking her to some unrelated site or into a thread that she was supposed to be interested in.

MacKenzie waited while the thread loaded, then started scrolling through it. Immediately, she was assailed with pictures of starving children. A cautionary tale of how poorly other countries were doing, she assumed. Stop worrying about the rich few getting transplants and start worrying about real problems that affected millions, like starvation and preventable disease. But the headings and the text around the pictures were not about poverty. Instead, they were discussions of children being kidnapped for organ transplants. MacKenzie quickly closed the tab, not wanting to read any more.

Her gaze was drawn to her attache, where the pictures from Amanda's computer still resided. She remembered the varying sizes of the bodies under the sheet. The ones that she had wondered whether they were women or children. She knew for a fact that children were not being kidnapped for organ harvesting. She had read statements to that effect, very strong ones, and she knew that it couldn't be the case. No one was stealing children for their organs. It was the stuff that nightmares were made of, which was why people were trying to use it to frighten each other, but it was not something that was actually going on. The organizations that were in the know said so.

She switched back over to her research. The articles that proved the transplant scare stories were just urban legend. She pulled a report from 1994 up on the screen and read a portion aloud to herself.

Since January 1987, rumors that children are being kidnapped so that they can be used as unwilling donors in organ transplants have been rampant in the world media. No government, international body, non-governmental organization, or investigative journalist has ever produced any credible evidence to substantiate this story, however. Instead, there is every reason to believe that the child organ trafficking rumor is a modern "urban legend," a false story that is commonly believed because it encapsulates, in story form, widespread anxieties about modern life.

Given the total lack of evidence for the child organ trafficking myth, its impossibility from a technical point of view, and the widespread, serious damage that it has already caused and is likely to cause in the future, the United States Information Agency respectfully requests that the U.N. Special Rapporteur give maximum attention and publicity to the information in this report, which demonstrates the groundlessness of reports of child organ trafficking and the impossibility of such practices occurring.

That was pretty clear. And that was the United States Information Agency and the United Nations. If they said that such a thing was just an urban legend, then she was satisfied that it was so. They had far more ability to investigate such a thing than she did. There was no child organ trafficking, and there never would be.

The atmosphere of MacKenzie's apartment was suddenly stifling. She needed to get out and to get some air. She couldn't stay there reading horrific things any longer. She needed to go out and do something to take her mind off of all of the rumors that something horrible was going on in the organ transplant trade. What she had thought was a simple case of escaping strict regulation and ending up having to deal with the consequences of that choice was now a simmering hotbed of rumors and crazy accusations and conspiracies.

She didn't want to deal with it or even to think of it.

She turned her computer off and picked up her bag. She picked up her cell phone and realized that the message indicator was flashing. She hit the voicemail button and dialed in her passcode and listened. It was Dr. Proctor. She wasn't sure when he had called her, but he said he was concerned about her and Lisa after seeing them at the gala and just wanted to make sure that everything was going okay. He left a somewhat rambling message, but MacKenzie decided she should call him back just to reassure him that everything was fine with Lisa.

She wasn't sure what she was going to say about herself. Maybe she could gloss over that part and just focus on her mother. Lisa was of Dr. Proctor's generation and he was probably more interested in her mental health than in MacKenzie's. That was why he had called MacKenzie, for the evaluation of someone who was closer to Lisa and could better judge how she was managing in the wake of her daughter's death.

MacKenzie rehearsed a few lines in her head before pushing the buttons to call Dr. Proctor back. She waited, thinking it was going to go to voicemail on his end, and then he picked up.

"Hello?" He sounded uncertain, as if he didn't know who it was. MacKenzie supposed he didn't recognize her number from just having called her once, and cell numbers didn't have any caller I.D. information associated with them.

"Dr. Proctor, it's MacKenzie."

"Oh, MacKenzie." His tone warmed. "I'm glad to hear from you. I know that the gala was a great success, and I see that your family has made a donation to the Forsberg clinic, like you mentioned they might. I just had a nagging feeling… the other day when you and I talked, and I told you that you should probably go to a private investigator if you wanted someone to look at the backgrounds of the doctors at the overseas Forsberg transplant hospital…"

"It's okay, Dr. Proctor. I understand that your time is precious, and you can't really be using it to search people halfway around the world. I did get someone who could help me in sorting them out, so you really don't have to worry."

"Oh? Who did you get?"

"I went through a private investigations firm, like you suggested."

"I see." There were a few seconds of silence and MacKenzie frowned, wondering if he actually disapproved of her going to a private investigator after he had said that was what she should do. Had it just been intended to be a brush-off and he didn't really expect that she would follow through like she had?

"It turns out that it's actually a lot harder to track international surgeons than you would think," MacKenzie told him. "You need all kinds of other information like birth dates and where they trained and social security numbers, that kind of thing. Because two doctors halfway around the world from each other can have the same name, or a doctor can change his name, or not show up as being credentialed in another country."

"I imagine so! As much as we say the world is getting smaller, it is still a challenge to track people across multiple countries or continents."

"Exactly. I'm glad that you didn't waste your time on it. Better that we leave that to the professionals."

She hoped that with that, his anxiety over brushing her off would evaporate and he would be able to be happy and go on.

"I guess your family has made that donation, so you must have been satisfied with what you found out. I just wonder if there was anything else that you were concerned about. Anything at all…?"

MacKenzie hesitated. Was he really interested in hearing more… really interested…?

"I don't know. I guess things are okay now," she said. Even to her own ears, it didn't sound very convincing.

"It sounds like there is still something. Do you want to share it? I worry about you, MacKenzie."

"I really shouldn't bother you. It has all been straightened out now. Like you said, we've made our donation to the clinic."

"But you still have doubts? I thought you had worked through all of that."

"I have. We have. It's just… well, there's one loose end."

She wouldn't tell him about the emails and the urban legends. But maybe she could show him the pictures. Maybe then he would understand why she had been so concerned. Like Walter, he might just explain them away. Maybe a doctor's explanation would be more satisfying than Walter's. Or maybe like Lance, he would suggest that she should follow up with someone on them. Not the police or FBI, but a medical organization. Some overseer that would do the work overseas and be able to provide an explanation. There had been some kind of outbreak, or accident, or tribal war. They would know because they would already be watching what was going on. They wouldn't be cut out of the loop and just guessing about everything like she was.

She took a deep breath, picking up her purse and her attache. If she showed the pictures to one more person, would she get one more interpretation? Or would he side with one of the other explanations, throwing more weight on one side or the other?

"Yes, please tell me about it. What is this one loose end?" Dr. Proctor coaxed.

35

She had thought when she arrived at Dr. Proctor's office that she would find it bustling with activity. She hadn't realized that she had spent her afternoon on web research on illegal organ trafficking and by the time she got to his office it was already after hours. There was no receptionist or nurse at the desk outside his office, no patients waiting, and the corridors of that wing of the hospital were almost deserted. But Dr. Proctor had invited her to go see him, so she knew she would find him still in his office when she got there.

She tapped on the door that stood slightly ajar and pushed it open far enough to poke her head in to alert him of the fact that she was there, without intruding on him if he were in the middle of something.

"Dr. Proctor?"

"Ah, MacKenzie. Come in."

He gave her a big, welcoming smile and motioned for her to enter. MacKenzie opened the door the rest of the way and sat down in the chair that he indicated.

"So… all of this fuss over the clinic…" He gave her a small smile and a shrug. "I suppose that progress will always bring with it controversy, especially when we are talking about transplants. There seems to be more demand for organs all the time, but the ethics of providing more and more organs to meet the demand becomes problematic."

MacKenzie nodded in response. The ethics became problematic? She could show him how problematic they had become. It was no longer just a matter of whether they had ventured into a gray area.

"Why don't you tell me what it is you are still having problems with?"

"When I looked at Amanda's computer after she died… I found some pictures."

Dr. Proctor raised his brows. "Pictures?"

"She took them while she was away for her transplant. Or what I thought at the time was just an innovative new surgery."

He waited for more. MacKenzie looked around. It was so quiet in that part of the hospital. She had never felt quite so isolated there before. It was like being in a school playground after all of the children were gone. Sort of uncomfortable and spooky.

"There isn't anyone who can overhear us," Dr. Proctor said. "It's just you and me."

"I know. It's just… I don't quite know how to talk about this. I haven't had much success in talking about it with anyone else."

"People don't believe you?" he asked sympathetically.

"People don't *want to* believe me, I guess," she agreed. It was an uncomfortable truth, and who wanted to deal with uncomfortable truths?

"I'll believe you, MacKenzie."

MacKenzie wasn't sure he would. He hadn't been terribly open to the idea that there was anything unethical—or worse—going on at the clinic up until that point.

She took a deep breath and tried to calm the racing of her heart and the tight knot in her stomach.

"Well, here it is." She delved into her attache to pull one of the pictures out. She looked at it for a moment herself, as if to confirm that nothing had changed, and it still showed just what it had the last time she had looked at it. Every time she looked at it. But it was exactly the same picture that she had studied so many times before.

Ingrained upon her memory. She handed it across the desk to Dr. Proctor.

He looked at it, and his eyes widened a little. MacKenzie waited for the explanation. "Oh, you see, these are from..."

"So..." He stared at the picture. "I was afraid of something like this." He shook his head. "From the time you first started asking questions, I feared that something like this could turn up."

MacKenzie nodded, waiting.

"Why don't you come around here, and I'll show you," he suggested. He opened his desk drawer to pull out a highlighter or marker.

MacKenzie got up and walked around the large desk to his side. Her attention was completely occupied by the picture Dr. Proctor laid down on the desk. What exactly was he going to show her that would change her perspective and put it in a new light?

"I always told Lisa and Walter you were a very smart girl. The reason you did not do as well as they hoped in school was because you were too bright. You were bored by it all. There wasn't enough to challenge you."

MacKenzie didn't know if that were true. She'd never been a star pupil. Not one of those who rose to the top and was always getting the highest marks. She'd done well, never struggling to pull off respectable grades, but she hadn't been passionate about her courses of study and did just what she needed to to maintain a good grade point average.

"You were always very quick to understand what was going on with Amanda's health. The medical words and the biology behind what we were seeing was always plain to you."

MacKenzie shrugged. "Biology was one of my favorite subjects in school. I enjoyed the dissections..."

He chuckled. "Exactly. Now, if you'll just get really close here..."

MacKenzie bent down, squinting at the photo. It didn't get any clearer being closer to it. The resolution and the lighting were too poor.

MacKenzie felt a prick against her belly and pulled back slightly, uncomfortable. She looked down and realized that Dr. Proctor had not pulled a highlighter out of his drawer, but a scalpel. He now held it against her, the sharp point just grazing her skin. She looked at him, her mind denying the reality of the situation, trying to come up with logical alternative explanations. A joke. A misinterpretation.

"I'm sure you remember the locations of the major arteries and organs in your abdomen," he said quietly. "An experienced surgeon like I am could map them in his sleep."

MacKenzie looked at the picture, hoping for some kind of revelation. He would point to it and indicate what had been done to the torsos of the victims in the photo. But they couldn't see the torsos, not through the sheet. There wasn't any marking or indentation on the sheet that showed what had been done to the people in that picture. Not that she could see, anyway.

"I told your parents that you would be upset about the fact that the kidney you donated to Amanda had failed. That they needed to keep you out of the loop about the second donation so that you wouldn't feel bad about it. It was more kind to just let you go on thinking that your kidney was keeping Amanda alive."

"Why would I feel bad? I know that transplants can fail. The body can reject the organ or it just stops functioning like it was supposed to."

"I said it because I didn't want you poking your nose into everything. I didn't want you picking up on anything that was going on that wasn't in the normal course. I couldn't be sure that you wouldn't twig to something if you were there."

"You kept me away," MacKenzie said.

She still wasn't understanding what he was saying. She was sure that she was misinterpreting his intent. He had always been good to Amanda and her family. He was a respected surgeon, one of the most prestigious in the hospital. She hadn't had enough sleep and she was reading something into his comments.

"Yes, I kept you away. And if Amanda had not contracted malaria…!"

"I wouldn't have known," MacKenzie agreed.

"They should have tested the donors," Dr. Proctor muttered.

"That was sloppy. Some people contract malaria without ever showing the signs."

"She got malaria from the organ donor?" MacKenzie asked, not sure she understood the leap.

"Of course. What do you think happens when you transfer an infected organ from one person to another?"

"But the donor was from Germany. How did she get infected that quickly?"

But she knew the answer without Dr. Proctor telling her. Looking down at the bodies in the picture. No white skin on any of them. No blond German woman.

"Who were they?" she asked Dr. Proctor. Her brain was starting to warm up, starting to understand that she had to get out of there before he killed her. So it was partially because she wanted to know the truth and partially because she wanted to stall, to come up with a plan that would get her out of danger.

No one knew she was there. She hadn't told anyone where she was going. She hadn't called Lisa to say that she would come by for dinner after visiting Dr. Proctor. She hadn't asked Lance to investigate him. She hadn't written it into her planner. No one looking at her room would have any idea where she had planned to go when she had left.

"Why does it matter?" Dr. Proctor said. "They were the people who were providing the organs that we needed so desperately. The people who could save Amanda and so many others. That was the important part. To get the much-needed organs for the Americans who were willing to pay for them."

"Their lives mattered just as much as the Americans," MacKenzie argued. "All life is… is sacred."

"Sacred?" He gave a little laugh. "Since when have you taken to religion?"

"I don't mean in a religious way. I mean… doesn't all life have intrinsic value?"

"If you saw the way these people lived, the things that they had done, you wouldn't have thought so. These people were refuse. They were just the packages the needed organs were being transported in."

MacKenzie felt like throwing up right there on his desk. How could he view human beings like that? He was a doctor; he was supposed to respect life. How could he have changed so suddenly from the kindly doctor to someone who was only in it for the money? MacKenzie tried to pull away from him, away from the scalpel, but he gripped her arm and pressed the blade more firmly against her.

"You can't get sentimental," Dr. Proctor insisted. "No more than you felt sorry for the animals that you dissected in biology. They were a learning tool. You didn't even recycle their parts. You just opened them up, looked at them, and tossed them out. If there was nothing wrong with that, what is wrong with transplanting organs to save lives? Not just Amanda, but others too."

"John Hopewell?"

He looked at her, raising his eyebrows. "Yes, John Hopewell. You got further than I had thought."

"He has malaria too."

Dr. Proctor nodded slowly. "That's not a surprise."

"They had the same donor."

"Yes. One kidney each."

"And any others? What about others who have died already? How many people were infected with dirty organs?"

"They would have died without a transplant. So you can't judge the correctness of what was done by whether they lived or died. All of them would have died without transplants."

"Amanda could have lived longer. She died from malaria. She wouldn't have had that without the transplant. She could have lived on dialysis, waited for an organ here in the States. Followed the proper protocol."

He pressed the knife into her. "You're so sure of yourself. So sure that you're right and that everybody else is wrong. You've just been manipulated by the system. When they tell you there's only one way to do things, you assume that they're telling you the truth. But they're not. There's plenty of room to do things differently. We could be saving a lot more people, if they would just listen."

"So is this all your operation? Your name wasn't on anything at the Forsberg Clinic. I didn't think you worked in transplants."

"They couldn't have done it without me. There are a lot of people who you wouldn't think were involved, but an operation like this takes a lot of manpower, a lot of different moving parts."

"My father?"

Dr. Proctor tipped his head, looking up at MacKenzie questioningly. "What about your father?"

"How long has he been involved with the clinic? How deeply? Has he been giving them money right from the start?"

"You need a lot of money to build a hospital and fund a business. Yes, he needed to put capital into it. But he wasn't the only one. There are a lot of funding sources. And the money required to fly these donors in from all around the world." He said it in a sarcastic tone. There was no one flying around the world. There were no donors from Germany or Iran. Wherever they were coming from, it was not around the world. They were islanders, or Chinese prisoners, or kidnapped children. A charter plane flying a couple of hours, not a whole day away.

MacKenzie closed her eyes, trying for a moment to push all of the emotion away, to keep it compartmentalized. She couldn't have it slowing her down and muddying her thinking at that critical moment. All of the grief and horror and disgust had to go away somewhere else. She stared down at the photo on Dr. Proctor's desk, but let her peripheral vision pick up the rest of his desk, trying to work out a strategy.

"What about this?" she asked, pointing to something in the dark corner of the photo, and then pulling her hand back so that Dr. Proctor could see it.

"What?"

She only needed him to look for a minute. She only wanted the momentary distraction, a shifting of his attention away from the scalpel he held against her body.

36

With the hand that had been pointing at the photo, and then drawn away, MacKenzie grabbed a rectangular paperweight of cut black marble with a commemorative plaque mounted on it and smashed it as hard as she could into Dr. Proctor's forehead.

She pulled his knife hand away from her body, aware that the blade had sunk deeper when she had hit him, rather than him pulling away so he could hold his head and protect his face. She tried to writhe away from the hand that had an iron grip on her arm, but it was harder than it should have been. He wasn't a frail old man. He was still in his prime and his hands had been strengthened by hours of surgery. She wrenched and twisted her arm, fighting wildly to get away before he managed to bring the scalpel back around to do further damage, hoping to capitalize on the blow to his face and the blood starting to drip down his forehead. She managed to wrench free and ran for the door, but he was right behind her, trying to trip her up, swinging the scalpel, and shouting at her.

MacKenzie got out the office door, into the office of the administrative assistant who acted as the gatekeeper and made for the next door. Her way was blocked.

Her brain was on fast forward, barely able to take in what she saw. A man blocked her exit.

Lance Reacher.

Was he the one who had been following her? Sending her email? He could have bugged her apartment under the guise of boosting security. She had no clue how he was involved in the racket.

Lance put out his hand to grab her and MacKenzie danced back.

"Kenzie. It's okay. What's—?"

He moved into the room and was distracted by Dr. Proctor's presence. As soon as his eyes darted to the side, MacKenzie slipped out the door behind him.

She heard an angry shout from Dr. Proctor, then a crash. She looked back but was unable to see what was going on inside the office. She had been home free. She could just run and leave it all behind. But she couldn't. Not if Lance could possibly be on her side. If there were even a chance of it, she couldn't run away and leave him there tangling with Dr. Proctor.

MacKenzie hesitated, then went back to the door and peeked in, worried that when she did so, she would be back in the line of fire. Both of them would grab her, and Dr. Proctor would be able to finish the job he had started. But she saw Lance holding Dr. Proctor off, refusing to let him get close to the door that MacKenzie had escaped through.

"Don't you have a gun?" she screeched.

Lance didn't look away from Dr. Proctor to see what MacKenzie was doing back again.

"Of course not," he said. "This isn't TV. I'm an investigator, not a cop. Get out of here. Call for help."

"I'll call. I have a cell phone."

"Go somewhere safe, then call."

MacKenzie ignored the instruction, digging into the handbag still slung across her body. She pulled out the phone.

"Give it up!" she shouted at Dr. Proctor. "You can't get away with this. You don't want to hurt anyone."

"Your belief that I can't get past an unarmed man is charming," Dr. Proctor said, advancing on Lance, who picked up a heavy binder and threw it at him. "But terribly misplaced. With a scalpel in my hands… I am the angel of life or death."

"Lance, be careful," MacKenzie warned. The phone rang through to the cell company's emergency operator, and then at her instruction, on to the city's emergency operator. MacKenzie described their location and answered the question about whether there were any weapons on the scene in the affirmative. She squeezed the phone tightly in her hand, wishing that she had chosen to pack a gun instead of just a cell phone. A cell phone might be fine for most emergencies she encountered, but not for a standoff with an armed assailant.

Dr. Proctor jumped forward and managed to get Lance's arm, making him jump and jerk back. He tried to grab Dr. Proctor before the surgeon could get another chance to bring the knife in. Dr. Proctor kept it low, aimed toward Lance's belly, rather than the overhand "Psycho" stabbing position.

"Careful," MacKenzie moaned.

Lance threw a stapler at Dr. Proctor, but the surgeon's reflexes were quick, and he batted it to the side. He suddenly jumped into Lance and, with his weight throwing Lance off balance and the knife still in his skilled hands, he managed to get a quick thrust into Lance's body.

MacKenzie screamed. She threw herself into the fray, even while her primitive brain warned her it was an exceptionally stupid move, but with the two of them both fighting off Dr. Proctor, the surgeon decided it was time to cut bait and ran for it.

MacKenzie didn't have any desire to chase after him. She turned to Lance. "Let me see. Move your hands." She pushed his hands back when he tried to stop her.

"I'm fine," Lance protested.

"No, you're not." Blood was flowing at an alarming rate. "Get down. Now. Lie down so I can put pressure on it."

She forced Lance onto his back and pressed both hands over the gash, using her weight to provide the pressure. But she couldn't seem to slow it.

"We're in a hospital," she said aloud to herself. "How do I get trauma doctors fast?"

She looked around the office, swearing. "Come on, Kenzie, think!" she ordered herself.

She took a chance on removing pressure for a moment, jumped across the room to pull the fire alarm switch, and grabbed the desk phone, throwing it on the floor beside Lance. She resumed the pressure with one hand and started hitting buttons on the phone. She needed someone, she didn't care whether it was security or the morgue, just as long as they could understand where she was and send help.

There was a tinny voice coming from the receiver. MacKenzie snatched it up. "Emergency in Dr. Proctor's office," she barked. "A stabbing. Send a trauma team now!"

"The fire alarm has been activated in that section," a calm male voice told her. "You need to evacuate the area."

"I pulled the fire alarm. Send paramedics. Emergency room doctors. Something. Right now!"

"The wing is being evacuated," he repeated.

"No! No, don't evacuate it, send help! I pulled it because I need help!"

"Ma'am, we have a protocol to be followed—"

MacKenzie shrieked. "Send help!"

"It's okay," Lance said. "Calm down, Kenzie. It's going to be okay."

She looked down at him. Lance's face was getting gray, but he smiled at her as if totally relaxed. "They always seem like they take too long," he said. "It seems like everyone is moving in slow motion. But they'll get here."

"How did you know? How did you get here?"

"Followed the followers." He grinned. "We knew that your father wanted you investigated, whether he was the one who had your apartment broken into or not. He had to go to another firm, so we watched to see who was watching you, and then we watched them..."

"Where are they?"

"They didn't come in. Must just be reporting on your whereabouts. But I didn't like the idea of you being in here alone, not knowing where you were or who you were talking to, so I came in..."

MacKenzie swore. She kept pressing on the knife wound, but Lance's clothes were soaked through. Dr. Proctor knew where every artery was in the human body. He had been fighting wildly, but he knew the human body like other people knew the bus routes or highway system.

"Stick with me, Lance," she urged. She could feel his body quivering under her touch and she didn't like his pallor. He licked his lips and tried to smile again, but his eyes kept sliding to the side and he couldn't seem to stay focused on her.

"It's fine," he assured her in a whisper.

"It's not fine. Where is my help? Where are they?"

Lance closed his eyes, not answering.

"Come on, Lance. Don't do that. Don't go to sleep." She nudged him, trying to keep him aware.

MacKenzie swore again. The fire alarm was still clanging loudly, getting on her nerves. She could feel Lance's resistance draining away, the tautness of his muscles relaxing.

"No, no, no..."

Finally, there were voices approaching. MacKenzie, kneeling over Lance's still body, shouted to hurry them along.

"Over here! Please help, now!"

They stopped talking and the footsteps increased in speed. In a moment, there were a couple of paramedics and a doctor, peering into the office to see if it was safe to enter.

"He's bleeding so fast," MacKenzie told them. "Come here, please. Help."

They were quick and sober, pushing in to examine Lance and to treat him, speaking to each other in quick mutters, calling for additional backup and equipment, saying nothing to MacKenzie. She moved back and sat on the floor, her back leaning against the secretarial desk, and watched them with warm tears running down her cheeks.

37

The next thing she knew, she was waking up in bed. MacKenzie lay there for a few minutes before opening her eyes, analyzing what she could remember and trying to decide how much of it had been a dream. Surely the part about Dr. Proctor being a villain could not be true. There was never a nicer guy. He'd always been very kind and attentive toward MacKenzie and her family.

Maybe the whole thing was a dream, all the way back to Amanda having malaria. Could there be anything more ridiculous? Amanda with malaria? Like she'd been serving in the war in India?

Eventually, MacKenzie had to open her eyes. She looked around for Amanda. She was in hospital, and that meant that Amanda must be there. Amanda was always the patient. The only time MacKenzie had ever been a patient had been when she had given Amanda her kidney. And she certainly couldn't do that again.

But there was no sign of Amanda. There was only Lisa, sitting in one of the visitor chairs beside the bed, just as she always sat next to Amanda's, when she was a patient there. MacKenzie blinked and tried to get Lisa's attention. Her mother appeared to be asleep sitting up.

"Mother," she whispered. She wanted to talk louder, but her voice was apparently not quite up to the job yet. "Mother. Lisa."

Lisa startled and her head came up, looking immediately for her daughter. She focused in on MacKenzie.

"Oh, MacKenzie. You're awake. That's very good."

"Why am I here?" MacKenzie asked. She was a little shaky and woozy, but wasn't quite sure why they would have put her in a hospital bed. She could have just weathered the flu at home in her own bed. Either in her apartment or at Lisa's house in her old room.

"You have a small injury," Lisa said. "I'm still trying to understand what happened. Something to do with Dr. Proctor...?"

"That was real?"

"Yes."

"Ooh..." MacKenzie shook her head. "I can't believe it. Really?"

"Tell me what happened."

"He was... he was the one who told you not to tell me about Amanda's transplant."

Lisa looked surprised. "Yes, that's right."

"They were harvesting organs. Not from live donors who had consented. But from people who... there is a black market for organ transplants... people who get kidnapped, children, death row inmates..."

Lisa's eyes widened. "No. That's just urban legend."

"No, it's not. It's happening. There are people being killed for their organs. For transplants like Amanda had. It's the truth."

"No, dear. No."

"That's how she ended up with malaria. Not because she got bitten by a mosquito. Because the person whose kidney she got had malaria. She was infected by the kidney."

Lisa frowned. She was still shaking her head, but she didn't protest verbally.

"Amanda took pictures while she was over there. Pictures of the bodies. They were on her computer."

"She would have told me that," Lisa insisted, eyes getting even wider.

"If she remembered. Maybe the anesthesia or the malaria fever mixed her up or made her forget it. But they were still on her computer."

"No there wasn't anything like that. I looked at her computer."

"You didn't look deep enough."

"You'll have to show me." Lisa's voice had a bit of an edge to it.

MacKenzie closed her eyes. "I can't. I don't have it anymore. Daddy had it stolen from my apartment."

"Walter wouldn't do that."

"You know how upset he was when I took the files."

MacKenzie met Lisa's eyes and Lisa looked away.

"I made photocopies, and he took those too. He didn't need them for filing taxes. He wanted to make sure that no one else saw them so that no one else would know what was going on."

Lisa frowned and didn't say anything. MacKenzie tried to twist to turn over and look at Lisa more easily and gasped at the pain that flared in her stomach. She clapped a hand over the spot, which was a bad idea and made her cry out.

"What is it, should I get the doctor?" Lisa started half out of her chair.

"No. No, it's fine." MacKenzie kept her hand over her stomach and probed it gently with her fingers. She could feel the bandage under her hospital gown. She remembered Dr. Proctor holding the scalpel to her stomach and threatening to cut her. He had cut her when she had hit him over the head, but it had been uncontrolled, not an intentional slash. She hadn't even noticed that she was hurt during all that had followed.

"Did they get Dr. Proctor?" she asked. "Did they arrest him and put him in jail for what he did?"

"They were looking for him. I haven't heard what happened. The police said they would come back and talk to you when you were ready."

MacKenzie let out her breath. "I'm not ready to talk to anyone yet. Except you. What about… What about Lance, is he okay?"

Lisa looked at MacKenzie, her mouth a long, thin line. Her eyes seemed very tired and shadowed. "MacKenzie, I don't even know who that young man was. How was he involved in all of this? You knew him? He was a friend of yours?"

"He was a private investigator. I hired him to do some background checks for me, and then he helped me with my apartment after it got broken into. And then… I guess he was following to make sure that I was okay after Daddy… tried to hire him."

"Hire him for what?"

"You'd have to ask Lance the details. He said that Daddy wanted… to know what I was doing. He had someone following me. He wanted to know who I was talking to, probably, make sure I wasn't going to cause any trouble for him, because of his lobbying."

Lisa didn't say anything. MacKenzie swallowed hard. She closed her eyes.

"Mom?"

"Yes, MacKenzie?"

"Lance? Is he okay?"

Her eyes were closed, and still she could sense Lisa shaking her head.

"Tell me he's not dead."

"The doctor said that the stab wound he sustained… it cut the aorta."

MacKenzie swore softly. "Why would he do that? I tried to stop it. I put pressure on it. I called for help. And the blood was just everywhere."

"They said you couldn't have done anything else. He bled out too fast."

MacKenzie was able to check herself out of the hospital pretty quickly. Her wound was only minor, unlike Lance's. She'd lost blood, but they'd given her a unit or two to top her off, and once everything was stitched up, she was ready to go. Her mother wanted her kept at the hospital for a few more days, but there was really no need. It was just a way to keep an eye on MacKenzie and make sure she was okay.

Her father was a problem. MacKenzie could only hold him off for so long. And the man was used to having his own way. Sooner or later, he was going to get it. So eventually, MacKenzie had to agree to meet with him, even though she was sure she was not going to like what he had to say.

Rather than picking out a coffee shop or somewhere that Walter would normally hammer out a deal or make his threats and demands, MacKenzie suggested a walk. It had probably been years since he'd strolled anywhere, and he seemed awkward and uncertain for once. MacKenzie was glad to have him off balance.

"I know you probably think I betrayed you with the donation to the Forsberg Clinic." He didn't sound apologetic, but he did sound uncertain.

MacKenzie lengthened her stride to keep up with him better. She disliked how much longer his legs were than hers and how it made her scurry to keep up. Long legs were one thing in a boyfriend, but quite another when she was trying to have a conversation. She tried to keep her voice light and matter-of-fact.

"Actually, I went to the clinic after the announcement and I got myself a copy of the agreement."

He looked at her, surprised. "You did what?"

"I wanted to know what was going on, so I snooped."

"Which is just what I told you not to do."

She nodded. "I know."

"And what did you think?" he asked grudgingly.

"I think you got an engraved invitation to go snooping on the island to see if you can figure out where Amanda took her pictures."

"It won't be there anymore."

"What? Why not?"

"It was just a little slapped-together shack. They could knock that down in a day. If they think that they're compromised, they'll get rid of all the evidence. It had a concrete pad floor, and that will be harder to get rid of, but they can just build something else over top. I'll go back there, and I'll look around the hospital and see where she was treated, and where they propose to put the new wing. And I'll look around the grounds, anywhere she might have gone on her own. But I won't find anything. I won't see what Amanda saw. They'll be far more careful after all of this."

"Are you going to go ahead then and give them the donation and build a new wing?"

"I'm studying their financials and their management policies. They might need someone with my skill set on the board."

MacKenzie looked at him, opening her mouth to object.

"And if they appoint me to the board, I can promise you there will be no… non-consenting donors."

"You think that's something the board of directors know about and can control?"

"It will be."

"And you'll keep working on changing the transplant laws."

"The current laws are stifling. Far too few transplants are being done here in comparison to more progressive countries in the world. I'm not saying we let them have a free-for-all. But things could be improved."

MacKenzie sighed and they walked in silence.

"What are your plans?" Walter asked.

MacKenzie took a quick look at him. "My plans? Why would my plans change?"

He didn't answer at first, letting the silence build up between them.

"Okay, I have been thinking about the future," MacKenzie admitted.

Walter nodded and waited.

"Dr. Proctor said a few times that he thought I should continue my education… in medicine. He said he thought I had a talent with it. And I always like biology and medical stuff at school."

"He told me a few times I should encourage your interest. But I happen to know… if I pushed you too hard in one direction, you'd just push back. Do you want to go into medicine?"

MacKenzie nodded slowly. "I kind of do. Maybe not a doctor at a hospital or clinic, but maybe… something in research. Or maybe pathology. This whole thing finding out about Amanda's transplant… it was kind of cool. The non-threatening parts. Figuring out that she had malaria. Finding out about the transplant industry and what people are dealing with. Yeah, I enjoyed that part. The research and digging up clues as to what had happened."

"It will mean a lot more education. You never were big on school."

"I know," MacKenzie agreed. "But mostly because I was so bored. If it's something that really interests me… that wouldn't be so bad."

38

One year earlier...

Amanda pushed open the door and walked into the outbuilding. Her toes curled when she stepped onto the concrete floor, cold on her bare feet. She walked through the building, looking around, her eyes searching in the dark, trying to make sense of everything.

She had heard people there earlier. She had seen doctors going in and out of the building. It didn't make sense, doctors using such a dismal, dark little building when they had a big, modern hospital available. She supposed it was some kind of garage or tool shed. But what tools would the doctors need that wouldn't be stored in the hospital? She hadn't seen a lot of cars driving around. She didn't think there were more than a handful of them on the island, just enough to transport patients and their families between the various buildings. The air strip to the housing settlement to the hospital and back.

It was still too warm in the shed. It was too warm everywhere she went, and she knew part of it was her fever. When the fever finally broke, maybe she would feel comfortable again but, until it did, she was going to be hot and cold and uncomfortable. That's how it always was.

She pushed open another door. Nothing seemed to be locked. It was just what it appeared to be, an empty warehouse, something left over that had been built before the hospital. Fallen into disuse.

Amanda looked around. The stench was terrible. What was it? Rats? some other kind of vermin? It definitely smelled like something had been caged there. Defecation and urine and the odor of sweat and bodies. Some wild animals, and the natives who took care of them. Amanda covered her nose with the back of her hand, trying to control her gag reflex. She walked through the room to the other side. The floor under her feet was sticky, and she didn't look down, didn't want to know what she was walking through. She'd clean off her feet when she got back to the hospital.

When she got into the next room, she stopped, startled. She realized she had walked into somebody's sleeping chamber. Was the warehouse used, then, to house servants? People who worked at the hospital or kept the grounds? She thought they would have their own huts on the island, like the one that Walter and Lisa were being housed in.

She was about to walk out, and then realized that the people were not sleeping. They were still as statues. Maybe they were statues, waxworks or something that the hospital was going to use for an information display.

The sheet pulled over them covered up their faces and their bodies. There were a few feet sticking out the bottoms of the sheets. Amanda pulled out her phone and took a couple of pictures. It was probably too dark for anything to show up when she uploaded them to the computer.

She got closer, peering at the statues. Why were they being stored in the warehouse? It couldn't be because it was cooler there. The hospital was better air-conditioned than the shed.

She got close enough to be sure that she had been right the first time, and the figures lying there were not statues, but people. But they still were not moving, not even the small movements of someone deep in sleep, the rise and fall of their chests, the whisper of breathing.

They were bodies.

Corpses lying all in a line and covered up so no one would have to look at them.

Amanda looked around in panic. Flies buzzed in the air and she felt nauseated. It was just the fever. The fever was making her hot and nauseated and she was probably hallucinating too. She wasn't really seeing anything there, she was back in the hospital in her own bed, fast asleep.

She tucked her mini flip phone into her bra. Kenzie was always laughing about her shoving things into her bra, but Amanda was so often in hospital robes with no pockets, that she'd had to find some solution. So she insisted on a bra under the robe. If she had to take it off for some physical examination or test, she would, but most of her doctors wanted to examine her kidneys, not her boobs, and they didn't care if she felt more comfortable wearing a bra under the hospital johnnies.

Amanda started to retrace her steps. She shouldn't have left the hospital. She shouldn't have left her room. She should have just stayed in her bed where she was told to, and then she wouldn't be having this hallucination about horrific things in the shed.

She left the building and walked back along the well-worn pathway toward the hospital. She tried to reason that the shed was just where they stored dead bodies. Like a morgue. Except that it obviously didn't keep them cool. She couldn't come up with an explanation for why they would transfer the bodies there, but obviously they did. She hoped that none of them were organ recipients she had met at the clinic's social events. She had been introduced to a few people who would be getting transplants around the same time as she would. Hopefully, none of them had ended up out there, in the shed.

"Here she is!"

A couple of men hurried toward her. They had on white lab coats and were coming toward her from the hospital.

"Amanda. What are you doing out here? You are supposed to stay in your room."

"I wanted to… get some fresh air." Amanda couldn't think of a better reason. She wasn't sure why she had come there in the first place.

"Come back to your room. You shouldn't be wandering. You could pull out your stitches."

She allowed them to take her by the arm and lead her back to her room. She was getting tired and wanted to lie down. She wanted to stop the nightmares and wake up again. The hospital would be cooler, and soon her fever would break and she'd be able to think straight again. In a few days, she'd be able to see her family again and go back to the States. Then everything would go back to normal.

EPILOGUE

Kenzie was focused on the forms in front of her, making sure she got everything down the way that Dr. Wiltshire would want it. She was still learning the ropes and didn't want the medical examiner to be disappointed with her work. She heard the man's footsteps coming down the hallway and blocked him out, trying to finish before she allowed him to interrupt her.

"Hang on. Just let me finish this part up, before I lose my train of thought."

He was quiet while he waited. He didn't interrupt, insisting that his request was more important than her form. He didn't pace around and sigh loudly or fidget. Eventually, she filled out the last space and looked up at him raising an eyebrow in inquiry.

He was a small man. Not quite as short as she, but below average height, with a slim build. He had dark hair, buzzed very short. His eyes looked slightly hollow, as if he'd been sick recently.

"You must be Kenzie," he said.

"I don't know if I must be," Kenzie said in good humor, "but I am. Kenzie Kirsch. And you are?"

"Zachary Goldman. From Goldman Investigations."

She was surprised. "A private investigator?" She looked him over more carefully, comparing him to the ten-year-old memory of Lance Reacher. Physically, there was little similarity between them. But Kenzie thought she could see that same acceptance and compassion that she'd felt from Lance all those years before. Like he'd had a few hard knocks of his own along the way and would understand about hers. He didn't give off the same aura as some of the chauvinistic cops who came down to her basement desk blustering and expecting to be treated like they were something special.

"Yes."

"And what can I do for you today, Mr. Private Investigator?"

"Zachary."

"Zachary," Kenzie repeated, smiling. "What can I do for you?"

"I need to order a copy of a medical examiner's report. Declan Bond."

"Bond." Kenzie remembered the case. Who could forget the poor little fellow? Especially when he'd been the son of a celebrity. "That's the boy? The drowning victim?"

"That's the one."

She shook her head, studying him. "Why do you need that one? It's closed. A determination was made that it was an accident."

"I know. The family would like someone else to look at it. Just to set their minds at ease."

"You're not going to find anything. It's an open-and-shut case."

"That's fine. They just want someone to take a look. It's not a reflection on the medical examiner. You know how families are. They need to be able to move on. They're not quite ready to let it go yet. One last attempt to understand..."

Kenzie remembered how she had searched for meaning in Amanda's case. She'd needed something else. Some kind of explanation for why Amanda had had to die.

"Okay, then... there's a form..." She went through her drawers to find him the right one. He didn't argue that he didn't want to fill out his own forms or thought they were somehow beneath him. He just started working on it.

She went on with her own administrative tasks while he filled it out. There were always plenty of forms to be filled and filing to be done. It took him longer than she expected to fill out the form, which most of the cops she dealt with barely scribbled a few details into. He put the pen away and put the form down beside her, allowing her to finish what she was working on. Kenzie finished hers and picked it up. She was surprised at his neat printing.

"You have nice printing!" She laughed at herself. "No reason why you shouldn't," she said quickly. "It's just that the majority of the forms that get submitted here are... well, to say they were chicken scratch would be insulting to chickens."

Zachary chuckled. "That's the difference between a cop and a private investigator."

"Neat handwriting?"

"Yeah. Cops have to fill out so many forms, they don't care. You can just call them if you need something clarified. Me... I know if I don't fill it out right, it's just going to go in the circular file." He nodded in the direction of the garbage.

"I wouldn't throw it out," Kenzie objected.

"If you couldn't read it? What else would you do?"

"I would at least try to call you."

Zachary pointed. "That's why I printed my phone number so neatly."

Kenzie smiled and nodded. "It's very clear," she approved. She gave him an appraising look, sensing that maybe there was some chemistry going on between them. Maybe he had printed his phone number so clearly for *another* reason.

"You'll call me?" Zachary asked.

"I'll let you know when it's ready to be picked up."

Zachary nodded. He hesitated for a minute before turning to leave. He smiled one last time, and then left. Kenzie suspected it wasn't the last time she was going to hear from Zachary Goldman.

Read more about Kenzie Kirsch and Zachary Goldman in *She Wore Mourning*, book #1 of Zachary Goldman Mysteries by P.D.

Workman and in *Doctored Death*, book #2 in the Kenzie Kirsch Medical Thriller series

Previews of both books follow!

BACKGROUND NOTE

The 1994 report that Kenzie read stating without reservation that child organ trafficking is an urban legend was:

> **The child organ trafficking rumor: a modern 'urban legend',** A report submitted to the United Nations Special Rapporteur on the sale of children, child prostitution, and child pornography by the United States Information Agency, December 1994, by Todd Leventhal, United States Information Agency Washington, D.C.
>
> Since January 1987, rumors that children are being kidnapped so that they can be used as unwilling donors in organ transplants have been rampant in the world media. No government, international body, non-governmental organization, or investigative journalist has ever produced any credible evidence to substantiate this story, however. Instead, there is every reason to believe that the child organ trafficking rumor is a modern "urban legend," a false story that is commonly believed because it encapsulates, in story form, widespread anxieties about modern life.
>
> Given the total lack of evidence for the child organ trafficking myth, its impossibility from a technical point of view, and the widespread, serious damage that it has already caused and is likely to cause in the future, the United States Information Agency respectfully requests that the U.N. Special Rapporteur give maximum attention and publicity to the information in this report, which demonstrates the groundlessness of reports of child organ trafficking and the impossibility of such practices occurring.

By 2016, black market organ trafficking, including child organ trafficking, was an accepted reality. Here is the abstract:

> **Child organ trafficking: global reality and inadequate international response.** Bagheri. Med Health Care Philos. 2016 Jun;19(2):239-46. doi: 10.1007/s11019-015-9671-4.
>
> In organ transplantation, the demand for human organs has grown far faster than the supply of organs. This has opened the door for illegal organ trade and trafficking including from children. Organized crime groups and individual organ brokers exploit the situation and, as a result, black markets are becoming more numerous and organized organ trafficking is expanding worldwide. While underprivileged and vulnerable men and women in developing countries are a major source of trafficked organs, and may themselves be trafficked for the purpose of illegal organ removal and trade, children are at especial risk of exploitation. With the confirmed cases of children being trafficked for their organs, child organ trafficking, which [was] once called a "modern urban legend", is a sad reality in today's world. By presenting a global picture of child organ trafficking, this paper emphasizes that child organ trafficking is no longer a myth but a reality which has to be addressed. It argues that the international efforts against organ trafficking and trafficking in human beings for organ removal have failed to address child organ trafficking adequately. This chapter suggests that more orchestrated international collaboration as well as development of preventive measure and legally binding documents are needed to fight child organ trafficking and to support its victims.
>
> KEYWORDS:
>
> Child organ trafficking; Organ trafficking; Organ transplantation; Trafficking of human being for organ removal; Transplant tourism

Did you enjoy this book? Reviews and recommendations are vital to making a book successful.

Please leave a review at your favorite book store or review site and share it with your friends.

Don't miss the following bonus material:
Sign up for mailing list to get a free ebook
Read a sneak preview chapter of Doctored Death
and a sneak preview chapter of She Wore Mourning
Other books by P.D. Workman
Learn more about the author

PREVIEW OF DOCTORED DEATH

KENZIE KIRSCH MEDICAL THRILLERS
Book #2

1

Will awoke in a dark room. He couldn't remember where he was. He wasn't sure what had woken him up, but something was wrong. Something was definitely wrong. He sat up and looked around, straining his eyes in the darkness. His breathing was irregular and he had a difficult time swallowing. Was he sick? He must be sick. It looked something like a hospital room.

He needed to talk to someone and find out what was going on. He slid his feet out from under the covers and put them on the floor. It was carpeted rather than tiled like a hospital room normally was.

He realized as he slid out of the warm spot he'd occupied on the bed that he was wet.

Something was definitely wrong. A grown man didn't wet the bed.

His legs were wobbly and weak. He held onto the bed as he tried to push himself upright. The room lurched around him. He couldn't find his balance.

He needed to get help. Someone outside the room could help him. If he could just make it to the door and out into the hallway.

He felt for the wall to steady himself. He kept banging his legs against furniture as he made his way around the room. A couple of times, he fell down to his knees and it was a struggle to get back up again. Eventually, he decided it was easier to crawl along the floor than it was to walk.

If he just knew where he was going.

He banged his head against something hard. It sent his brain spinning. Blackness gathered closer in to him. A warm trickle ran down his temple. As he lay on the carpet, giving in to the hopelessness of the situation, a line of light appeared across the room. It was too bright, making him squint. The line grew into an elongated rectangle. A partially open doorway?

Will was relieved. Someone was there. Someone had come to check on him and they would tell him what was wrong and help him back to bed where he could rest his head.

But it wasn't a nurse that came in to see to him. He felt a cold nose and warm snout against his hand and arm. A dog. It moved to his face and sniffed and breathed its warm breath on him, investigating his face, licking him in greeting and cleaning away the blood.

He murmured words to it. He didn't know the animal's name, but it brought him comfort to have another living being there with him. He wasn't alone.

The dog barked a couple of times. That would bring help. Then it lay down alongside him. It was warm and soft.

Will closed his eyes and breathed out.

2

Kenzie was awakened by the insistent beeping of her clock. She reached over to turn it off, forcing her eyes open. Friday. And she had the weekend off, provided nothing untoward happened that required her at the Medical Examiner's office. One more day. Saturday she could sleep in. She sat up, hoping that would help to wake her enough to get her day going. She ran her fingers through her wildly curly dark hair to push it away from her face.

She felt the bed beside her to see if Zachary was there, but she knew he wouldn't be. It would have been more than rare for him to still be in bed when she woke up. It had only happened once or twice in the months Zachary had been sleeping there. After the assault, it had been different. His sleep patterns had become completely erratic and he was frequently unable to get out of bed or to keep from falling asleep where he sat on the couch or in front of the computer. But he was back to his normal routine, and that meant that he was up before her. Sometimes hours before.

Kenzie pushed herself to her feet and staggered to the ensuite bathroom. She went to the bathroom and then started the shower. She rubbed her hands over her face and looked at herself in the mirror while she waited for the water to warm up. A cold shower might wake her up faster, but she preferred her creature comforts; she wasn't getting in until it started to steam.

+++

After a quick shower, Kenzie tidied her spiraling hair into some order, put on her makeup, including the red lipstick that would have to be reapplied after breakfast. But she loved the way it looked, so she put it on anyway. She pulled on her usual work uniform. A blouse and slacks topped with a short blazer. Comfortable shoes, since she would be on her feet much of the day. Then she left the bedroom and went down the hall to the living room and kitchen area to see how her partner was.

"Morning, Zachary."

He didn't look up from his computer.

Kenzie hadn't picked Zachary Goldman for his looks. He was a small, slender man with close-cropped black hair. He had been feeling pretty good over the summer, but she thought he might be losing weight again. His cheeks, which had filled in since his last depressive cycle, looked a little thin and his eye sockets hollow. He hadn't shaved yet, and might not. He frequently kept a scruffy three days' growth of beard. It made him look like a homeless man. Intentionally so. People looked away from him, discounted him, which made his surveillance jobs much easier.

The reason Kenzie was with him was because he was kind and cared about people and he made her laugh. He was also one of the few people she could discuss her job at the Medical Examiner's Office with. He was interested in the medical mysteries she helped to solve, not disgusted by them.

There weren't a lot of people she could look at autopsy photos with over dinner.

"Zachary." Kenzie leaned over his shoulder and gave him a peck on the cheek.

He gave a small start and looked at her. He smiled. "Oh, you're up." He stretched and massaged his neck. "I didn't hear you."

"Up and dressed and ready for breakfast," she pointed out, in case the private investigator didn't notice these clues. "Are you ready for something to eat?"

He stood. "Sorry, I didn't hear you in the shower or I would have put some coffee on."

"It won't take long." Kenzie picked up a couple of mugs from the side table, one empty and one half-full of lukewarm or cold coffee. Zachary was pretty good about keeping them away from his computer to prevent any accidental spills. Not so great at remembering to pick them up again later.

She carried them into the kitchen and, after dumping the one in the sink, put them into the dishwasher. She started the coffee maker and put a couple of pieces of bread into the toaster.

Zachary went to the fridge and got out the margarine and marmalade for her. They moved around each other, used to the flow of the morning routine. Kenzie put a granola bar in front of Zachary's chair. His meds made eating in the morning difficult, but he could usually manage one of the chocolate chip granola bars, and the doctor said that anything he could get down was better than nothing.

They both sat down once the coffee was finished brewing and the toast popped.

"How did you sleep?" Kenzie asked. She couldn't remember him getting up.

Zachary had a sip of the hot coffee and started to unwrap the granola bar. "Not the best night. Restless. But I got a few hours in."

"Good. I didn't hear you up."

He nodded. "I tried to be quiet. Don't like you to be tired at work."

"I know. But if you need me..."

He gave her a smile. The one he always gave when he was comparing her reaction to how his ex-wife Bridget would have treated him. Criticizing him from disturbing her beauty rest instead of inviting him to wake her up if he needed her. The bemused smile that said he wasn't sure he deserved to be treated so kindly.

Zachary broke off a corner of the granola bar and put it in his mouth. "Think you'll be busy today?"

"Things have been quiet lately. I just don't know if that means they are going to continue to be quiet or we are building up to something big."

"Hopefully quiet. But not too quiet. Enough that you won't be bored. But no mass murders."

"Exactly," Kenzie agreed, taking a couple of bites of her marmalade toast. "I don't think there's any need to worry about me getting bored. People aren't going to stop dying."

Order *Doctored Death, Kenzie Kirsch Medical Thriller #2* by P.D. Workman at pdworkman.com.

PREVIEW OF SHE WORE MOURNING

ZACHARY GOLDMAN MYSTERIES
Book #1

CHAPTER 1

Zachary Goldman stared down the telephoto lens at the subjects before him. It was one of those days that left tourists gaping over the gorgeous scenery. Dark trees against crisp white snow, with the mountains as a backdrop. Like the picture on a Christmas card.

The thought made Zachary feel sick.

But he wasn't looking at the scenery. He was looking at the man and the woman in a passionate embrace. The pretty young woman's cheeks were flushed pink, more likely with her excitement than the cold, since she had barely stepped out of her car to greet the man. He had a swarthier complexion and a thin black beard, and was currently turned away from Zachary's camera.

Zachary wasn't much to look at himself. Average height, black hair cut too short, his own three-day growth of beard not hiding how pinched and pale his face was. He'd never considered himself a good catch.

He waited patiently for them to move, to look around at their surroundings so that he could get a good picture of their faces.

They thought they were alone; that no one could see them without being seen. They hadn't counted on the fact that Zachary had been surveilling them for a couple of weeks and had known where they would go. They gave him lots of warning so that he could park his car out of sight, camouflage himself in the trees, and settle in to wait for their appearance. He was no amateur; he'd been a private investigator since she had been choosing wedding dresses for her Barbie dolls.

He held down the shutter button to take a series of shots as they came up for air and looked around at the magnificent surroundings, smiling at each other, eyes shining.

All the while, he was trying to keep the negative thoughts at bay. Why had he fallen into private detection? It was one of the few ways he could make a living using his skill with a camera. He could have chosen another profession. He didn't need to spend his whole life following other people, taking pictures of their most private moments. What was the real point of his job? He destroyed lives, something he'd had his fill of long ago. When was the last time he'd brought a smile to a client's face? A real, genuine smile? He had wanted to make a difference in people's lives; to exonerate the innocent.

Zachary's phone started to buzz in his pocket. He lowered the camera and turned around, walking farther into the grove of trees. He had the pictures he needed. Anything else would be overkill.

He pulled out his phone and looked at it. Not recognizing the number, he swiped the screen to answer the call.

"Goldman Investigations."

"Uh... yes... Is this Mr. Goldman?" a voice inquired. Older, female, with a tentative quaver.

"Yes, this is Zachary," he confirmed, subtly nudging her away from the 'mister.'

"Mr. Goldman, my name is Molly Hildebrandt."

He hoped she wasn't calling her about her sixty-something-year-old husband and his renewed interest in sex. If it was another infidelity case, he was going to have to turn it down for his own sanity. He would even take a lost dog or wedding ring. As long as the ring wasn't on someone else's finger now.

"Mrs. Hildebrandt. How can Goldman Investigations help you?"

Of course, she had probably already guessed that Goldman Investigations consisted of only one employee. Most people seemed to sense that from the size of his advertisements. From the fact that he listed a post office box number instead of a business suite downtown or in one of the newer commercial areas. It wasn't really a secret.

"I don't know whether you have been following the news at all about Declan Bond, the little boy who drowned...?"

Zachary frowned. He trudged back toward his car.

"I'm familiar with the basics," he hedged. A four- or five-year-old boy whose round face and feathery dark hair had been pasted all over the news after a search for a missing child had ended tragically.

"They announced a few weeks ago that it was determined to be an accident."

Zachary ground his teeth. "Yes...?"

"Mr. Goldman, I was Declan's grandma." Her voice cracked. Zachary waited, listening to her sniffles and sobs as she tried to get herself under control. "I'm sorry. This has been very difficult for me. For everyone."

"Yes."

"Mr. Goldman, I don't believe that it was an accident. I'm looking for someone who would investigate the matter privately."

Zachary breathed out. A homicide investigation? Of a child? He'd told himself that he would take anything that wasn't infidelity, but if there was one thing that was more depressing than couples cheating on each other, it was the death of a child.

"I'm sure there are private investigators that would be more qualified for a homicide case than I am, Mrs. Hildebrandt. My schedule is pretty full right now."

Which, of course, was a lie. He had the usual infidelities, insurance investigations, liabilities, and odd requests. The dregs of the private investigation business. Nothing substantial like a homicide. It was a high-profile case. A lot of volunteers had shown up to help, expecting to find a child who had wandered out of his own yard, expecting to find him dirty and crying, not floating face down in a pond. A lot of people had mourned the death of a child they hadn't even known existed before his disappearance.

"I need your help, Mr. Goldman. Zachary. I can't afford a big name, but you've got good references. You've investigated deaths before. Can't you help me?"

He wondered who she had talked to. It wasn't like there were a lot of people who would give him a bad reference. He was competent and usually got the job done, but he wasn't a big name.

"I could meet with you," he finally conceded. "The first consultation is free. We'll see what kind of a case you have and whether I want to take it. I'm not making any promises at this point. Like I said, my schedule is pretty full already."

She gave a little half-sob. "Thank you. When are you able to come?"

After he had hung up, Zachary climbed into his car, putting his camera down on the floor in front of the passenger seat where it couldn't fall, and started the car. For a while, he sat there, staring out the front windshield at the magical, sparkling, Christmas-card scene. Every year, he told himself it would be better. He would get over it and be able to move on and to enjoy the holiday season like everyone else. Who cared about his crappy childhood experiences? People moved on.

And when he had married Bridget, he had thought he was going to achieve it. They would have a fairy-tale Christmas. They would have hot chocolate after skating at the public rink. They would wander down Main Street looking at the lights and the crèche in front of the church. They would open special, meaningful presents from each other.

But they'd fought over Christmas. Maybe it was Zachary's fault. Maybe he had sabotaged it with his gloom. The season brought with it so much baggage. There had been no skating rink. No hot chocolate, only hot tempers. No walks looking at the lights or the nativity. They had practically thrown their gifts at each other, flouncing off to their respective corners to lick their wounds and pout away the holiday.

He'd still cherished the thought that perhaps the next year there would be a baby. What could be more perfect than Christmas with a baby? It would unite them. Make them a real family. Just like Zachary had longed for since he'd lost his own family. He and Bridget and a baby. Maybe even twins. Their own little family in their own little happy bubble.

But despite a positive pregnancy test, things had gone horribly wrong.

Zachary stared at the bright white scenery and blinked hard, trying to shake off the shadows of the past. The past was past. Over and done. This year he was back to baching it for Christmas. Just him and a beer and *It's a Wonderful Life* on TV.

He put the car in reverse and didn't look into the rear-view mirror as he backed up, even knowing about the precipice behind him. He'd deliberately parked where he'd have to back up toward the cliff when he was done. There was a guardrail, but if he backed up too quickly, the car would go right through it, and who could say whether it had been accidental or deliberate? He had been cold-stone sober and had been out on a job. Mrs. Hildebrandt could testify that he had been calm and sober during their call. It would be ruled an accident.

But his bumper didn't even touch the guardrail before he shifted into drive and pulled forward onto the road.

He'd meet with the grandmother. Then, assuming he did not take the case, there would always be another opportunity.

Life was full of opportunities.

CHAPTER 2

Molly Hildebrandt was much as Zachary expected her to be. A woman in her sixties who looked ten or twenty years older with the stress of the high-profile death of her grandchild. Gray, curling hair. Pale, wrinkled skin. She wasn't hunched over, though. She sat up straight and tall as if she'd gone to a finishing school where she'd been forced to walk and sit with an encyclopedia on her head. Did they still do that? Had they ever done it?

"Mr. Goldman, thank you for seeing me so quickly," she greeted formally, holding her hand out for him to shake when he arrived at her door.

"Please, call me Zachary, ma'am. I'm not really comfortable with Mr. Goldman."

Telling her that he wasn't comfortable with it meant that she would be a bad hostess if she continued to address him that way, instead of her seeing it as a way of showing him respect. He hadn't done anything to deserve respect and was much happier if she would talk to him like the gardener or her next-door neighbor.

Not that there was any gardener. Molly lived in a small apartment in an old, dark brick building that was sturdy enough, but had been around longer than Zachary had been alive. The interior, when she invited him in, was bright and cozy. She had made coffee, and he breathed in the aroma in the air appreciatively. It wasn't hot chocolate after skating, but he could use a cup or two of coffee to warm him up after his surveillance. Standing around in the snow for a couple of hours had chilled him, even though he'd dressed for the weather.

Molly escorted him to the tiny living room.

"And you must call me Molly," she insisted.

She eyed the big camera case as he put it down. Zachary gave a grimace.

"Sorry. I didn't come to take your picture; I just don't like to leave expensive equipment in the car."

"Oh," she nodded politely. She didn't ask him who he had been taking pictures of. That wouldn't be gracious. She would have to imagine instead, and she would probably be correct in her guess.

They fussed for a few minutes with their coffees. Zachary wrapped his fingers around his mug, waiting for the coffee to cool and his fingers to warm. It felt good. Comforting. He waited for Molly to begin her story.

"You probably think that I'm just being a fussy old lady," she said. "Imagining something sinister when it was just an accident."

"Not at all. Why don't you tell me why you don't think it was an accident?"

"I'm not *sure* at all," she clarified. "Maybe they're right. Maybe it was an accident. It isn't that I doubt their findings..." she trailed off. "Not really. I know they had to do an autopsy and all that. We waited for months for them to come back with the manner of death. I thought that once they ruled, everyone would feel better."

"But you still have doubts?"

"I'm worried for my daughter."

Zachary blinked at her and waited for more.

"She's not well. I had hoped that once they released the body... and after the memorial... and after the manner of death was announced... each milestone, I thought, it would get better. It would be easier for her, but..." Molly shook her head. "She's getting worse and worse. Time isn't helping."

"Your daughter was Declan's mother."

"Yes. Of course."

"What's her name?"

"Isabella Hildebrandt," Molly said, her brows drawn down like he should have known that. "You know. *The Happy Artist.*"

Zachary had heard of *The Happy Artist.* She was on TV and was popular among the locals. Zachary didn't know whether she was syndicated nationally or just on one of the local stations. She had a painting instruction show every Sunday morning, and people awaited her next show like a popular soap. Most of the people Zachary knew who watched the show didn't paint and never intended to take it up. She was an institution.

"Oh, yes," Zachary agreed. "Of course, I know *The Happy Artist.* I didn't put the names together."

"When it was in the news, they said who she was. They said it was *The Happy Artist*'s child."

"Sure. Of course," Zachary agreed. He rubbed the dark stubble along his jaw. He should have gone home to shave and clean up before meeting with Molly. He looked like he'd been on a three-day stakeout. He *had* been on a three-day stakeout. "I'm sorry. I didn't follow the story very closely. That's good for you; it means I don't have a lot of preconceived ideas about the case."

She looked at him for a minute, frowning. Reconsidering whether she really wanted to hire him? That wouldn't hurt his feelings.

"You were going to tell me about your daughter?" Zachary prompted. "I can understand how devastated she must be by her son's death."

"No. I don't think you can," Molly said flatly.

Zachary was taken aback. He shrugged and nodded, and waited for her to go on.

"Isabella has a history of… mental health issues. She was the one supervising Declan when he disappeared, and the guilt has been overwhelming for her."

That made perfect sense. Zachary sipped at his coffee, which had cooled enough not to scald him.

Molly went on. "I think… as horrible as it may sound… that it would be a relief for her if it turned out that Declan was taken from the yard, instead of just having wandered away."

"That may be, but how likely is that? Surely the police must have considered the possibility, and I can't manufacture evidence for your daughter, even if it would ease her mind."

"No… I realize that. I'm not expecting you to do anything dishonest. Just to investigate it. Read over the police reports. Interview witnesses again. Just see… if there's any possibility that there was… foul play. A third-party interfering, even if it was nothing malicious."

"I assume you know most of the details surrounding the case."

"Yes, of course."

"How likely do you think it is that the police missed something? Did they seem sloppy or like they didn't care? Did you think there were signs of foul play that they brushed off?"

"No." Molly gave a little shrug. "They seemed perfectly competent."

Zachary was silent. It wouldn't be difficult to read over the police reports and talk to the family. Was there any point?

"The only thing is…" Molly trailed off.

As impatient as Zachary was to get out of there, he knew it was no good pushing Molly to give it up any faster. She already knew she sounded crazy for asking him to reinvestigate a case where he wasn't going to be able to turn up anything new. For no reason, other than that it might help her daughter to come to terms with the child's death. He looked around the room. There were no pictures of Molly's husband, even old ones. There was no sign she had raised Isabella or any other children there. There were several pictures of a couple with a little child. Declan and Isabella and whatever the father's name was. There was one picture of Declan himself, occupying its own space, a little memorial to her lost grandson. There were no pictures of anyone else, so Zachary could only assume Isabella was an only child and Declan the only grandchild.

"Declan was afraid of water."

Zachary turned his eyes back to her. He considered. It wasn't totally inconceivable that a child afraid of the water would drown. He wouldn't know how to swim. If he fell in, he would panic, flail, and swallow water, rather than staying calm enough to float. Molly wiped at a tear.

"How afraid of the water was he?" Zachary asked.

"He wouldn't go near the water. He was terrified. He wouldn't have gone to the pond by himself."

"How tall was he?"

Molly gave a little shrug. "He was almost five years old. Three feet?"

"How steep were the banks of the pond and what was the terrain and foliage like?" He knew he would have to look at it for himself.

"I don't know what you want to know… there wasn't any shore to speak of. Just the pond. There were bulrushes. Cattails. Some trees. The ground is… uneven, but not hilly."

Zachary tried to visualize it. A child wouldn't be able to see the pond as far away as an adult would because of his short stature. If his view were further screened by the plant life, the banks steep and crumbly, he might not be able to see it until he was right on top of it. Or in it.

"It's not a lot to go on," he said. "The fact that he was afraid of water."

"I know." Molly used both hands to wipe her eyes. "I know that." She looked around the apartment, swallowing hard to get control of her emotions. "I just want the best for my baby. A parent always wants what's best. Growing up… I wasn't able to give her that. She didn't have an easy life. I wonder if…" She didn't have to finish the sentence this time. Zachary already knew what she was going to say. She wondered if that rough upbringing had caused Isabella's mental fragility. Whether things would have turned out differently if she'd been able to provide a stable environment. Molly sniffled. "Do you have children, Mr.—Zachary?"

Zachary felt that familiar pain in his chest. Like she'd plunged a knife into it. He cleared his throat and shook his head. "No. My marriage just recently ended. We didn't have any children."

"Oh." Her eyes searched his for the truth. Zachary looked away. "I'm sorry. I guess we all have our losses."

Although hers, the death of her grandson, was clearly more permanent than any relationship issues Zachary might have.

In the end, he agreed to do the preliminaries. Get the police reports. Walk the area around the house and pond. Talk to the parents. He gave her his lowest hourly fee. She clearly couldn't afford more. He wasn't even sure she'd be able to pay on receipt of his invoice. He might have to allow her a payment plan, something he normally didn't do, but something about the frail woman had gotten to him.

He put in an appearance at the police station, requesting a copy of the information available to the public, and handing over Molly Hildebrandt's request that he be provided as much information as possible for an independent evaluation.

"You got a new case?" Bowman grunted as he tapped through a few computer screens, getting a feel for how many files there were on the Declan Bond accident investigation file and how much of it he would be able to provide to Zachary.

"Yes," Zachary agreed. Obviously. He didn't encourage small talk; he really didn't want Bowman to start asking personal questions. They weren't friends, but they were friendly. Bowman had helped Zachary track down missing documents before. He knew the right people to ask for permission and the best way to ask.

Bowman dug into his pocket and pulled out a pack of gum. He unwrapped a piece and popped it into his mouth, then offered one to Zachary as an afterthought.

"No, I'm good."

Bowman chewed vigorously as he studied each screen. He was a middle-aged man, with a middle-age spread, his belly sagging over his belt. His hairline had started receding, and occasionally he put on a pair of glasses for a moment and then took them off again, jamming them into his breast pocket.

"How's Bridget?" he asked.

Zachary swallowed. He took a deep breath and steeled himself for the conversation. Bowman looked away from his screen and at Zachary's face, eyebrows up.

"She's good. In remission."

"Good to hear." Bowman looked back at his computer again. "Good to hear. It's been a tough time for the two of you." His eyes flicked back to Zachary, and he backtracked. "I mean it's been tough for her. And for you."

"Yeah," Zachary agreed. He waved away any further fumbling explanation from Bowman. "So, what have we got? On the Bond case?"

"Right!" Bowman looked back at his screen. "I've got press releases and public statements for you. medical examiner's report. The cop in charge of the file was Eugene. He likes red."

Zachary blinked at Bowman, more baffled than usual by his abbreviated language. "What?"

"Eugene Taft. I know, it's a preposterous name, but he's never had a nickname that stuck. Eugene Taft."

"And he likes red."

"Wine," Bowman said as if Zachary was dense. "He likes red wine. You know, if you want to help things along, have a better chance of getting a look at the rest of that file, the officers' notes and all the background and interviews. If you have to apply some leverage."

"And for Eugene Taft, it's red wine."

"Has to be red," Bowman confirmed.

"Okay." Zachary looked at his watch. "Can you start that stuff printing for me? Is there anyone downstairs?" He knew he would have to run down to the basement to order a copy of the medical examiner's report. Just one of those bureaucratic things.

"Sure. Kenzie should be down there still."

Zachary paused. "Kenzie. Not Bradley?"

"Kenzie," Bowman confirmed. "She's new."

"How new?"

"I don't know." Bowman gave a heavy shrug. "How long since you were down there last? Less than that."

Zachary snorted and went down the hall to the elevator.

As he waited for it, Joshua Campbell, an officer he'd worked with on an insurance fraud case several months previous, approached and hit the up button. He did a double-take, looking at Zachary.

"Zach Goldman! How are you, man? Haven't seen you around here lately."

"Good." Zachary shook hands with him. Joshua's hands were hard and rough like he'd grown up working on a farm instead of in the city. Zachary wondered what he did in his spare time that left them so rough and scarred. He wasn't boxing after work; Zachary would have been able to tell that by his knuckles. "Hey, how's Bridget doing? Did everything turn out okay…?" He trailed off and shifted uncomfortably.

"Yeah, great. She's in remission."

"Oh, good. That's great, Zach. Good to hear."

Zachary nodded politely. His elevator arrived with a ding and a flashing down indicator. Zachary sketched a quick goodbye to Joshua and jumped on. He was starting to regret agreeing to look into the Bond case.

The girl at the desk had dark, curly hair, red-lipsticked lips, and a tight, slim form. She was working through some forms, those red lips pursed in concentration, and she didn't look up at him.

"Hang on," she said. "Just let me finish this part up, before I lose my train of thought."

Zachary stood there as patiently as possible, which wasn't too hard with a pretty girl to look at. She finally filled in the last space and looked up at him. She raised an eyebrow.

"You must be Kenzie," Zachary said.

"I don't know if I must be, but I am. Kenzie Kirsch. And you are?"

"Zachary Goldman. From Goldman Investigations."

"A private investigator?"

"Yes."

He didn't usually introduce himself that way because it gave people funny ideas about the kind of life he lived and how he spent his time. Most people did not think about mounds of paperwork or painstaking accident scene reconstructions when they thought about private investigation. They thought about Dick Tracy and Phillip Marlowe and all the old hardboiled detectives. When really most of a private investigator's life was mind-numbingly boring, and he didn't need to carry a gun.

"And what can I do for you today, Mr. Private Investigator?"

"Zachary."

"Zachary," she repeated, losing the teasing tone and giving him a warm smile. "What can I do for you?"

"I need to order a copy of a medical examiner's report. Declan Bond."

"Bond. That's the boy? The drowning victim?"

"That's the one."

She looked at him, shaking her head slightly. "Why do you need that one? It's closed. A determination was made that it was an accident."

"I know. The family would like someone else to look at it. Just to set their minds at ease."

"You're not going to find anything. It's an open-and-shut case."

"That's fine. They just want someone to take a look. It's not a reflection on the medical examiner. You know how families are. They need to be able to move on. They're not quite ready to let it go yet. One last attempt to understand..."

Kenzie gave a little shrug. "Okay, then... there's a form..." She bent over and searched through a drawer full of files to find the right one. Zachary had filled them out before. Usually, he could manage to do an end-run and Bradley would just pull the file for him. Officially, he was supposed to fill one out. He didn't want to end up in hot water with the new administrator, so he leaned on the counter and filled the form out carefully.

She went on with her own forms and filing, not trying to fill the silence with small talk. Which Zachary thought was nice. When he was finished, he put the pen back in its holder and handed the form to Kenzie. To the side of the work she was doing. Not right in front of her face. She again ignored him while she finished the section she was on, then picked it up to look it over.

"You have nice printing," she observed, her voice going up slightly. She laughed at herself. "No reason why you shouldn't," she said quickly. "It's just that the majority of the forms that get submitted here are… well, to say they were chicken scratch would be insulting to chickens."

Zachary chuckled. "That's the difference between a cop and a private investigator."

"Neat handwriting?"

"Yeah. Cops have to fill out so many forms, they don't care. You can just call them if you need something clarified. Me… I know if I don't fill it out right, it's just going to go in the circular file." He nodded in the direction of the garbage can.

"I wouldn't throw it out," she protested.

"If you couldn't read it? What else would you do?"

"I would at least try to call you."

Zachary indicated the form. "That's why I printed my phone number so neatly."

Kenzie smiled and nodded. "It's very clear," she approved.

"You'll call me?"

"I'll let you know when it's ready to be picked up."

Zachary hovered there for an extra few seconds. He was enjoying the give-and-take of his conversation with her but didn't want her to accuse him of being creepy. He wasn't the type who asked a girl out the first time he saw her.

He gave her another smile and walked away from the desk. Maybe next time.

Order *She Wore Mourning, Zachary Goldman Mysteries #1* by P.D. Workman at pdworkman.com.

ABOUT THE AUTHOR

P.D. Workman is a USA Today Bestselling author, winner of several awards from Library Services for Youth in Custody and the InD'tale Magazine's Crowned Heart award, and has published over 90 mystery/suspense/thriller and young adult books, including stand alones and these series: Auntie Clem's Bakery cozy mysteries, Reg Rawlins Psychic Investigator paranormal mysteries, Zachary Goldman Mysteries (PI), Kenzie Kirsch Medical Thrillers, Parks Pat Mysteries (police procedural), and YA series: Tamara's Teardrops, Between the Cracks, and Breaking the Pattern.

Workman loves writing about the underdog, who the reader may love or hate. She has been praised for her realistic details, deep characterization, and sensitive handling of the serious social issues that appear in all of her stories, from light cozy mysteries through to darker, grittier young adult and mystery/suspense books.

> P. D. Workman, does not shy from probing the deep psychological scars of childhood trauma, mental illness, and addiction. Also characteristic of this author, these extremely sensitive issues are explored with extensive empathy, described with incredible clarity, and portrayed with profound insight.
>
> — —KIM, GOODREADS REVIEWER

Some of Workman's titles have been translated into Spanish, French, Portuguese, German, and Italian.

Workman began writing at an early age and is a prolific reader as well as writer. She is also passionate about teaching and learning, expresses her creativity through art and cooking, and loves exploring the Calgary parks and green spaces where the Parks Pat Mysteries are set. She was a legal assistant for many years and has done extensive charitable work.

Workman was born and raised in Alberta, Canada, and is married with one adult son.

Please visit P.D. Workman at pdworkman.com to see what else she is working on, to join her mailing list, and to link to her social networks.

If you enjoyed this book, please take the time to recommend it to other purchasers with a review or star rating and share it with your friends!

facebook.com/pdworkmanauthor
twitter.com/pdworkmanauthor
instagram.com/pdworkmanauthor
amazon.com/author/pdworkman
bookbub.com/authors/p-d-workman
goodreads.com/pdworkman
linkedin.com/in/pdworkman
pinterest.com/pdworkmanauthor
youtube.com/pdworkman

Find P.D. Workman's books at

PDWORKMAN.COM

Scan the QR code below